REVIEWS FOR *The Meek*

"If the Dork Diaries, The Stand, and Are You There God It's Me Margaret, were put in a blender with a deadly virus, this novel might be the result. Think of the 'realistic rebuilding of society' qualities of The Stand (without the paranormal or creepy elements), the 'young women coming of age' qualities of Are You There God, It's Me Margaret, and the easy-to-read lively diary format and likable, relatable qualities of the Dork Diaries. That might give you a bit of a feel for what you can expect with this book. What an engaging story. And so relevant to the Covid-19 pandemic! I especially appreciate the two strong female voices telling the story, and their character development. I look forward to the next book in the series!"

"This novel grabbed my attention from the first and kept me engaged throughout the book. I finished it in record time and was left wishing the story continued. I cannot wait for the sequel! A unique approach to a very timely issue, the format was successful. Even though it might be considered a young adult genre, anyone would find this a good read. I highly recommend this to anyone who enjoys a good solid novel."

"I read this during the worst days of Covid. It reminded me that even during a crisis people have the potential to be leaders and make ethical and level headed decisions for their communities."

"I have never liked the "Mad Max" apocalyptic movies and books with all their violence and unbelievable characters. "The Meek Shall Inherit" was, to me, a much more believable story of what a small group of real people would do if suddenly they were the only people still living. The letters of two late teen girls form the story of three families, who come together to form a community to survive. How they work together, build trust, and confront unknown threats tells a story of the strength of the human spirit. The book apparently is aimed for the young adult reader, but this 79-year-old man loved it."

"I've told everyone I know about this book. The concept is great, the storytelling superb, and the ending -- WOW! I can't wait for the next one."

May all your journeys
end well!
Cynthia Neira

COMPANIONS
OF THE
JOURNEY

All content by authors Julia White and Cynthia Siira
Edited by Rebecca Chedester Dussault
Cover design by Laura Myers
Map Resources from U.S. Census Bureau
Published in the United States of America

ISBN: 9798386200800

What happened to Mom? That is the most often asked question from readers of *The Meek Shall Inherit*. Julia and Cynthia spent the last year or two poring over maps and virtually wandering the U.S., following Mom as she traveled with her companions in their journey to get home.

This book is dedicated to our readers and their curiosity.
Thank you!

"Death and sorrow will be the companions of our journey; hardship our garment; constancy and valour our only shield. We must be united, we must be undaunted, and we must be inflexible."

Winston Churchill, 1940

DANGER

VIRUS OUTBREAK

KEEP OUT!

Prologue

Who was a stranger anyway? Are they always the people our parents told us not to talk to or avoid? Sometimes we spend whole days and weekends with people who are strangers at first, but are they still strangers at the end? How long does it take to become an acquaintance, a companion, a friend? Simply spending time together doesn't always change that relationship, maybe it's something deeper...something in our souls that connects and fits together with someone else's. And what tells you this shift has happened? How do you know to trust people and when do strangers stop being strange and change into something else....

Chapter 1

March - Arizona

Tim kicked the front tire of his Corolla and cursed as pain shot through his foot. Now what? He hated this! Dad had said to wait at home and not leave until they got back. Mom and Dad had gone to pick up Granddad, but it had been almost two weeks since they'd left, and he didn't know what to do. Time passed so slowly and it seemed like ages since he'd seen them and who knew what was going on in the world. He sure didn't. It was all because of stupid K-Pox.

He hated K-Pox! When the K-Pox virus had started rapidly spreading in late February, he and his parents had followed directives and stayed isolated at home. He'd gotten so tired of being home with only his parents. Talk about boring. And talk about parents being irritating! Don't go outside. If you do go outside and see someone, wear a mask. Wear two masks. Don't talk to anyone. Stay home. Stay home. Stay home. He was sick of staying home. He was scared and sad and frustrated and wanted to cry, was actually tired of crying, and had no idea what to do. He picked up a rock and threw it as hard as he could. And then another and another. He threw rocks and cursed until his arm was sore and he'd run out of rocks and curse words. He wiped away tears, kicked the car tire again. Stupid car! It could get him to Granddad's house but couldn't bring them back. Stupid K-Pox!

Tim knew more than he'd ever wanted to know about Kongla Pox. It had been the sole item on the news and the talking heads had stopped only when the electricity went off in early March. At first there'd been plenty of information about Kongla Pox or K-Pox the "Red Death," the extremely contagious airborne virus mutation which had the symptoms of Smallpox and Ebola. It had moved through populations so quickly and was so deadly researchers hadn't had time to create an immunization to stop it.

Tim still had the article on the dining room table about Dr. Herman Fitzgerald, leading virologist at Hayden College of Medicine who reported, "K-Pox, the deadly airborne virus, is now known to be the most lethal virus ever to strike mankind." The virus was first noted in the village of Zambulu where all 87 inhabitants died. The virus spread quickly from one village to the rest of the world. Tim had wondered where the hell Zambulu was anyway and how the virus got to other countries. It didn't seem fair.

People all over the world were dying in huge numbers. The TV people had freaked out and had given panicked reports about the unbelievably rapid increase in deaths. There'd been some violence but not as much as there might have been as people were dying so fast. The last newscast Tim had heard said that about 90 percent of all people on earth were likely to die, maybe even more, and live broadcasting would stop until things got better. Which they didn't. TV stations had played old movies and then there was nothing. Tim had found radio stations with weird people broadcasting and then nothing there as well.

Those who had K-Pox were required to put the skeletal *K-Pox Keep Out!* signs on their doors so people would know who had it. One of the last things the government did was to send signs to every address so everyone would have one, just in case. Tim had tried to ignore their K-Pox sign which he'd placed under information notices where he couldn't see it.

He'd read the gruesome and scary details of dying with K-Pox. He didn't really want to know those details. Not anymore. He couldn't get the frightful images out of his mind. The virus attacked the respiratory system and lymph nodes causing painful lesions to form on the skin, in the mouth, and on the scalp. Sufferers had high fever, fatigue, nausea, vomiting, pain, and disorientation. The body's organs would break down and blood would leave the body through the eyes, nose, ears, and gums. Limbs would swell and skin darken as blood seeped into the epidermis. Many died within days but for those who didn't, it was a painful death before the heart gave out. K-Pox was a death sentence—a terrible way to die. When they'd begun their isolation Tim and his parents had been glad they were spared. That was then. And now his world was silent.Since the quarantine started, Tim and his dad had been to the grocery store twice. The first time they'd gone was after the store had officially closed and they could tell people had broken in as there weren't full shelves. Tim had felt weird taking stuff and he could tell his Dad had been uncomfortable too, but they'd needed food. They'd seen a few other people walking out with items, staying far away and not looking at each other. Tim had been surprised there weren't more people taking food or that there was any food left at all. So was everyone else in hiding, too sick to go out, or already dead? Scary thought.

The second and last time they'd been to the store they hadn't seen anyone anywhere. There'd been some food left–mostly cans of stuff nobody really wanted. They'd found a couple bottles of water rolled under a counter. But mostly they'd taken boring canned food like stews and tomato sauce and weird canned fish products he wasn't sure he'd eat. Dad had told him he couldn't be too fussy and they'd take what food was available. They had loaded up what they could in their car and had driven home. That had been right before Dad and Mom had gone to Granddad's.

The few times he had been on the road lately he thought he might have seen a few people, but they disappeared quickly. One time he saw a car on a side road going away from him. It was like everyone was disappearing from the face of the earth. And K-Pox signs. He hated those signs. They'd gone up on his friends' houses. About a week ago he'd knocked on Carlos' door and no answer. No car in the drive. He'd gone to see if Lucas was ok and saw the K-Pox sign so didn't knock. He'd also noticed their car wasn't there. Tim wondered if they'd gone somewhere. Where would they go if they were sick? And what if they died in the car before getting there? Maybe someone else had taken their car. But to drive it, you'd have to get in the house to get the keys, and going inside was almost certain death. Not worth it for only a car. Just another one of the stupid mysteries of stupid K-Pox. He hated it!

Were there no more people in town? Or in the county? Or in the state? Or anywhere? He'd heard very little human noise in ages. The few times he had heard vehicles he'd been surprised that the sound of car and truck tires and their engines were so loud when rolling on pavement. You can hear a vehicle from a long way away. He hadn't noticed that before. Earlier in the pandemic he and his parents had occasionally heard gunshots. They'd kept quiet in their house and kept their guns loaded and ready. But nothing human lately. Nothing. No one.

Tim tired of throwing rocks and went inside. He was hungry but wanted to eat something not in a can. He'd eaten his self-rationed stash of chips and candy and didn't want to go out for more. Not by himself. Tim wandered into the kitchen. The power had gone out days ago and the stuff in the freezer was going to go bad so Tim decided to eat those things first. He grabbed the last two thawed hot dogs, picked the mold off the last piece of bread, slathered it with catsup and mustard, and threw himself down on the couch. Cold hotdogs weren't too bad. He could've used the grill but it was too much work. He wanted to watch TV but had no power. He wanted to message or text or snap or even call someone but now it was totally out of the question with all communications down. He wanted to talk to friends to see how they were, but he was afraid his friends "weren't" anymore and that was beyond sad. But more than anything he wanted to talk to his parents. He really seriously wanted to talk to his parents. And Granddad. In person. But he couldn't. Not anymore.

Back in February when all this started, Granddad had refused to move in with them. He was determined to stay in his home by himself—he said he was only in his late 70s and not going to be dependent on his daughter. So Mom and Dad had driven to see him every couple of days and he'd been fine. But the trips had become more hazardous due to some violence around town, and they were using up gasoline so Mom was going to insist that he come back with them. They shouldn't have to deal with the threat of thugs or being out in public and be more liable to catch K-Pox just because he was stubborn. He'd have to deal with it. Besides, they'd need to share their scarce resources, especially food. They had driven off almost two weeks ago.

Tim finished his hot dogs and was still hungry. He was always hungry. He felt he never had enough to eat. He knew he couldn't just eat whatever he wanted though and was careful about his food supply. As a consequence he was getting thinner and thinner. Even before the pandemic he'd tried to put on weight. He hated when people commented on how thin he was. Like he didn't know he was skinny. It wasn't a choice. And now he was even thinner! Mom had told him when he stopped growing, he'd put on weight. Not to worry. And before the pandemic he'd actually started gaining. Then food became scarce so that stopped that.

He'd had his growth spurt in middle school. By ninth grade he was already taller than most of his peers and as skinny as a rail. Now he was in his senior year and a little over six feet. He was tired of being asked if he played basketball. He didn't want to play basketball, and if he had ever gone out for the team, the coach would've asked him to resign immediately. He was horrible at it. Mostly because he didn't like playing. What he did like was hiking and camping, not activities with crowds of people looking at you waiting for you to make a mistake. He might not be good at team sports, but he could do a mean cartwheel. His friends thought it was funny that this tall lanky guy could cartwheel across the yard like a gymnast, but he could.

Tim thought about what else there was to eat. He was so hungry, although some of his stomach pain was probably due to thinking about his parents. When they'd driven off to get Granddad, they were supposed to come back and then they'd all make a decision on what to do next. Should they stay in town or move out to a deserted farm somewhere? Should they look for other survivors and all work together to survive or hide from people they didn't know? Or…or…or…Who knows what they would've decided. They had never come home.

Granddad lived thirty miles away. With so little traffic it should have taken Mom and Dad only an hour or two to get him and return home. They definitely should have been back the same day. At first Tim wasn't too worried when they didn't show up the same evening, and he'd enjoyed the time by himself. But then they weren't back the next morning and he'd begun to worry. Maybe when they got there Granddad wasn't feeling well and they'd decided to stay until he got better. Or maybe he got really sick and they tried to find medical help. Or they started home but had car trouble. Tim imagined Dad trying to fix the car and someone shooting at them. He didn't continue that line of thought.

After his parents had been gone for three days, Tim hadn't been able to stay home, even though Dad had told him to. He'd gotten into his old Corolla and driven to Granddad's house. It had been so eerie driving on the roads and seeing so few people. Weeks ago he and his dad had seen a few cars on the road and occasionally people in their yards or walking out of a store, arms piled with items. Not now. Driving to Granddad's he'd not seen any people anywhere. No moving cars. He'd seen cows in fields munching on grass, a few dogs and cats crossing the road, and birds flying about, but no other life. It had been very creepy. Even though he hadn't seen anyone he had felt there were people watching him as he drove by. After all, if he was alive, other people would be too, right?

When he'd pulled into the driveway, both Granddad's and Mom and Dad's cars were there and full of Granddad's stuff. Tim saw they had planned on coming home. But they couldn't. The K-Pox sign was on the door. He'd grabbed the doorknob and struggled to get in but the door had been locked. He stood outside, banging on the door and yelling for them to open up and let him in.

Finally he heard his parents' voices. They pleaded with him, "Tim, we have K-Pox. We can't let you in. You have to leave. Please move away from the door. We don't want you to get it too. Please go. You have to! We couldn't stand it if you died too. Please, please go home. You'll be safer there. Please!"

He had refused to go away. He would stay there and bring food to put outside the door for them. He wouldn't leave them. He wouldn't. Tim had still hoped they'd all be able to go home together. He had even prayed for that to happen. He wasn't sure prayer worked (as the whole world was praying and people were still sick and dying) but he'd given it a chance. And so he'd slept in the driveway in his car for a couple of days, talking to Mom, Dad and Granddad when they were well enough to talk. No, he wouldn't leave them. But they made him promise to keep on and never give up and to go find other people and live his life if the worst happened.

Then the worst happened. They stopped bringing in the food.

He'd waited outside for several days, calling to them to come out, to answer, to be alive. But they didn't respond. Everything was quiet. Scary and sad and quiet. Finally Tim had to understand, had to acknowledge, that his parents and Granddad were gone. He didn't think his heart could survive the pain, the desperation, and the all-encompassing fear. All he wanted to do was curl up and die too. But he knew he couldn't. He knew what he needed to do and what they'd told him to do and what he'd promised to do, but right now he couldn't do anything. Not yet. He'd finally driven home, but all he could do now was sit and eat and cry and throw rocks and curse.

Tim knew he needed a plan. Before they'd gotten so sick, Mom and Dad had told him he'd need to leave home if no friends or neighbors showed up. They didn't want him by himself. But he didn't know where he'd go, or why he'd even bother to go. He didn't want to abandon their home. And he wanted to say goodbye again. He wanted to say all the things he didn't say through the locked door.

He decided since he couldn't talk to them anymore, he'd write them a letter. Tim struggled over his letter for several days. Writing wasn't easy for him with his learning disability, and he used the dictionary to look up some words. He felt he must have written the letter over and over a million times to get it right, and finally it looked ok. His handwriting was never good but it was the best he could do. He put the letter in an envelope, drove back to Granddad's house, and slipped the letter under the door.

Dear Mom and Dad and Granddad,

I wish I could see you and talk to you some more. If your dead I think I'd like to join you anyway. It's really lonly and scary without anyone. I miss you. So now I have to decide what to do by myself. I don't want to do this. I can't just sit in the house and run out of food. I don't want to die at home by myself. I need to find some other people. I'm very lonly. I need someone to talk to. So when I make my desision, I will leave a note at home. Then you will know what I decide. In case you get better and come home.

I want you to know I love you very much. I'm sorry I was angry all the time when you were here. I know you care about me. I just wanted to do what I wanted to do. Rules seemed stupid. Now I'd stay on house restriction for months if you would come home and I could see you again. I'd tell you I love you and play games with you and help bake cookies and decorate the Christmas tree and do all the things you wanted me to do with you and I refused to do cuz I wanted to spend time by myself. Well, I've spent enough time by myself now. Before K-Pox I spent time in my room by myself, but I knew you were in the next room. I could count on you. You were there. And you loved me. Not having you here is the worst feeling in the world.

I'll be here another day or two. Please come home.

I love you.

Tim

He gently touched the door with his palm, then slowly walked away and slid into the front seat. He put his hands on the steering wheel and stared at the house for a long time, tears streaming down his face. Leaving his letter at Granddad's made their being gone very real. They were truly gone, and they weren't coming back. He was on his own. He didn't think he could cry any more than he had done already, but apparently there were always more tears. Tim wiped his face on his sleeve and winced at the mess. "Dammit! Now I have to wash my stupid shirt!" He pulled out of the driveway and drove home blinded by tears.

So now here he was kicking the car, throwing rocks, swearing into the wind, finishing up hotdogs, working on a bag of cookies, and wondering what to do. Sitting on the couch with cookie crumbs all over his t-shirt, Tim had never felt so lonely and scared before. He knew he had to go somewhere. Somewhere with other people. He hoped he wasn't the last person in the world. How horrible would that be! But more importantly, what was he to do next? Part of him wished he could just sit there and quietly die. He had seriously thought about giving up. He'd even told his parents he would. But they'd made him promise that he would find other people and carry on. That he would live the best life he could and not give up. They made him promise. And he didn't want to break his promise.

Several hours later the sun had gone down and Tim was still sitting on the couch with several empty cookie bags crumpled at his feet. "Ok, I gotta leave. I'm not stayin here by myself." His voice sounded loud in the quiet of the dark room. He got up and pulled the curtains shut, reached for the battery powered lantern, and turned it on. There may be no one outside in the dark, but just in case, he didn't want the light to advertise he was still here. By himself. It was creepy being by yourself, but it was even creepier thinking of someone lurking outside in the shadows peering in at you.

He didn't know where he'd go, but he would go. So first things first. What to take and what to leave. He started with the stuff he and his father had used for camping and piled it up in the middle of the living room floor: his backpack, sleeping bag, pillow, hiking clothes, first aid kit, lighters/matches, lanterns, food, a road atlas, and anything else he could find.

There were so many things he wanted to take. So many memories. He wandered through his parents' bedroom, ran his hand over his mother's clothes, held onto his father's shirt sleeves, and wished they were there. He opened his mother's jewelry box. She'd never liked a lot of jewelry but what she had, lay sparkling on their small velvet shelves. He couldn't leave her jewelry there for someone else to take. He couldn't. He knew his mom had really loved her mother's ruby ring and had worn it on special occasions. He didn't want someone stealing it. The ring was hers. He decided he'd bury the really good jewelry just in case someone came to ransack the house. He gently wrapped her jewelry in one of her soft scarves and slipped it in an empty shoe box.

Digging the hole for the jewel-filled box in the dry hard-packed ground was tougher than he thought it would be. And digging made way more noise than he thought possible; the shovel scraping against the hard earth, the metallic chunking against the occasional rock. He realized how loud everything was when there were no other people around. Finally the hole was deep and wide enough. Tim looked at his mother's jewelry one more time before burying it, touching the sparkling smoothness, thinking how it had looked on her. The last time she had worn the ruby ring she'd told him the story about her mother wearing this ring. He felt bad now because he had rolled his eyes and had told her, "Yeah, you told me a million times!" She'd just laughed and said, "And I'll probably tell you a million more times!" His heart ached as he looked at the ring. Somehow burying what had been important to his mother was too painful. He pulled a long chain from the jewelry box and strung the ring onto the chain. He slipped it over his head and tucked it inside his shirt. Now he felt he had his mother with him, over his heart. Where she would always belong.

He walked back into the house and grabbed the guns and ammo. The shotgun, the .22 rifle, and the .38 pistol had been out and loaded since the beginning of the quarantine. Those guns were definitely going with him. He looked at his pile of miscellaneous items in the middle of the living room and felt a sense of satisfaction. The dreadful ache was still there, would never go away, but just knowing he had a plan and he'd be doing something his parents had wanted him to do was better than just sitting on the couch and feeling sorry for himself and wishing for death.

He wondered what time it was. He glanced up at the clock on the kitchen wall. How was he going to tell time when he was hiking? He couldn't use his phone anymore. No place to charge it and maybe no satellite transmissions. He went back to his parents' room, got his Dad's watch out of the top dresser drawer, and strapped it to his wrist. Dad's watch and Mom's ring. They'd go with him everywhere he went. He liked that. He took a shower with the diminishing water barely trickling out of the shower head and washed his dirty clothes in the sink. He threw his clothes over the shower curtain to dry, went to his room and threw himself down on his unmade bed. He thought of another good thing about leaving tomorrow. He wouldn't have to wash his sheets. They were pretty rank. He slept better than he had in a long time.

In the morning Tim wasn't as confident as he'd been the night before. He was leaving hours later than he'd planned. The decision to move on was more daunting in the bright light of day, and he was reluctant to leave everything so familiar and secure. He looked at all the things he had yet to pile in the car and one more time he considered staying. "No, I've gone over all this a million times. I'm going!"

He draped his still damp clothes on the back seat to dry and packed the car until it was stuffed with the things he had chosen to bring. He glanced around the house. The cookie bags were still on the floor so he picked them up and threw them in the trash. He looked around one final time, walked out, locked the door, and slid behind the steering wheel.

With the car purring quietly in the driveway, he wondered what direction to head in. He hadn't planned where to go, had no destination other than "not here." He had almost a full tank of gas to get him started on his road to nowhere, somewhere, wherever. He shifted in his seat and looked around. Which way? Right or left? A large flock of dark birds flew overhead. "Ha! I'll follow the birds! They gotta to be goin' somewhere!" He put the car into drive and turned right.

Chapter 2

March - California

I can't believe I went on this trip. Why didn't I just stay home? WHY? Resa screamed at herself in her head and slammed her hand on the steering wheel in frustration.

I thought this work trip would be fun! A trip to LA and then a quick meeting in San Bernardino where I could take a few days of my own time to explore and visit the McDonald's museum. It was the first time I went on a trip by myself in years. And the kids love McDonald's! I wanted to show them pictures when I got home. Now those pictures are just a ridiculous reminder of me wasting precious time.

Sightseeing and a little "me time." Of all the stupid, idiotic things to do. WRONG CHOICE THERESA JEAN! Arrggg! This is why moms don't take days off, everything falls apart! This virus has turned the world upside down! But I DIDN'T KNOW! I didn't know it was going to get this bad, this quick! Or that all transportation would stop! When I got to the airport and my flight home was canceled, I even slept in those horrible chairs, thinking I would just hop back on a plane in the morning. But nope! It was even more chaotic when I woke up. And now I have NO CELL SIGNAL AND NO WAY TO CONTACT MY FAMILY!

Meg is probably freaking out. Oh Meg, my sweet girl. I know she's a teenager and always saying she can take care of herself, but this is too much. And Mitchell! He's only 12. He's probably terrified....and Sam is HORRIBLE at explaining stuff. Good grief...when he tried to explain the tornado that went through a town 30 miles away...he just freaked the kids out more. I have to get home. I have to get home! I just have to stay calm. STAY CALM RESA!

Resa had been having the same conversation with herself for almost 100 miles. She couldn't shake the overwhelming sense of regret and despair careening from deep inside her chest. It welled up inside her like volcanic lava, threatening to overflow and wipe out any coherent thought she struggled to grasp at the moment. All she wanted to do was scream into the wind until she was hoarse, collapse into pieces, and weep through all the pain and anguish. NO! She had to keep moving no matter how excruciating it was. She could fall apart later. After she got home and wrapped her arms around the bodies of her precious babies. No, not bodies. Not BODIES! Why did she even think that word? What was wrong with her? They were fine. Meg and Mitchell were fine. Sam was there with them, and they were all alive, hunkering down, quarantining like the news said, doing exactly what they needed to do to survive until she got there. They were fine. Everything was fine. It had to be.

For the four hundredth time, Resa swiped her hand across her face, smoothed down her right eyebrow and rubbed her temple. Sam always used to tell her she was going to lose an eyebrow that way, but she barely noticed any more. And besides, eyebrows were the least of her worries now that the whole world was falling apart. She would shave her eyebrows…heck! She would shave her whole head if it would make her more aerodynamic and let her move faster. She'd always heard if March came in like a lion, it would go out like a lamb. But this month came in like a DRAGON and there was no gentle end in sight! Right now she just needed this tank of gas to last until she could find an open gas station or place with another car.

Resa glanced at her phone on the seat beside her. One puny little bar taunted her from the screen. Still not enough signal to send a text or an email. Not even one more bar to let her tell her family everything was going to be ok, and she was coming home as fast as she could manage. This entire LA trip had been a mistake. Well, it wasn't a mistake at first, but now all she could do was kick herself for leaving when she did. But like everyone else, no one had thought K-Pox was serious. It was something happening in other countries, not in the U.S. It was exaggerated, right? Never in the history of EVER, would anyone have believed this reality. It was like some surreal Hollywood movie.

Resa sighed out loud. It didn't matter. It didn't matter what they had believed or what had happened in the past month. K-Pox WAS happening, and people were getting sick and dying. The survivors were either going into hiding or having a corruption field day, robbing and looting and being overall idiots. But who cared about them! Her only focus now was to get home.

Resa's thoughts wandered as she looked out over the horizon. After her restless night at the airport, she had awakened to the sounds of desperation. People were crying and yelling at any airline worker they could find. All flights had been canceled. Permanently. She had quickly gathered her belongings and only stopped at an ATM for cash on the way to the rental cars. She checked the family account balance and saw charges to the local Sav-More Foods. The recent activity made her feel better somehow. If they were shopping, they were alive and well. She hoped they saw her cash withdrawal as a relief too. She would try to send any message to her family that told them she was alive.

The car rental counters had been almost deserted except for one lone attendant at the last place open. She had stood in line behind a single man and an elderly couple waiting in front of her. Her cell phone service was completely dead in the basement of the airport, but she thought she would have another chance to call once she got on the road.

The man ahead of them in line had walked away with a key in his hand, which Resa thought was a good sign. When it was the couple's turn, the woman had stood off to the side while her husband stepped up to talk with the attendant. The woman had offered Resa an orange to eat while they waited, and she made small talk as if the world wasn't falling apart around them. It had been nice to be distracted, if only for a few minutes. The woman introduced herself as Isla. She and her husband, Alec, had been in California on vacation and now they were traveling home to Arizona. They'd been on a hiking and fishing retreat in the national park and had completely disconnected from the world for the last couple of

14

weeks. Isla said they had quite the shock when they emerged from their vacation cocoon! Isla told Resa about her daughters and their families, including all the names and ages of their grandkids. Resa had smiled at how chatty this woman was, even in a crisis. Resa's mom had been that way too and while it felt annoying when Resa was a teenager, the familiarity of it had been surprisingly comforting to her now.

Alec finished at the counter and walked over as Isla smiled at him. They moved to the side as Resa stepped up to the counter. The weary attendant looked at her with sad and regretful eyes.

"I am so sorry ma'am, but we don't have any more cars to rent. We just gave out our last one and all the other companies are out too. We're closing. We've all been told to go home."

Resa's heart had tumbled to the floor and shattered in despair. She felt her control slipping away as she frantically asked if there were any other options, maybe a bus or a train or a crop duster, anything! But there was nothing.

Resa had taken a deep shaky breath and collapsed on the chairs in the waiting area. As she took a long drink from her water bottle and considered what to do next, she heard a voice calling her name.

"We overheard what the young man told you," Isla had said. "We were the ones who got the last car. But we don't really need it and we'd like you to take it instead."

"But how are you going to get home?" Resa had asked, confused.

"We have a car we drove at the beginning of our vacation and it made it here just fine," Alec explained. "But the check engine light came on this morning and we weren't sure if it would be safe to drive the rest of the way, especially since we were worried about gas stations being closed and who knows what's going on in-between. Our daughters wanted us to get a rental. But you're trying to get home to your kids and you have much farther to go, so we want you to have it. We'll be just fine with our old Buick. It's taken care of us so far!"

"And besides," Isla added, "our daughters are only a couple of hours away and will come and get us if anything happens."

"Good thing we have our CB in the car. It used to be a fun conversation piece, but it may just come in handy again. And people think old fogies hanging on to their vintage stuff is just sentimental. We'll show them," Alec winked.

Resa was stunned by their generosity. She was a complete stranger and at their age, they would be in much more danger if their car broke down, right? Well, maybe. They'd just been on a hiking trip by themselves. But still. Resa started to protest.

"We insist dear," Isla had dropped the keys into Resa's hand.

"Let me draw you a map to our vacation house in Colorado in case you're headed that way. It's kind of out in the middle of nowhere, but it should be a good place to stop and rest if you need it. Sorry I'm not a better artist! Gardening is more my preference." Isla had smiled and patted Resa's hand.

"Thank you so much. I don't know how to thank you." Resa's words had been shaky and broken and she wiped away a stray tear which had escaped down her cheek.

"We'll be praying for you the whole time," Isla had said.

Resa didn't have the heart to tell them she was not a praying woman. She had given it up years ago when God seemed to turn a deaf ear to her pain. But she would take any help she could, spiritual or otherwise, to get home quickly right now.

Resa had given Isla a firm hug. After losing her parents, she imagined this is what it would have been like if her mother was still here. Someone to look out for her while she worked so hard to take care of everyone else.

When they stepped apart Isla had said, "If you do end up at the vacation house, don't forget our names as the code to get in."

Resa wasn't quite sure what Isla meant, but she knew she was grateful and anxious to get going.

"I'll never forget you as long as I live," Resa answered firmly.

"Let's hope that's still a long while yet," Alec replied as he gave her arm a squeeze. Resa nodded one last time and grabbed her bags as the whoosh of the doors led her outside into the sticky heat of the sun.

16

When she had driven away from San Bernardino, the bells on the college campus had been ringing and ringing. She had heard on the radio they were ringing bells for the death tolls, but she couldn't believe it was so many. It had to be a mistake. What an eerie sound…hollow, echoing tolls...reverberating through a town buzzing with the energy of frightened people hiding or trying to escape.

Resa had barely noticed the buildings as she whizzed by on her way out of town. There was very little traffic, and she flew through more than a few stop signs. She stopped for gas in Barstow at the outlet mall. The deserted pumps were still working despite the stores being abandoned by employees. The sounds of yelling and wheels whirring across pavement drew her attention away from the gas tank. A group of skateboarders were hanging out and doing tricks down the deserted walking path. She had wanted to scream at them. The whole world was falling apart! Go home to your families! Didn't they know what was happening?

Resa blinked rapidly, refocusing her eyes on the road ahead of her and away from the memories of her panicked departure. Had that only been yesterday? The gray cement cut like a flat sword across the landscape and the yellow line stretched far into the horizon. She gripped the wheel harder, her knuckles turning white. The carefree attitudes of the teenagers and the tender way Isla and Alec had been together made Theresa wistful, sad, and honestly, fiercely angry.

While Sam's job helped with bills, his decision to spend more time at the office instead of home created even more distance in a marriage which was already strained and painful. Resa shook her head. Too much pain to bear right now. Feeling like her life had been flipped on its side again was causing all those same feelings of panic, fear, and desperation to bubble up, but she had to shove them down. Waaaay down.

Resa intentionally shifted her thoughts to picturing her kids. Meg's quiet smile. Mitchell's loud energy. How were they doing? WHAT were they doing? Had the schools shut down? They were saying on the radio everything was closing to try to control the spread of the virus. Was Mitchell staying out of trouble if he couldn't see his friends? Was Meg angry at her for leaving and not making it back? Were they all terrified? The constant unknowns were enough to eat her alive from the inside if she let them.

The green mile marker whizzed by on the side of the road. One mile at a time, one mile at a time. Resa could almost hear the miles ticking by one after another...tick, tick...*clank*... Wait! What was THAT sound?? Resa jerked her eyes from the road to the dashboard where ugly red and yellow lights were flashing on and off on the display.

"What the. . ??" she sputtered as yet another light started to glow.

"No, no, no, NO! NO!" Resa protested loudly at the car's dashboard.

She frantically looked at the sign zooming up on the side of the road.

Needles, AZ
10 miles

"Ten more miles! Ten! Then I can find a repair shop or get another car, or something. Come on! Just ten more!" Resa's heart began to hammer. This couldn't be happening. All she needed was this car to last the four days it would take to get home. Four days!!! And now she was pleading for ten miles.

"Comeoncomeoncomeon...COME ON!"

Resa fought against the panic which dug its icy claws into her back. She pressed down on the gas pedal to push the car faster. Her brain told her to slow down, but the terror of being stranded hijacked all rational thought. The faster she could get to Needles, the faster she could get this all sorted out.

But the car did not respond to her pleas. Thin gray smoke started to show up in wisps in her rear view mirror. The clanking from under the hood kept getting louder. It was almost as if the engine itself had started to knock against the frame of the car.

Needles, AZ
8 miles

"Come on, Come on!" Resa felt like she was pushing the car forward by sheer will, but it wasn't enough. Suddenly the car started to jerk and jolt, like the controls had been taken away from her. Even though her foot pushed the pedal to the floor, the speed was dropping. 80 mph to 65 mph to 40…All she could do was hold on to the steering wheel as smoke billowed over the hood. Tears threatened as Resa realized no matter how much she willed it to be different, this car was a goner. Determined to cover as much ground as possible, she steered until the car was slowly sputtering and gasping for its last breath. It finally crawled to a stop on the side of the road. All the years of watching movies where cars exploded propelled Resa out of the car. She grabbed her bags and jogged quickly up the road until her heavy breathing caused her to flop her suitcase on the ground and collapse into a seated position on top of it.

Resa sat in shocked and horrified silence. Her plans lay destroyed and shattered, AGAIN! Resa pulled in one shaky breath after another until she felt her heart slightly settle back into a semi-normal rhythm. She glanced back at the smoking car, but it remained intact. Apparently it wasn't going to blow up after all. She couldn't believe her luck. This was the car that Isla and Alec had rented because they thought theirs was going to break down and look where she had ended up!

"Well. I guess it's me and you, legs."

She closed her eyes and did what she had always done when she felt off balance or chaos was threatening to overtake her…she pictured home. Meg would be studying and video chatting with Jenna, but she'd start rolling her eyes at Resa's silly dancing in the background. Mitchell would be laughing at something that happened with his friends and he would not be able to tell her the story without cracking up. Sam would walk through the door and have flowers for her like when they were first married. Resa slowly breathed in and out.

"You can do this," she said out loud. Resa slowly stood up, dusted herself off, and reached for her suitcase handle.

Chapter 3

March - Arizona

Well, perhaps following birds wasn't such a great idea, Tim thought. He slowed the car down as he watched the birds land on the scrabbly overgrown lawn only two blocks from his house. He wasn't really sure why he thought he'd follow birds anyway. In those few short blocks he'd decided he would head north. After spending his entire life in southwest Arizona, he wanted to go to the total opposite end of the country so he was going to head northeast. He was going to Maine.

He'd been mulling the idea around for the last several days, and the more he thought about it, the more he liked it. And then he saw the birds heading north (well, sort of north) it had confirmed his decision. But when they landed on the neighborhood lawn he knew following birds was a stupid idea. A road atlas was much better. He pulled it out and looked at the nationwide map. If he took the back highways he could get to Maine in a week or so. If...he could get gas the whole way and if his car didn't break down.

He waved goodbye to the birds as he pulled back onto the road. He decided he'd stay off the main roads and go around big cities. He didn't want to run into violent people with weapons. While he knew how to use his guns, he didn't want to risk his life for Ramen noodles or the last roll of toilet paper.

Thank goodness they'd had enough toilet paper. Earlier they'd stockpiled an ample stash of paper towels and Kleenex and napkins, so it wasn't an issue at the moment, but it would be if things didn't change. Tim thought it was funny how there was never a run on paper plates or vitamins even though they got used a lot too. It was like the jokes about people running to the stores for bread, milk, and toilet paper when a storm was coming. Only this time it was for K-Pox.

Maine would be fun. He'd always wanted to be snowed in somewhere. That was another reason to go there. Maine had snow in the winter. Oh, and Maine had moose, meese, mooses; there should be a better plural for moose than "moose." It was one funny looking animal and he really wanted to see a moose, a real one. He'd seen them on TV, but TV didn't count. He'd watched all those North State Law shows a bunch of times. Being a game warden was a cool job. He'd like to do that someday. But he guessed the job wouldn't be around anymore. Probably not enough people breaking the laws to need police. Perhaps not enough people period! But maybe eventually. He could always hope. Not hope for law breakers, just for the job of being a warden and watching over the animals.

Tim refocused on the road and his thoughts wandered back to the car. He'd been driving and not really paying attention to what he was doing. Perhaps he'd better focus and keep his mind on driving. It was too easy to daydream with so little traffic. His parents and his teachers were always on him about paying attention to what he was doing. He couldn't help it if he had lots of interesting things to think about. Way more interesting than schoolwork or remembering to do chores. But right now he did need to remember where he was and how he was going to get to Maine. He pulled into a parking lot and looked at the map again. He decided to head to Flagstaff and noted the highways he'd take to get there. He'd go around the western side of Phoenix and stay on the small highways.

As he pulled back on the road he looked again at the gas gauge. He wasn't sure he'd have enough gas to get to Flagstaff. He never used to pay attention to how much gas it took to get anywhere. When he needed gas he just bought more or asked to borrow his parents' car. Gas had always just been there. And now it wasn't. He figured he'd head to Flagstaff and then look for another car with both keys and gas. He would hate to leave his car behind though.

He viewed the scenery as he drove. Long flat stretches of land slowly turned mountainous as he headed north. Many of the heat loving plants would be in bloom soon. He was leaving Arizona during his favorite time of year, the desert blooming with flowers and the temperature only about 80 or so. He really hated summer. So much heat for so long. And he did not even want to think about living in his house without air conditioning. It'd be unbearable. 100 degree temperatures with no AC. No way. Tim was already hot in his car and according to his dash thermometer it was only

70 degrees outside. Even though the sweat was dripping down his face he didn't turn on the car AC as it would take away from his gas mileage. He opened all the windows and let the air blow through. The dry desert air smelled fresh and clean. No truck or car exhaust.

Tim slipped back into planning what he'd do in Maine and how he'd get food and if and when he'd go hunting there. He returned to reality and wondered where he was. He hadn't really been paying attention to the road signs. He was so used to his GPS telling him when and where to turn, he just drove without thinking, but now his phone wasn't working and no GPS. He saw a road sign that didn't make sense and pulled the car over to the side of the road and got out his road atlas. Where exactly was he? He'd gone through Wickenburg and then was supposed to take Hwy 89 north. He wanted to go around Prescott, but he missed a turn somewhere and was heading northwest instead of northeast.

"AAAAA!" Tim yelled. "I can't believe I just did that! I'm such an idiot. Now what am I going to do? Besides talk to myself!"

He was so mad at himself. Why did he daydream so much? Couldn't he just pay attention? Even when it was important! Like gas wouldn't last forever and here he goes and gets himself lost. He just couldn't afford to be stupid! He knew he had better sense. He had to get better.

He continued to fume and tried to come up with a plan. He looked at his watch. It was almost noon. Might as well have lunch and figure it out while eating. He saw a small country store up ahead on the right and decided to eat there. He slowly pulled off the road and looked carefully around as he drove behind the store to hide the car. If someone was going to drive by, he didn't want them to see him. Though he'd been driving all morning and had seen no one, it didn't mean there weren't more people. After all, he was still here. He moved his hand to his pistol beside him on the car seat just in case.

After waiting a few minutes to make sure no one was going to come out and shoot him, Tim got out and looked around. A small milk crate had been thrown out of the back of the store. It would make a good chair. He set the crate against the wall of the store in the little shade he could find. He walked back to the car and pulled out his crackers, tuna, and can opener. He was glad he liked tuna and wasn't allergic to peanut butter. They were his main meals now. He'd go into the building after he ate and see if there was anything left he could use. But right now he was going to eat. He was starving. He sat on the crate crunching on his crackers and tuna and thought about his friend Jeromy. He had hated tuna. Tim wondered what Jeromy was eating now.

He smiled as he remembered his friends. He wondered what had happened to them. He missed them so much. All the goofy stuff they did. All the video games they'd played, movies they'd watched, cars they'd wanted to own someday, girls they'd liked or thought were cute. He really missed having someone to hang out with, someone to talk to. It was so lonely being by yourself. He used to like shutting himself up in his bedroom to be away from his parents and playing hours and hours of online video games with his friends. But now he'd give anything to be able to talk to Mom and Dad. To his friends. To anyone friendly. Especially to his parents. But he pushed the thought away. It hurt too much.

He remembered this old movie his parents had watched where some old guy had talked to a volleyball because there were no people around. Tim really didn't want to get to the point where he was going to be like some old guy and talk to a ball or a doll or anything weird.

Something cold touched his elbow. "AAAA!" Tim yelled sharply and dropped his tuna cracker. He thought of his gun on the front seat of his car and how it was too far to get to. He turned to see a mid-sized golden-haired dog who shoved his wet nose into Tim's elbow again, ate the dropped tuna cracker, and then rolled on his back to get his tummy petted. The dog squirmed and whined and tried to lick Tim's tuna scented hands and face as Tim reached down to pet him.

"Hey fella, where'd you come from? Are you hungry? Do you need someone to play with?"

The dog bounded up and ran in big circles around Tim, tail wagging and ears up. Tim didn't know much about dogs but he could tell this one was happy.

"How'd you get here? Why are you out here by yourself?" Do you want something to eat? I have tuna and peanut butter. I wonder if dogs like peanut butter. Do you like peanut butter? That's mostly what I have."

He laughed as the dog bounced around him and on him and then ran in more circles.

"Hey boy, let's go in the store and see if there's anything in there for you to eat."

The dog ran ahead and bolted into the store through the hole in the screen door. He obviously lived there. Tim opened the screen door and as his eyes got used to the dim light, he quickly scanned the area for the owner or any living body. Since the dog was bouncing all about, Tim doubted there was danger here. Or another person. Tim looked around more closely. Dog food bags were opened and the food strewn about on the floor. A large number of buckets had been filled with water though most of them were now empty. There was a little water left in one bucket. It was clear someone cared for the dog but had to leave him and wanted to provide him with everything he would need, for as long as they could.

"Poor boy! Did your folks have to leave you? Did they get sick? And you're all by yourself? Aw! Poor lil dude!"

"Lil dude" was still bounding around the store as though he wanted to show Tim all his things. This had been one of those small country stores which had a limited amount of items but a wide variety of things one might want but didn't want to drive into town to get. Like chips and candy or band-aids or a screwdriver. Whoever had owned this store had cleaned out the perishable goods so it didn't have the overwhelming stink of rotten food the last food stores he'd been to had. This store smelled a lot like dog. Tim searched the mostly empty shelves for what he and the dog might need.

He'd decided almost immediately he was taking the dog. There was no way he could possibly leave that happy, fluffy, bouncy dog by himself. Look how happy he was to see Tim. And Tim was so happy to see another living friendly soul he could almost cry.

The dog stuck close to Tim as he peered into the backs of shelves, under the cabinets, and behind the cash register. He gathered up a dog leash, food and water bowls, dog toys, some batteries for his lantern, ten bottles of fruit punch from back in the storeroom, three large bags of dog food which hadn't been opened, and some canned food for dogs and humans. He didn't have much room in his car for the new items, especially for the bags of dog food. Tim wasn't sure about taking a roll or two of poop bags. Do you pick up doggy poop when there are so few people around to step in it? He grabbed a couple of rolls, just in case.

Tim looked at the dog and the dog looked back at Tim, eyes bright and tail wagging furiously. Tim squatted down and held onto the dog in a big hug.

"Man, I'm so glad to see you. You know that? Hey, you wanna come with me, right?"

The dog wagged his tail so hard his whole body moved back and forth. Tim laughed as his face got slobbery swipes of a dog tongue.

"Ok. I think that's a yes. I'm going to have to trade some of my things for our new stuff. What shall we leave here?

Tim looked carefully through what he'd packed. He would keep his camping and hiking gear including the camp stove and fuel. Some items he really hated to leave. Like some of his parents' favorite things, things he'd have liked to have in his new house in Maine. His Dad had really liked his power tools, but they required electricity so he reluctantly left a drill and sander on a high shelf in the store. Next to the tools he left his mother's thick fluffy bath towels they only used for company and kept the thinner, more utilitarian towels. Though where he'd take a bath he didn't know. Then he looked at his big box of video games and sports card collections. He sighed. Having a dog would require him to have more space for dog stuff. And if he had to choose between dog food and the video games or sports cards (hoping there'd be some way of playing the games again and maybe he could download them if/when the electricity came back on) the choice was easy.

He stood in the center of the store and looked around one more time.

"I'm gonna leave a note for your people. If they come back they'll want to know what happened to you." He found a pencil, a slip of register paper, and some tape. On the paper he wrote,

"I have your dog. He is going with me to Maine. He wants to go with me cuz he's lonly. I'll take good care of him. I promise. Tim"

He taped it to the door of the near empty storage room.

"Ok buddy! I think that's it. Let's go to Maine!" Tim opened the passenger door and the dog jumped in, sat down, tail wagging, and waited for Tim to get in the driver's seat. Tim moved the gun out from under the dog's wiggling bottom. Just what he needed was for the dog to shoot one of them in a fit of happiness. He stuffed the pistol down beside the seat, ruffled the dog's ears, and started the car.

Tim turned back down the road in the direction he'd just come from and started looking for the turn-off he'd missed earlier. He was in a much better mood than when he had first pulled into the store lot. He looked at his happy, panting passenger and grinned.

"Hey buddy, I'm not going to have to talk to a ball! I can talk to you. But you have to have a name."

As he drove, he looked back and forth between the road and the dog, noting details about his new friend. Shortish golden-brown hair with long droopy ears and a sort of fluffy tail. He wasn't as big as a lab but bigger than a beagle. Those were about the only dogs he could reference as his friends had those breeds for pets. The dog stepped on Tim's lap and tried to lick his face. Tim pushed him back into the passenger's seat.

"Hey, you stay there. You can't jump on me when I'm driving!"

Tim pulled over, dug out the leash and fixed it so the dog was able to move around but not get into Tim's lap. And back on the road they went.

"So what's your name? You didn't have a name on your collar so I guess I can name you." He looked at the dog again and the dog pulled at the leash trying to reach Tim. "You're a crazy dog, man!"

This was a serious thing he was going to do, name his dog. He'd always wanted a dog. But his mother had told him if he wanted one, he would be the one to take it for walks twice a day and pick up the dog poop. *She* was not going to do it. A lot of moms did, but she would not. She asked him if he really wanted to be walking or exercising a dog in the Arizona summer heat? He knew himself well enough to know he'd promise to do it, but when it came right down to it, he knew he wouldn't. He loved his AC and hated the heat. So he gave up begging for a dog. But here he was, with a dog, and he'd have to take care of him properly. At least he was moving further north so he wouldn't have to walk in extreme heat. Extreme cold eventually instead. Well, he'd do it. It was worth it to have his first dog.

"You know what? You kinda look like that dog, Max, on The Grinch Stole Christmas. You're about the same color and you have floppy ears. You wanna be called Max?"

Max wagged his tail, panting and drooling.

Tim grinned, "I think I shoulda kept one of Mom's big fluffy towels for you to sit on. Oh well, too late. I guess we'll just use these old towels instead. Perhaps I can pick up something else later for you to sit on."

As he drove further north the temperature dropped to 61 degrees. Tim closed the windows of the car except Max's window so he could smell whatever it is that dogs smell, and Tim looked for a place to park for the evening. Being closer to Flagstaff there were more houses and stores and greater chance to run into people. He slowed down and looked carefully for a place where he might find more water and be hidden for the evening, and where he and Max could sleep in safety.

Tim felt a surge of happiness and a good bit of relief knowing he wouldn't be spending another night alone. He'd have a friend and a watchdog. And he'd be able to relax better. Perhaps he should keep the leash on Max while they slept so he wouldn't wander off and get lost. Or leave. Tim had his new friend now and didn't want to lose him. He looked at Max.

"You don't want to leave do you? You want to stay with me, right?" Max wagged his tail.

"Good! Flagstaff tomorrow. And we'll find a grocery store and get us some food."

He found a parking lot next to a grassy patch with trees that looked like a good place to make camp for the night and pulled in. He walked Max on his leash and put out bowls with kibble and water. Tim grinned as he watched Max wolf down his supper. He then opened cans for his own supper, giving bits to Max as he ate.

The sun was sinking lower in the sky and before it got dark, Tim prepared for the night. He didn't want to spend the night in his car as he was too tall to get comfortable in the front seat, and the back seat was packed with stuff. He got out his sleeping bag and unrolled it in the grass next to the car. He put Max on a long chain and attached it to the car's rear-view mirror so he could sleep next to Tim. Max snuggled up next to him. Tim felt better now than he had in weeks. Not so alone. He didn't think he'd mind this new adventure as long as he had his new friend to adventure with. Having a companion was important. They both fell quickly and deeply asleep under the bright Arizona stars.

Chapter 4

March - California to Arizona

Resa trudged the eight miles to Needles. She hoped yet feared she would see cars on the road. She desperately wanted a ride but was terrified of who might show up. Didn't really matter, she hadn't seen any traffic in hours.

The first three miles went by steadily. It was the last five miles of heat, however, that threatened to melt her body into the pavement. Her shoulders felt bruised from her backpack and her hand cramped from gripping the suitcase handle as it rolled along behind her. It clanged into the back of her numb legs and twisted on its wheels when it hit a pothole. Anger and frustration surged through her every time she had to stop and readjust. She was ready to explode when the town sign finally loomed up ahead. Resa sighed deeply. She passed a closed gas station and then a restaurant with skull and crossbones signs in the windows. It was one thing to hear about those awful K-Pox signs on the radio, but it was completely different to see so many. The hollow eyes gaped at Resa. There was only death behind them. Resa shuddered and hurried away. She was still alive, for now.

The back of her neck tingled as she felt an unnatural stillness to the town. The sound of the plastic suitcase wheels skating across the pavement, the squeak of her sneakers, and panting of her breath were the only sounds she heard. There were no signs of people, no sounds of cars in the distance. Her relief at arriving was quickly replaced with bone-deep weariness and anxiety about where she would rest for the night.

Ahead there were two hotels. Surely one would be open. The entry door of the first hotel didn't budge. Resa peered in through the glass and saw a dark, deserted lobby. Birds crowed at her from the carport roof as she walked to the second hotel. Resa gasped when she saw the doors had been smashed and the lobby looted and destroyed. Discarded sugar packets and plastic coffee stirrers lay on the ground like breadcrumbs leading away from the carnage. The tingling in the back of her neck spread down her spine. She needed to get somewhere safe. In the distance she saw a sign for another motel and crossed her fingers.

The Sunset Motel was well past its prime, but thankfully, the front door swung open easily. Her already frayed emotions turned to panic as an overweight, greasy man leered at her from behind the front desk. Maybe her hopes had been too lofty.

"Do you have rooms still available... for me and my brothers waiting outside?" Resa stood straighter to keep the shakiness out of her voice. The last thing she needed was for him to think she was alone and vulnerable.

"One room. No power. Two hundred cash," he grunted. Resa dug the money out of her purse and was cautious when he had handed her a key card. She saw the black handle of a pistol sticking out of his waistband and immediately stepped back from the desk. Resa figured he was charging her twice what the room should cost, but she desperately needed a shower and a place to recover behind a locked door. On a table by the desk she noticed local brochures and accordion-folded U.S. maps. She looked back at the man who was busily opening another package of coconut covered snowballs and slipped one of the maps into her waistband. Resa left the office to find her room and locked the door behind her.

She immediately pulled out her cell phone to check her signal. Still only one tiny bar. Resa growled when the obnoxious computer voice told her it was not able to complete her call. No one had responded to her messages or emails, but she kept trying.

After sending another text message she stood with her hands on her hips and surveyed the room. There was no way she was trusting that flimsy lock to keep out unwanted visitors. Her eyes landed on a saggy dresser leaning against the wall. Her muscles strained, but she was able to shove the dresser securely against the door. Better. Thank you cardio dance classes, she thought. Resa checked her phone again. Nothing. She hoped with all her heart her messages had gotten through. She was coming guys!

Resa plodded to the bathroom and turned on the shower. She shivered as the tepid water washed away the grime from the airport and the long, dusty road. She threw on pajamas then toweled off her damp hair as she spread out the U.S. map on the bed to look for alternate routes, she might need to take to get home. She also marked Durango, Colorado, for Isla and Alec's vacation house. Resa couldn't imagine wanting to stop there too long, but it might be a safe haven should she need it. Feeling somewhat accomplished with her plan, Resa threw back the covers, curled up on her side, and wept silent tears into the scratchy pillow as she drifted off to sleep.

In the wee hours of the morning, Resa was jolted awake by the sounds of angry screaming outside. She sat up in a panic then crept over to the space below the windowsill and peeked out the side of the shabby curtain, making sure she didn't draw attention to her room.

In the parking lot a man and woman were standing next to a truck, forcing open its door. Glass glistened on the asphalt from the broken window. The truck must have belonged to the greasy hotel owner because he was yelling at them to back up and pointing his black handled pistol at them. The man near the truck raised his gun and screamed it was either the truck or his life. Resa gasped. The woman crept around to the tailgate, climbed up into the truck bed, and aimed her shotgun at the owner. Resa crouched lower and watched as the yelling became more intense. The owner fired, the sound of the blast ricocheting off the walls. The man by the truck ducked, but the woman coolly fired directly into the owner's chest. Horrified, Resa watched his blood splatter on the wall behind him and his body hit the pavement with a dull thud. The man yelled at the woman to get in the truck and drive. He opened the door and jumped in the passenger's seat. The truck's taillights gleamed menacingly as they sped away into the night.

Shaking, Resa sat and watched for any movement from the owner who lay motionless on the ground. Tears streamed slowly down her face, but she was too frozen with fear to wipe them away or to move away from the window. Resa knew the man must be dead, but she couldn't believe it happened. No one deserved to die like that.

Resa spent the rest of the night on the floor unable to move, her arms clenched around her tucked up legs. She dozed off when her weary body could no longer stay alert. When the sun woke her the next morning, Resa stiffly uncurled. Her back ached, her head throbbed, and her stomach growled. The last thing she'd eaten was the orange Isla had given her at the airport. Resa rummaged through her backpack, found a granola bar which she ate hungrily before turning on the shower again, and tried to muster up the energy it would take to start her journey again today. When she stepped out of the shower and looked in the mirror, she didn't recognize the woman with gaunt cheeks and dark circles under her eyes looking back at her.

"It's not a beauty contest, Resa," she muttered. She filled her water bottle and quietly surveyed the contents of her open suitcase. She'd need to lighten her load and keep moving as fast as possible. It was a survival show now.

She'd leave behind her work clothes. She could always use moisturizer and tinted sunscreen, right? The cheap mascara was out though. Didn't need to rub that out of her eyes for the next week, she thought. Resa grabbed her few remaining clothes and packed them in her backpack. She tucked the maps in the front pocket along with the half sheet of paper Isla had given her. Resa's plan was to sneak into the main office to locate information on a local car rental. She shuddered when she realized it would take her past the corpse of the murdered owner. Steeling herself against the gruesome sight, she tucked her hair up under her favorite ball cap, hiked the backpack up on her shoulders, opened her door quietly, and ran for the lobby.

Resa almost tripped over the owner's pistol which had skidded across the sidewalk. Luckily he'd walked away from the front doors so his body didn't block the entry. Resa couldn't help but look down at his blue and gray bloated face and her stomach churned as his hazy eyes stared back at her. Ants and flies were beginning to swarm around the gaping hole in his chest. She grimaced, shook her head, and ran inside, the grisly image imprinted on the inside of her eyelids.

Resa rifled through pamphlets on the side table then spotted a phonebook in the corner. She flipped through the yellow pages and ripped out listings for car rental places in the neighboring town of Kingman. On her way past the counter, Resa saw a stack of towels on the floor. She knew it wasn't exactly a white sheet, but she felt guilty leaving the man's body completely out in the open. She reached for the towels and a twenty-dollar bill caught her attention. Its crumpled corner was sticking out of the drawer where the owner stuffed her cash last night. She hesitated but knew money could come in handy. Resa slowly opened the drawer and discovered a box of bullets on top of loose cash. She moved the bullets to the side, pulled out twenties totaling the exact amount she'd paid for her room, and quickly shoved the money in her pocket. No doubt the bullets were for the pistol now lying in the parking lot.

Resa wasn't afraid of guns. She'd grown up in a small town and gone hunting numerous times. Resa paused only a second then tucked the towels under her arm, grabbed the bullets, and headed outside to pick up the pistol. This world had become a place she no longer recognized, and she couldn't take any chances.

34

She draped the towels over the man's robust frame. At least his face was hidden from view and it might stave off the bigger animals for a little while.

"Rest in peace," Resa whispered. Then she took off in a dead run back towards Route 66, each step taking her further away from the nightmare she left in her wake. Resa ran until her lungs burned and the buildings looked shabbier. She realized most of the buildings along this stretch of road had been empty long before K-Pox. They were past sentinels of a brighter, more prosperous time. On the horizon, she made out a small blue circle that looked like a familiar gas station sign. She started to walk and jog, the sign growing bigger as the sun got hotter. Resa almost cheered with joy when she saw the gas station was still open. Loud generators dotted the outside parking lot and seemed to be powering some of the gas pumps. There were a few people milling around and filling up their cars. Resa opened the door to the small store and saw two small fans blowing the thick air around in heavy clouds of heat. Suddenly her thirst and hunger overwhelmed her.

Behind the counter was a small man with skin wrinkled from years of sun and desert wind.

"Water?" she asked. He directed her towards the dark coolers that were warm, but still organized. She paid for four large bottles of water and whatever snacks might sustain her until she reached the next town. As she took her change, the outside door thudded open and a tall woman walked in holding a very energetic toddler by the hand.

"Can you help me?" Resa asked the man at the counter. She pulled the yellow pages out of her pocket and pointed to the car rental listings.

"I'm desperate to get home. Would any of these places have a car I could rent or buy?" Resa was willing to promise someone a small fortune to have a car that worked.

"Everyone's gone," the man said matter of factly.

Resa felt her resolve start to slip.

"Is there anything else? A train? A bicycle shop? Anything, AnyONE who could help me? Please, I *need* to get home to my family. My kids…I'm their mother, you know? I need to be there and I have to go all the way across the country." Resa completely lost it. Tears poured down her cheeks and her voice had become a high pitched, broken jumble of syllables and panicked words. "Please. There has to be someone, something, somewhere!"

She closed her eyes and took a deep breath. She rubbed her hands over her face and tried to stop her body from trembling. She knew she'd walk home if she had to, but that could take months!

"Excuse me, miss?" A gentle voice piped up behind her. Resa turned her head and saw the woman standing behind her with the toddler, now happily chewing on a granola bar.

"Where're you headed?" the woman asked.

Resa tripped over her words, trying to re-organize her thoughts.

"I'm trying to get home to my family. On the east coast. Laurel, Pennsylvania. But I'll go anywhere that takes me closer east. Anywhere. But my family is in Laurel…" Resa's voice cracked as her last words trailed off.

"Could you wait just a moment?" The woman handed cash to the man behind the counter and walked outside. The toddler let out a whoop of glee when she let go of his hand so he could run across the parking lot to a blonde woman. Resa watched the two women talking while they stood by the gas pump and gestured towards the store. The blonde woman seemed to nod in agreement. Then the tall woman who'd told Resa to wait, walked quickly back inside and gestured for Resa to join them outside.

"I'm Madison and this is my wife, Casey," she said, walking Resa over to the car. We live in Dolan Springs, which is northeast of here. We can't take you far because we're trying to get home ourselves, but we'd be happy to take you as far as Kingman. There might be a few car rental places still open. That ok with you?" Madison asked as she stopped next to the hood of the car.

"If you don't mind riding in the back with Mr. Fussy, who is bound to whine at you for most of the ride," said Casey dryly. "This is Tommy by the way," she said, nodding her head and grinning at the boy doing ninja kicks into the garbage can.

"I'm Resa, and I would be so incredibly grateful, thank you." Resa's shoulders dropped with relief as she watched Madison move items from the back seat to the trunk.

"You can put your pack anywhere it fits," Madison told her before sliding into the passenger seat. Resa tucked her backpack awkwardly at her feet.

"You're not a bloodthirsty vampire, are you?" Casey said smilingly, closing the driver's door and looking at her in the rear-view mirror. Madison gave her a quick side look and nudged her with her elbow.

"Not today," Resa attempted a half smile, "Just a hot mess."

"Aren't we all, right now," Casey replied solemnly. Shortly into the trip, Resa realized they weren't kidding about Tommy whimpering.

"He doesn't like being strapped in," Madison explained over Tommy's protests. The hour-long trip didn't give much opportunity for conversation. To distract Tommy from fighting with his carseat straps Resa continually plopped snacks on Tommy's tray.

"Did you have a list of places in Kingman?" Casey asked over Tommy's muffled wails. He was currently trying to stuff as many goldfish in his mouth as possible.

"Looks like there's one called Hanson's Travel and Car Rental off Main Street. Would it be the easiest to find?" Resa said, trying to read the crinkled yellow pages while also bouncing a fluffy rabbit toy across Tommy's tray. She was rewarded with a cracker-stuffed laugh.

Once in town, Casey found the rental place without difficulty. It was a small box-shaped building off the main drag with painted red bricks and a striped awning.

"We'll wait and make sure it's open," Madison said. Resa wrestled her legs and her bag out of the back seat and walked to the front door.

Once the door opened, she waved goodbye to Madison and Casey and then stood in yet another lobby of another place to beg for help. As she recounted the events of the past few days to the owners, she figured Darcy and Drew Hanson must think she was crazy. Who would help a half crazed woman who could barely speak without tearing up, apologizing, or shaking violently? But just at the moment when Resa began to apologize again, Darcy gently signaled Resa to stop.

"We have one car left and we want you to take it. No charge. Just go ahead and take it as far as you can."

"What do you mean?" Resa asked, shocked. "I can pay the one-way rental fee or whatever price you think is fair."

"No, No. Systems are down, so I can't enter your information and money doesn't seem to matter anymore. And honestly, I'm not sure how far you're going to get, but I want you to be able to try." Darcy murmured something to her husband before he slipped out the back door. Then she turned to a tall lanky teenager who'd been standing halfway in the doorway to the kitchen area and whispered something to him too before he disappeared from sight.

"The radio said gas stations are closed because they're out of gas and a lot of places have no electricity or no one left working. So, please take the car. My husband will fill up an extra gas can for you. It'll be in the trunk," Darcy explained.

The distant sound of a car engine grew louder as Resa processed the mix of experiences she'd had in the last two days. With the crunch of tires, a light blue car pulled up and Drew got out of the driver's seat. The bell above the door jingled as he strode inside.

"It's all gassed up and ready to go. You should be able to get to Flagstaff. There might be stores there with supplies still. Just be careful and don't trust anyone. We heard there's riots in the bigger cities…. like hell has come to earth early." Drew handed Resa the keys and nodded grimly.

"Daniel got you a basket of food to take along too." Darcy took the small cloth-covered basket her son handed her as he came back through the doorway and slid it across the counter.

"It's a couple sandwiches, some fruit, and a can opener," Daniel said in a deep voice. "I hope you like canned peaches."

"We know it's not much, but it's something. I'm sorry we can't share more," Darcy added.

"I...I... don't know what to say," Resa stuttered, flustered once again by the generosity of strangers. She felt like all she had done was stutter and sputter today. Horrible flashbacks of the motel seeped into her thoughts, but she tried to focus on the kindness and generosity in front of her. Maybe those were things even the darkest horrors couldn't destroy.

Darcy told her about a sporting goods and camping store in Flagstaff.

"Outdoor Explore is the place you'll want to stop and stock up on supplies."

"If they have any left," Daniel muttered quietly beside her.

Resa managed a nod and another quick thank you before she was back outside and sliding into the driver's side of her new miracle. She pulled out her maps, smoothed them onto the seat beside her and pulled the gearshift down to drive. She let out a huge exhale when she finally watched the 'Thanks For Visiting Kingman' sign slowly fade away.

The road was open and wide, bordered by layered rock, scraggly brush and cacti, and mountains rising far into the distance. It was early afternoon when she left, and she was determined to get in a few hours of driving before dark. She was worried about missing turns or not seeing street signs after dusk. The last thing she needed was to get lost.

Resa pulled over to the side of the road when her stomach started to growl again and reminded her that survival included eating. She had to have strength for the journey ahead. She stretched her legs and ate a sandwich from the basket. As she walked back and forth, drinking water and trying to calculate how many more hours she'd be on the road, a caravan of military vehicles appeared over the slope of the hill. The ground trembled and Resa was surprised to see the trucks fitted with large guns and the flatbeds stacked with large crates. Where were those trucks headed? One of the drivers, face completely obscured by helmet and dark sunglasses, turned towards where Resa stood. They raised a hand in a small salute and Resa couldn't help but raise a hand to wave back. Godspeed, she thought, may your journey bring peace. Resa hurried back to her car, anxious to get back on the road.

Resa drove a few more hours before she got sleepy and pulled over in a secluded location to rest for the night. She curled up on her side in the back seat and drifted into a fitful sleep. At first light, Resa woke, walked out the kinks in her neck and shoulders by taking laps around the car, and got back on the road. Maybe at this pace, I'll be home by St. Patrick's Day, which is about a week or so away right? Resa asked herself. She felt like time was slipping through her fingers.

Once the sun hit mid-morning, she started seeing signs for Flagstaff. Thank goodness. There were also large billboards for Outdoor Explore. Resa thought of the military caravan and her palms started to sweat thinking of how desperate times encouraged desperate behavior. She tried not to worry about who might be lurking at the stores.

Suddenly she saw overturned cars on the road ahead. A few cars were smashed into each other and one had wisps of smoke still rising from its blackened frame. Trash littered the pavement and shards of glass reflected the afternoon sun. Resa pressed down harder on the gas and hoped the glass wouldn't give her a flat tire.

"Oh please, oh please, oh please," Resa whispered as she drove past the cars and further on past yawning holes in buildings which used to be front doors and windows. The destruction seemed to lessen as she drove towards the northeast side of town and could see signs for Outdoor Explore looming in the distance. However, she decided to stop at the small grocery store she saw ahead on the right.

Might as well be brave in this smaller place first, Resa thought. And it would be quicker. She'd already made a short list in her head.

Resa slowly pulled into one of the employee spots on the side of Howard's Fresh Market, looked around for anything suspicious, and then dumped out her backpack so she could fill it with groceries. No need to carry everything around all at once. Resa reached in the side zipper pocket and her hand hit the butt of the pistol she'd taken from the motel. She should get used to carrying it. A world in chaos was a scary one.

Resa shut and locked the car door and scanned the deserted parking lot. The front doors of the store were cracked, but not shattered. Cautiously, she pulled the door open and stepped inside. The messy store smelled like rotten food, but it looked like there were still items here and there on the shelves.

Resa walked towards the aisles of non-perishables. She picked up a can of green beans then noticed the sign for canned fruit was another aisle over. She turned into the next aisle when a clatter of boxes and a patter of feet startled her. She looked up and down the aisle but couldn't find the source of the noise. It sounded like something small but fast running towards her. She'd been too busy worrying about scary people to even think about scary animals! What if it was a rabid racoon or something bigger? Resa ducked down, backing up to look for something she could use as a weapon. She felt the weight of the pistol in her backpack and took off one shoulder strap so she could easily access the gun in the side zippered pocket.

And of course, she'd turned into the paper goods aisle! The shelves were almost bare, but maybe there were paper plates she could throw as a distraction. There were a few boxes of plastic storage bags and a couple misplaced boxes of crackers. Well, Toasty Crackers sure weren't going to scare anyone. Resa was questioning whether she should make a run for it. Suddenly, a wet nose hit the back of her leg and Resa yelped as she stared in shock at the friendly brown eyes gazing back into hers. Resa exhaled, relieved.

"Well, hello there!" Resa exclaimed. "Where did you come from?" The wiggling body of the waggling dog almost bounced. She stretched out her fingers for him to smell when a shadow moved off to her side. Resa straightened too quickly and had to blink rapidly to clear away the black circles swimming at the edges of her vision. She found herself staring at the lanky form of a hesitant looking young man. Her mouth ran dry as she watched him slowly reach to his side and place his hand on a gun.

Chapter 5

March - Arizona

Tim stood stock still in the grocery store aisle, hand resting on his pistol in its holster. What should he do? Who was this woman? And where had she come from? He had purposely waited in the parking lot to see if anyone was around, pistol at the ready, and hadn't seen anyone. And now there was this person. He thought he'd be alone. He was supposed to be alone. Now what was he supposed to do? She didn't look dangerous. She looked like someone's mom. And Max liked her. And she seemed to like Max. Now what?

"Who are you?" Tim lowered his voice and tried to sound threatening and not like he was scared stiff, which he was.

The woman stood straight, blinking rapidly from where she had been bent over talking to Max.

"I...I'm Theresa," she said quickly, "I was just looking for some food and supplies. I don't want any trouble."

The woman held one hand up in surrender, but he noticed the other hand was reaching around to her pack. He wondered if she was reaching for a gun.

Tim watched her suspiciously as Max was still wagging his tail and jumping excitedly, putting his paws on her chest. She started slowly backing up, her eyes darting from side to side, probably looking for a place to run or maybe just to stop Max from jumping on her. She had to lower her arms to push Max off.

"Down, boy. Good boy," she whispered to Max, not moving her wide eyes away from Tim even when Max jumped up again.

"I don't want trouble either," Tim said quickly. "I just need food for me and my dog." Did she think he was going to shoot her? No way. "I'm not going to hurt you. I'm just gonna get food for me and Max and we'll be out of your way. I don't want any trouble." He tried but wasn't able to keep his voice from shaking as he was so nervous. What was he going to do if she had a gun too?

Her face softened but her posture stayed alert. "Your dog's name is Max? That's a good name. I had a neighbor who had a dog named Max. He used to love playing fetch with a frisbee." She looked down again as Max jumped up and down, wanting these people to stop standing there and play with him.

"I named him for the Grinch's dog. From the TV show. I just found him yesterday and he wanted to come with me. I didn't steal him! He didn't have a collar or a name tag. Max, come here!" he ordered. The dog blithely ignored Tim's command and kept bounding back and forth between them, trying to get one of them to play. Tim was disappointed Max hadn't come to him when he was called. Perhaps he didn't know his name yet. And he wasn't much of a guard dog, at least not with this lady they didn't know.

"My kids love the Grinch movie, the cartoon one, not the new ones. We watch it every Christmas." Her head tilted with curiosity as she asked, "Is your family here with you?"

"No. I'm by myself." Tim thought quickly he should have said he had lots of people with him so she wouldn't know he was alone. Too late now. Besides she had kids who watched the Grinch. How bad could she be? "Where's your kids?"

"I'm trying to get home to them." Her voice shook a little at the mention of her kids. "I live out east but was on a trip and my flight got canceled, so now I'm driving. I just stopped here to stock up on supplies, like you are. And then I'll keep going." Her brows creased together, like she was worried.

"How far east? Where's your home?"

Tim wondered if she was going to one of those states in the middle of the US. He never could remember which ones they were. Or maybe she was going all the way to the Atlantic.

She hesitated, "I live all the way out east," then said slowly. "It's a small town. I doubt you've heard of it."

"I'm heading to Maine. I always wanted to go there so Max and me are gonna go to Maine and see what's there." He shrugged. "I hope we make it. But I don't know. Things aren't too good anywhere." He nodded towards the window indicating the whole country.

Max bounced back to Tim. The more they talked, the more relaxed Tim felt with the woman, but he noticed she kept looking nervously at his hand still resting on his pistol. He didn't think she

44

was a danger so he moved his hand off the pistol and crouched down and petted Max's ears. Max rolled on his back and Tim rubbed his belly. Tim smiled as he thought Max was definitely not a guard dog.

Tim noticed her watching him petting Max and she smiled.

She took a deep breath. "Well, it sounds like we're going the same direction. What'd you say your name was?"

Tim looked up from Max. "I'm Tim. What's your name? I forgot if you already told me."

"I'm Theresa Shultz, but most people call me Resa. It's nice to meet you Tim."

"Resa. Sounds like Reese's Pieces. Those are my favorite," Tim said.

"I like them too. We'll have to grab some if we find any." Resa smiled.

Tim was glad she finally stopped looking at him and started looking at the shelves.

He decided Resa was a good person. She'd smiled a little at him. She had kids. She liked dogs. She seemed friendly even though she was really nervous, like he was. Max definitely liked her, but Tim didn't really know Max that well yet either. So he was going to have to go with gut instinct and gut instinct said Resa was ok. He hoped they could talk longer. He liked talking to an actual person.

Tim continued to pet Max but also watched Resa out of the corner of his eye. He wanted to know what she'd do next.

Finally she said, "Well, it's about time to eat and I could take a small break from driving. Should we eat something together and talk about the route you're going to take? I have some maps you can look at."

"Yeah, ok. I didn't really have a route planned. I'm just heading northeast cause that's where Maine is. And I'll stay away from big cities. I wouldn't a been here but I need food and Max needs to eat too. I got a lot of peanut butter but need more stuff. Should we get our lunch from here?" He looked at Resa and then around at the looted store.

"I found some canned veggies. I was going to check for canned fruit and maybe crackers. That is, before Max distracted me." She smiled sadly as she pointed to the box on the shelf, "Those are my daughter's favorite kind of crackers. I hope she's still able to get some back home." She sighed then said, "I have my maps in my car. I can grab them and meet you up front?"

Tim said, "I haven't had time to get stuff yet. Can we eat and then I can shop? I need to get Max some stuff, like maybe treats and food. Oh, and I do have a road atlas in my car we can share. If you wanna look at it."

Tim wished he could ride with someone, and not be on his own. He wondered about riding with her, but he'd just met her and that was probably not a good idea. They could drive separately but go together maybe? Or just go their separate ways? But she kind of reminded him of his mom. She didn't look like her but she just seemed like a mom. She was about his mom's age, probably in her 40s (he reminded himself to *not* ask her age). She had frizzy brown hair pulled back in a ponytail but some of the hair was coming out of the clip. Like his mom she was about average height and had brown eyes. But Resa was thinner and looked like she exercised. Mom didn't like exercise and was a little heavier. She was always on a diet of some type which never really worked. But just because Resa reminded him of his mother didn't mean she was like her at all. Perhaps Resa had killed a bunch of people just to get their car. He didn't think so but he couldn't know for sure. Well, they'd eat and see what happened. Besides, she liked Max and Max liked her. He didn't think dogs would like really bad people, would they?

Resa responded, "Sure. Sounds like a plan to me. I haven't finished my shopping yet either, so we can chat a little bit and then figure out what supplies we'll each need. I'm sure there's enough to share." She walked slowly up the aisle and grabbed the box of crackers she had pointed to earlier.

Tim noticed as Resa walked further up the aisle away from him she kept an eye on him. "Hey," he called to her, "I'm not gonna shoot you. You don't have to be afraid, ok?"

He felt uneasy knowing she might think him dangerous. He didn't like that feeling. "I'm not dangerous," he added.

He looked at her and hoped she believed him. Then because he felt awkward, he reached down to put the leash on Max so he'd stay close. Max bounced along happily as Tim walked around the store picking up lunch things. He went over to the bench, sat at one end, Max beside him, and waited for Resa.

He watched as Resa turned down another of the aisles and came back with a couple packages of beef jerky along with tuna and more supplies. She sat on the opposite end of the bench and dumped the food out between them. Resa dug through her backpack and Tim tensely watched, wondering if she was going to pull out a gun, but it was just a can opener.

He relaxed and felt a little silly, but how was he to know? He'd just met her. She opened the can and handed him a plastic fork. They opened the crackers, tuna, mayo, pickles, green beans, mixed fruit, and beef jerky and sat in silence as they ate their meal.

"I miss ice," Resa said suddenly. She pulled out a bottle of water from her backpack. "It'd be nice to have a cold drink."

Tim fed a piece of jerky to his begging dog. "I miss ice cream. I miss a lot of stuff." He mostly missed his parents, but he wasn't going to say that. He'd cry if he did and he wasn't going to cry. "Do you miss your kids?"

Resa's eyes immediately started to fill with tears, "I miss them more than anything. I'm so mad I left home when I did, and I'm so afraid they're scared and worried." She blinked back her tears before they had a chance to fall. "I have to get home." Resa's words came out quickly, but she squared her shoulders and sat up a little straighter. "I thought I'd take Route 66 across most of the country since it would keep me off the main highways. But I could take Highway 89 since I need to go north too. Have you thought about how you're getting to Maine? Those same routes would work for you too."

"Do you think your kids are dead?" Tim could have kicked himself as soon as he said it. What was he thinking to ask her that? He was always too impulsive. He was always told to *think* before he spoke. Which he was still trying to learn. But he knew people could die. Family could die. "I'm sorry. I shouldn't have said that. I'm sorry." He watched tears fill her eyes. "I didn't mean it. I'm sure they're fine. And I'm sure they miss you. Ok? I didn't mean it."

What had she been saying to him before he so stupidly asked his stupid question. Boy, was he stupid! Something about highways to get to Maine. And for her to get home.

"Route 66. Yeah. Yeah, that'd probly be good. I'd planned on taking 89 but 66 would work too." He had no idea where Route 66 was or where it went, but he'd agree with her. Anything to stop her tears. He looked away while she pulled herself together.

Tim glanced at Resa. She sat very still and stared at nothing, like one does when thinking. Or recovering from another person's stupid remark.

"I honestly don't know if my family is still alive, Tim, but I do know I'll only find out if I get home, so that's what I'm going to do. So. Route 66..."

She spent the rest of the time eating and telling Tim about the road that was the first one which went all the way from Chicago to California, but Highway 89 would take them northeast to Maine and the east coast. She was explaining how there may not be many, or any, gas stations along the way so perhaps they could figure out how to siphon gas from other cars.

"Hey, you wanna come with me? Max and me have space in my car if we move stuff around. And we'd both have someone to talk to and more people are better to have in case we run into bad people. Having someone else around would be better. I could help be protection."

Resa studied him carefully for a few minutes before she answered.

"Honestly, I want to think about the idea a little more before we decide. Two people would definitely be more helpful with the driving, and I'd feel better with someone else if we have to hike for some reason. Hopefully that won't happen, but you never know," she looked at him with kind eyes, "and two guns are definitely better than one." Resa patted her backpack meaningfully. "I only have a little gas left in my car. I was hoping maybe I could get a new car here." She

48

thought for a minute and said slowly, "But maybe I wouldn't need to find one if we ride together. You have gas in your car?"

"Yeah, I got about half a tank. A little less, maybe."

So she did have a gun in her backpack. He wasn't being suspicious after all! But he didn't blame her. She probably didn't trust him totally either. How could she? He was bigger and stronger than she was and he had a dog. Well, maybe Max wasn't too scary. But he might have been. Anyhow, knowing she had a gun was good to know.

Resa nodded, "Ok. Let me give it some thought. Thank you for being so generous. You seem like a very kind young man, Tim."

After eating, they cleaned up their trash and walked up and down the littered aisles picking up things they thought they'd need, discussing the merits of each item. Tim turned up his nose at water chestnuts, but Resa said they were crunchy, tasted good heated up, and could be used in salads and other cooking. He picked up bottles of hot sauce she would have left on the shelf. Tim ran back to get a cart to put their things in and they filled much of the cart.

"Do you feel weird taking all this stuff?" Tim asked.

"I do feel sort of weird, I guess," Resa admitted, "but there's no one to pay. And we need it to survive, so we do what we must. Do you feel weird about it?"

"Yeah. I mean my parents always told me not to steal. And here we are with a cart full of stuff. But it doesn't really seem too much like stealing. There's no one here."

Resa sighed. "I know. Many of the old rules don't apply anymore." Resa glanced at Tim walking beside her. "You must have good parents though."

"Yeah. They are." Tim strode ahead. He didn't want to talk about his parents. Not yet.

He walked up and down the next aisle by himself to get his emotions under control, but he didn't like being by himself. Even just walking down this aisle by himself was too lonely, and he turned to go back to Resa. He was glad Max was bouncing back and forth between aisles which helped Tim feel less awkward when he wandered back to Resa. He decided to ask her about the poop bags. Maybe she knew whether he should pick up dog poop or not.

"Um. Could I ask you a question?" Tim wandered up to Resa carrying a container of doggie bags. "Do you think I should pick up Max's poop in the bags? Cause if I do, where do I put the bags? I was thinking it might be better just leaving it on the ground cause it would disappear after a while instead of being in plastic which isn't good for the environment. What do you think?"

Resa nodded in agreement. "Sounds like you've thought this through. I think you're right to just let him go and not worry about it. But you could take a couple of rolls, just in case we end up somewhere where you'll want them. You never know. But right now, I agree. There isn't any sense in adding more plastic to the earth."

They walked out to the parking lot with the full cart, Max panting happily beside them. It was later in the day than they'd realized. Tim hadn't wanted to get back on the road this late. He'd wanted to get an early start. Now it was late afternoon and if he were by himself, he'd stay in the parking lot again. He wondered if he should tell Resa he didn't want to drive til tomorrow.

"Well Tim, I guess we spent more time shopping and talking than I thought. I think it'd be better to have a fresh start in the morning, no matter what we decide," Resa said as if reading his mind. "How about if we both sleep in our own cars tonight and figure out what we're going to do in the morning. We talked about going to the Outdoor Explore store to pick up more things. We could do that in the morning and then get on the road?" She looked up at him questioningly.

"Sounds good to me. What time in the morning do you wanna leave?" He hoped it wouldn't be too early. He didn't like doing too much in the mornings. He liked doing stuff at night after everyone else was sleeping. But he figured Resa was going to be like most parents and expect him to get up and not sleep in. Especially on a day when they had to travel. But he'd get up early every morning of his life (well, almost every morning) if he had a person to talk to.

"Let's play it by ear. I expect you won't be sleeping too late with Max wanting to get up and get moving." She smiled at Max.

50

"Yeah, right. I didn't think of that." Tim was reminded of his Mom telling him he'd have to walk his dog. She was right. So much for sleeping in. Oh well, Max was worth it. He reached down and scratched Max behind the ears.

He watched her walk to the other side of the parking lot to her vehicle. She didn't pull her car over to his. He was glad. He liked knowing she was there but wasn't sure about having her right next to him. Yet. There'd be plenty of time later. And he was still getting used to people again. Nice to have around sometimes, but a little nerve wracking as well.

In the early evening Tim thought he'd try to teach Max to return a frisbee. Tim quickly realized this might take awhile. He threw the frisbee, Max chased after it, and then panted, drooling all over it, but didn't bring it back. When Tim walked over to retrieve the slimy disc, Max grabbed the frisbee in his mouth and ran away with it. He eventually let Tim take the frisbee from him, so Tim would throw it again, dog slobber spinning off it, and the process went on until they were both tired.

He could see Resa getting her supper ready, and he realized he didn't want to eat by himself.

"Hey! Resa! Do you wanna eat supper together?" he called out.

"Sure!"

He gathered his crackers, tuna, mayo, pickles, a can of peaches, and Max's food and wandered over to Resa's car. After they ate he took Max around the parking lot so he could pee on things. Funny how dogs do that. He should get a book on raising dogs.

He wandered back to Resa's car so they could talk some more. He wasn't ready to go back to his car yet. He felt comfortable around Resa, she was kinda like an aunt or maybe a friend's mom. They sat in the darkening evening and talked about family and things they'd done. Resa talked about taking her two kids to the local amusement park when they were young and how they both got sick from the rides and threw up. He talked about when he and his Dad got lost when hiking and how long it had taken them to get home. Mom had been really nervous until they called and told her they were ok. All kinds of stories about the people they missed most.

51

Tim could tell Resa wanted to know about his parents. At first he didn't think he could tell her; it hurt too much. But as the stars got brighter and they were surrounded by the dark, he was able to talk about those days. How he'd waited for them to come home and they hadn't. And how when he went to Granddad's he found they had K-Pox so he brought them food and talked to them through the door and how finally he had waited outside the door until he knew they were gone. In his telling he broke into heavy sobs. He didn't think he had that many tears left in him but he did.

In between sobs he kept saying, "I'm sorry. I'm sorry! I don't mean to cry!"

Resa sat down next to him and put her arm around his shoulders and murmured, "There's nothing to be sorry about. You cry all you want to. It's an awful thing and I'm so sorry and sad this happened. I'm so sorry."

Tim felt the tears wouldn't ever stop, but was finally able to control himself, and his sobs slowly faded to rough breaths. Resa got up and went to the car. She brought back paper towels and handed him the roll.

"I always need tissues when I cry," she said as she wiped tears from her own eyes.

"Thanks," he muttered as he wiped away the tears and blew his nose. "I miss them so much."

"I'm so sorry. They sound like wonderful people."

"They were." Tim didn't want to talk anymore. He was worn out with the whole long day and crying and everything. "If you don't mind, I'm going to bed. I'm tired." He put Max on the leash and walked slowly to his car.

He laid the sleeping bag and mat out and Max curled up next to him. It felt comforting knowing he had a person and a dog to travel with now. Tim looked up at the stars, twinkling brighter without city lights to dim them. It took him a long time to fall asleep. He had to push the painful memories from his mind. He forced himself to think about tomorrow and felt both excited and anxious about what the future held.

Chapter 6

March - Arizona

Well, it's official, Resa thought. THIS is the most uncomfortable position in the world. In the backseat of the car, Resa tried to shift her arms and legs into a more semi-comfortable position so she could sleep a little longer. She had stirred awake when the first rays of sunlight peeked over the horizon, but she wasn't ready to face the day. Her night had been restless after meeting Tim yesterday. Well, every night was restless. She may never sleep a full night again. She rubbed her eyes and tucked her hands under her head. Was she making the right decision to team up with this stranger she'd just met? Sure, dogs can tell you a lot about a person, but maybe this dog was trained to fool strangers so this 'Tim' person could...could what? Steal from her, leave her for dead? She had already been around people like that. Resa shuttered. She could have been the one left cold on the motel pavement. Besides, she couldn't imagine soft-spoken, quick talking Tim as a criminal mastermind who would leave her lifeless body in the desert somewhere. If he was one of her kids, wouldn't she want someone kind to take a chance on them?

Resa sighed. No more avoiding it, time to get up. She was tired, but antsy. The longer she lay in this car, the more minutes ticked by when she wasn't driving towards Laurel. Resa's body groaned as she sat up. She half crawled, half stumbled out of the back seat and stood up to stretch her shoulders and back. The rising sun already promised heat to warm the day. She looked across the parking lot towards Tim's car. It was still there, but Tim and Max were nowhere to be seen. Maybe they went back to the store for more things. Or maybe they went to tell their gang of murderers and pirates she was here all alone...

Oookaaay Resa, get it together, she told herself. After the kind and compassionate responses she'd had on this trip, she should be more trusting of people. Maybe they just took a walk. Resa couldn't imagine Tim sitting still for very long. Aaah, to be young and full of energy.

Resa sleepily grabbed a water bottle, a package of instant coffee, and applesauce. She missed hot coffee and fresh fruit and warm oatmeal...she missed a lot of things. Pans! Camping pans, she thought as she scribbled it on the growing list of supplies they'd hopefully get at the camping store. Her list had been pretty short when she left Kingman, but she honestly hadn't had much luck with cars so far. Who knew how long the next car would last and where they could find gas? Now her focus shifted to include anything she might need for camping and hiking her way home.

Resa heard thudding footsteps and saw Tim walking across the parking lot, still wearing yesterday's clothes. She wondered if he showered recently. It might make it interesting if she was going to ride across the country with him. Mitchell always made quite the sensory impression after baseball practice. Tim was kicking a few rocks here and there as Max bounded in front of him. Resa felt a wave of sadness, thinking about how much Mitchell had wanted a dog and how they'd said no. She sighed. Just keep going.

"Morning," Resa called out when Tim was closer.

"Hey!" Tim answered, shielding his eyes from the ever-brightening sun. "I moved things in my car so we can fit your stuff in too."

After Tim told Resa about his parents last night, she'd felt like their destinies were intertwined. Extreme circumstances drew people together in strange ways, she supposed. The chaos in the world had stripped away the luxury of getting to know people slowly. She couldn't leave him to fend for himself and she could use the extra support. They'd decided riding together was a good option, but she still mentally reserved the right to run like hell if she needed to.

"I don't have much," Resa said, thinking of the past times she'd wanted new things to "keep up" with everyone else. And now, all her belongings fit in one single backpack. "I want to pick up a hiking backpack at the outdoor place."

"Alright. I left space in the back seat but we gotta leave room for Max. I made him a bed behind the passenger seat. I'm gonna take some of my other stuff and leave it here."

Tim gathered an armful of his belongings from the backseat and headed towards the store, his hands and elbows catching loose items while he tried to balance the bulky load and walk. She wondered what Tim was taking inside, but by the way he strode quickly away without offering an explanation, she was pretty sure he didn't want to talk about it.

Resa finished up her breakfast and carried the extra gas can over to Tim's car just as he walked outside. She left the keys to her rental car on the dashboard and wished the next driver a safe journey home. She hated to leave the other car behind since it was given out of kindness. She especially hated to leave even the small amount of gas in the tank, but she couldn't siphon it into this car. She didn't know how. Maybe the camping store would have a kit or something they could use later. They filled the tank with the extra gas she'd gotten from the Hansons and then put the empty container in the trunk. Tim walked to the driver's side door.

"Do you mind if I take the first shift driving?" Resa asked quickly. "I'm more focused in the morning and I would really appreciate your help reading the maps." To be honest, she didn't feel entirely safe letting a teenage stranger control where they were going, but she didn't want to tell him that. She also didn't want to tell him she felt better driving instead of riding when she was stressed.

"Yeah, ok." Tim looked a little surprised, but handed her the keys, and walked to the passenger side instead.

Resa slid into the driver's seat of Tim's car, moved the seat closer and adjusted the mirrors.

"Ready Max?" Tim asked as he scratched Max's ears. Max leaned the top half of his body onto the middle console and stretched his paws out in front of him.

"As ready as we'll ever be," Resa murmured. With that thought, she took a deep breath and pulled out onto the road.

"I don't think this camping store is far away. I saw tons of signs for it yesterday." Resa pulled out the cash register receipt with her scribbled notes. No more making lists on her phone. It was almost dead and she was trying to save the battery. Who knew when she might get a signal again, but she would keep sending messages.

"What are you going to get? I've already got a hiking pack and most of the stuff I need but I'll see what else they have. I could use some bug spray, matches, dehydrated food, things like that," Tim said.

"I thought of those things too. And sunscreen, phone charger packs, lighters, first aid kit, hand sanitizer, and camping stuff like sleeping bags and cooking items. I got toothbrushes and toothpaste at the last store, along with some other hygiene stuff. I haven't been camping in years, but I might have to get pretty good at it soon." Resa tried to sound like she was making a joke, but her voice sounded thin. She couldn't shake the band of anxiety tightening around her chest as she thought of all the miles ahead of her.

"I already got a cooking stove and pan and I'll carry it since I'm used to carrying more weight in my pack. But you'll need your own plate and utensils. Want me to help you find stuff?"

"Sure. Sounds good," Resa replied. She hoped they could grab everything quickly and keep moving.

"There it is, right there," Tim said, pointing towards another giant sign with a smiling family on it and a huge arrow pointing to a building a short distance away.

"Great, thanks. They could have used a bigger sign," Resa said jokingly and could see a small smile on Tim's reflection in the window.

The parking lot was empty as Resa drove up to the front door and parked. Yep, lots of rules no longer applied when you were the only people around. Max jumped out of the back seat and sniffed around, but stayed close to Tim.

They walked in the front doors and exchanged looks of surprise. Torn up cardboard, fishing lures, drink tumblers, and pocket flashlights were strewn all over the front entryway. They could see clothes hanging haphazardly on the racks, but many were in piles on the floor. The glass in the vending machines near the door was shattered and a single Snickers bar hung halfway in the last slot.

"Well, I guess we'll get what we get," Resa said before grabbing two hand baskets miraculously still in the holder.

"Yeah," Tim nodded, and they both wandered through the maze of camo hats, open packages of dried fruit, trail mix, and splintered sunglasses.

Surprisingly, it didn't take as long as Resa had thought to find things. Most were close-ish to the aisle they were supposed to be in; they were just on the floor or a different shelf. Tim and Resa decided they would both get good hiking boots. The trick was finding the right size. Resa thought she was out of luck because she only found one which fit, but then she remembered a lonely boot when they walked in that might have been the same color.

"Aha!" Resa exclaimed, holding up the matching boot by the front doors as Max bounded in her direction. He seemed happy for her too.

Tim's basket was full of lighters, batteries, compasses, rain ponchos, kindling containers, snacks, and other treasures he found along the way. Resa had grabbed interesting things like bear spray, biodegradable soap, gaffer tape, and a hygiene trowel! Who knew they had such things? She didn't know when she'd be in a store like this again, so she didn't want to regret not taking something.

"Let's set up our backpacks outside," Tim suggested. "I got a new one too. There's no way I could've afforded this before, but it's free today! You're gonna want to make sure your pack isn't too heavy for you to carry. That's easy to do. I can always carry a little more if we need to," he offered.

"I suppose things will get lighter as we go along and use some things up." Resa appreciated Tim's concern and knew he had a younger back, but she had to be strong for this journey too. She'd walk until her legs could no longer hold her.

Resa had picked a backpack with a built-in water pack; it would free up some room for other items in the pockets. They both put on their new boots, threw their old tennis shoes in the back of the car and started packing their backpacks.

Resa tried to remember how she packed grocery bags in her first job at Sav-More Food. Was this the same? She remembered something about building walls around the sides so she didn't squash the items in the middle. She stacked her camping plate and utensils, collapsible mug, and lantern around the sides, then tucked in food, water purification tablets, filters, hiking socks, multitool, and a variety of other things. She tried her best to be organized, but in the end she threw in whatever she could and smooshed it down to make it fit.

After tying up her pack, Resa put on the sports watch she'd found on the back of a sunglasses display. She rolled up her blanket and small pillow with her sleeping bag and strapped it to the bottom of her pack. When she was done packing, she took Tim's advice to walk around and make sure she could carry everything. Tim helped her get the pack adjusted and she walked around the parking lot a few times making minor adjustments as the pack shifted with her movement. Then she filled up her water compartment with as much water as she thought she could carry and tried walking again. The pack was heavy, but bearable. They loaded the car with their new acquisitions and Resa got back into the driver's seat.

As she pulled out of the parking lot, she realized she was starting to feel better about the decision to join this kid on her journey. He was kind and considerate, and he actually seemed to know quite a bit about camping. Back on the road Resa asked Tim where he'd learned so much.

"Dad and I used to go camping and hiking a lot. We both liked being away from work and school," Tim grinned. "We had a whole bunch of places we were gonna go and we used to compete for how long we could go without showering. Mom opened the door with a clothespin on her nose one time when we got home cause she knew we were gonna smell really bad. Dad and I totally cracked up." Tim laughed as he remembered that day. Resa hoped Tim wouldn't want to have the same competition with her.

Tim lapsed into silence as the dull whirr of the tires and Max's gentle snoring arose from the back. The dusty road was lined with cacti and forests of trees whose branches were made of prickles and spiky, pancake-shaped leaves. It certainly was different here than the trees that creaked in the wind and the green grass back home, Resa thought. There were mountains in the distance. Would they make it there before nightfall?

Tim had drifted off to sleep and she glanced down at the gas tank, biting her lip as the needle was falling below the quarter tank mark. She wasn't sure how much longer they could go if there were no gas stations in service. Tim blinked his eyes awake and stretched his long arms and legs in the small space.

"So how many kids did you say you had, Tre...Resa?" Tim asked as the view out the windows grew rockier and the land started to form itself into high sculptures of stone.

Resa glanced at a sign for an upcoming gas station. Pleeeeease let it be open.

"I have two wonderful and amazing kids. My son, Mitchell, is 12 and my daughter, Meg is around your age. She'll turn 18 in September."

"Yeah, my 18th birthday is May 20th." Tim said, "Me and my parents were gonna go bowling. I love bowling. I'm not very good, but it's fun." He laughed. "Mom is way worse than me. She gutter balls all the time."

"Meg and her friends got a little beach house for a weekend this summer to celebrate graduation. They've all known each other since grade school."

Resa had a sudden wave of grief for all the families she had shared a life with, coming and going from sporting events, PTO bake sales, volunteering. She and Tim were talking as if life might get back to normal, but she honestly wondered if anyone was left to be normal with.

Tim had turned his face towards the window, but Resa could see the sadness in his face in the reflection. It mirrored her own sorrow. She slowly drove off the next exit and headed towards the gas station she saw in the distance. Even before the car pulled to a stop, Resa's stomach took a sickening drop. Dust was caked on the handles of the gas pumps and the edge of an OUT OF ORDER sign fluttered in the wind on the station door. The car idled as Resa and Tim stared at the dusty station.

"Ok. Maybe there's another place up ahead." Resa tried to say in a tone more hopeful than she felt.

Max whimpered in the back seat.

"If you want to take Max out, I'll just wait here. Sounds like he needs to go."

Tim got out and opened up the back door. Max ran around Tim in a circle before they ran off to explore.

When Tim got back, Resa pointed the car back to the highway and they watched the miles tick by. The gas indicator light inevitably lit up. Resa and Tim both scanned the horizon for gas stations that might be open and stopped and checked a few cars on the side of the road to possibly take instead. Resa didn't get too close to the cars that still had people in them. The smell was enough to make you lose your lunch, even from far away. They passed a sign for Bitter Springs. Yep, 'bitter' sounds about right, Resa thought as the sign disappeared into the distance. The lights on the dashboard dimmed and flickered and the engine started to sputter. Resa and Tim both tensed as the car began to lose speed.

"I'll try to get up to the look-out point and we can at least rest before we figure out our next steps."

Resa struggled to fight back her feelings of dread and defeat. How would she ever make it home at this rate? The car slowly coasted to a stop next to a magnificent view of marble-colored mountains and canyons, but the view was blurry as Resa's eyes watered and sharp anger rose up into her chest.

"Uggggh! I *hate* that we only got this far!" Resa said sharply and gripped the steering wheel until her knuckles turned white. When she peeled her hands away she curled them into fists in her lap and took several deep breaths to lessen her frustration. She pushed down on the brake and put the car in park so it wouldn't roll anywhere.

"I think maybe there's a town not too far away. I saw a sign. Maybe we'll run into more people or find another car. We'll probably only walk a little while. It's a good thing you found those boots!" Tim said quickly.

Resa turned a watery half smile toward him. "Yes, I'm sure you're right. This is just a short detour," she sighed, "Do you want to save your keys?" Resa asked, finally opening the door to step out of the car. Tim let Max out and he ran around and bumped her with his nose, wagging his tail and bouncing. She would so much rather be a blissfully unaware dog right now.

"I'll be right back," Tim said, taking his keys from her and whistling to Max before heading off for a short walk.

Resa stretched her arms above her head and tried to absorb the peacefulness of the landscape into her bones. The layers of rock stretched into the distance. How could such beauty stand firm when everything else felt like it was crumbling around her? By the time Tim and Max walked back, she was munching on some trail mix and dried fruit.

"So I guess we'll just keep heading along this road," Resa said. "We can walk for a while then camp tonight and do it all over again tomorrow. Just as long as we keep moving. Sound ok to you? Do you know how to set up the tents?"

"Yeah, they're the pop-up ones. Dad always said those were easier than the ones with the separate poles. We'll have to do it before it gets too dark though so we can clear the area and set up a fire if we want one."

Tim smiled as he watched Max snuffling after a beetle across the rocky terrain before he made himself a sandwich and got Max's food out of the backseat.

After lunch, they rearranged their backpacks. Tim decided to take only his pistol as he couldn't carry the other two guns and their ammo. Resa could tell Tim was sad to leave his car. He took the car key off his keyring and put it above the visor, writing a quick note to stick on the dashboard.

"I'm sorry about your car Tim. I'm sure it's hard to leave it behind. What did the note say?" Resa asked.

"I just wanted to let the next owner know it's a good car if they wanna take it. Not broken or anything, just needs gas. Maybe someone who needs it will find it."

They were both determined to believe in hopeful things. That was a good sign, Resa thought. When they started walking, Resa *was* thankful for the new walking boots. After an hour of hiking, she didn't have a blister or anything. She had also grabbed a wide brimmed hat and sunglasses and was glad for those too.

After a few hours, they stopped for a rest and talked about setting up a camping site when Max perked up his ears and sniffed into the wind.

"Do you hear that?" Resa asked Tim as she wiped sweat off her forehead. Her shoulders ached from the weight of the pack. They heard a slight whirring in the distance.

"Sounds like a motor," Tim replied, looking at Max as his body grew more tense.

"Maybe we should get off to the side of the road," Resa suggested, thinking back to the caravan of military vehicles passing her when she left California. She felt apprehensive. Those burned out cars and looted houses in Flagstaff didn't just happen on their own.

"And maybe we should be ready…just in case," Tim said pointedly, reaching down to put Max on his leash and then pulling out his gun from the holster. He kept it casually at his side, but his body looked strained as the motor sound grew closer.

The thought of facing dangerous people was terrifying, but Resa knew Tim was right. She fished her gun out of the side pocket of her backpack and pointed the barrel to the ground. She knew she'd protect them both if she had to.

An ATV appeared over the cusp of the hill, slowing as it got closer. In the seat was an older man with gray hair tumbling to his shoulders. He came to a stop.

"Well, hello there, folks!!! My name's Gary Walter, and I just live up the road a piece. Not gonna hurt ya," he said, glancing at the guns in their hands.

That's what all criminals say, Resa thought. She glanced sideways at Tim and he shrugged. It was hard to know who to trust.

"Hello," Resa said tentatively. "What brings you out and about today?" Maybe conversation would give them time to decide whether or not he was harmless.

Gary Walter smiled wide and stepped off the four-wheeler. Tim stepped closer to Resa.

"Oh, I been out looking for supplies at my neighbors' houses." He pointed to a few cans and paper goods in a basket on the back of the ATV. "They're gone, but I thought I'd store everything in one place and then share if they come back. Where you folks from? You traveling on foot?"

Resa didn't want to give too much information, but she didn't get any scary vibes from him so far. He just seemed like a friendly local.

"Our car ran out of gas, so we decided to start walking," Resa answered. "I'm Resa," she said.

"I'm pleased to meet ya!" He answered, stretching out his hand to shake hers. "You can call me GW. I heard on the radio the gas stations were runnin' dry. Leffler's gas station is out and it's the only one around here for miles" GW made a concerned face. "If you'd like Ma'am, I'd be quite happy to invite you and your friend here back to my house for dinner and a safe place to rest? No tricks. I'm a family man." GW grinned up at Tim and then gave Max a little wave as Max wagged his tail.

"Would you mind giving us a minute to discuss it?" Resa said.

"Sure. No problem at all. Take your time," GW said agreeably. Resa and Tim stepped away so they could have a private moment to confer.

"It's going to be dark soon. What do you think about going for dinner and then maybe we could set up the tents close by his property if it felt safe?" Resa asked Tim. "He seems ok."

"Yeah, I guess he doesn't seem dangerous. Besides, it's two against one if he's living alone. But if there's a crowd of creepy people at his house he's calling 'family,' I say we run," Tim said seriously.

"Agreed."

They turned back to GW to tell him the news and he happily moved his supplies so they could ride back to his house together.

After dinner, Resa thought maybe the horrible people at the motel were a fluke and she could lower her guard a little. After all, GW had welcomed them into his home, said he'd restock their supplies, and had shared a hot meal with them. Of course he hadn't stopped talking the whole time, but maybe that was because he hadn't seen anyone in weeks. He even offered them rooms in his house, but they said they would be ok in their tents for now. GW told them he'd lost his wife to cancer a couple years ago and his son had recently died from some type of infection. He'd been left to tend his property all alone, which had been ok until K-Pox hit. Now he wasn't sure which of his neighbors were still around.

Resa could barely keep her eyes open after dinner, but she managed to help Tim put up tents in the yard where GW said it would be safe and dry. As she snuggled into her still new-smelling sleeping bag, she was thankful for friendly strangers. Yeah, she thought, drifting off to sleep, he seems ok.

Chapter 7

March - Arizona

Tim stared at the ceiling of his small tent; it was very dark. Really dark, like dark, darkest dark. Very black nights were one of the many things he was still getting used to. And tonight there was no moon so the night was truly black. Only star light. Beautiful but scary and very dark. Life was so weird. Nothing was the same anymore. He tossed and turned, trying to sleep but his thoughts kept running back over the last few days. It was only a couple of days ago when he'd left home and found Max and then met Resa and then slept in a parking lot. And now tonight he was sleeping in some strange guy's backyard with Max.

Max definitely made sleeping less comfortable, but more comforting. If that made any sense. Life was so weird. He didn't think he'd ever fall asleep. Tim flipped over on his side and stared at an equally black tent wall. Tim turned again, and Max shifted but didn't wake up. It was going to be hard to go to sleep with everything that had happened today.

It was only this morning that he'd awakened at the grocery store with Max licking his face, and he'd started traveling with Resa. He liked having Max and Resa to travel with. They were pretty good companions, since he couldn't have his parents. Resa was like a parent. He was glad she didn't mind taking charge. He wondered if he was supposed to be the man of the group, and if so, what was he supposed to do? He wanted a say in decisions. Like it was irritating when she just decided to take the first shift driving his car. He had wanted to tell her no, that he wanted to drive first, but had decided not to say anything because he didn't want to argue. It didn't make any difference anyway, as the car had run out of gas and now neither of them could drive it. Anyway, he just didn't want to make any more major decisions on his own for a while. He needed more time.

Going to Outdoor Explore had been fun. They didn't take a lot of food as it was heavy and they'd decided to scavenge food from stores and deserted houses along their route east. There'd been next to nothing left in the gun section. Apparently people had wiped the stores out of weapons. What did all these people think was going to happen? We'd all turn into people-eating zombies? Or we'd need to kill each other for stuff? It depressed Tim just thinking about it.

Max had been good in the car yesterday. He'd spent the time either sleeping or panting in Tim's ear. Tim was becoming aware that dogs do not have good breath. He wondered if there were breath mints for dogs. If so, he'd have to get Max some. Tim liked having his dog though, smelly breath and all. Max was already his best friend. It didn't make any difference they'd just met. Tim smiled as he thought about Max and the frisbee. Tim was sure he'd soon learn how to catch and return. Next time they were near a bookstore he'd pick up a book on how to train dogs. Resa said she thought Max was still young, maybe not even a year old so this would be a good age to start training.

After a break today he and Max had run up and down the road, just to burn off energy. No vehicles on the streets. Just them running. So weird not having cars. When they'd got back, Tim poured a bottle of water in Max's bowl and they both quickly downed their bottles. Tim saw Resa shoot him a worried glance and then remembered water was going to be scarce. Tim had sighed. This was going to be so hard. No water? He'd still been thirsty and could probably have drunk all the water they had in one day. And he'd just finished running and was sweating up a storm and there was no shower. And he had stunk! Ugh! He had dug through the car, found the alcohol wipes and deodorant, and slipped behind the car to clean up. Scraping a little hole in the grass with his boot he had put the used wipes in it and covered the hole. It'd be embarrassing to stink in the car. He'd decided he wouldn't run anymore if they were going to get right back in close confines. Didn't want to be too sweaty in a small car. Hopefully deodorant won't be a hard commodity to find in the future. What did people use before that was invented? Maybe everybody just smelled bad.

They had watched the gas gauge get lower and lower, and the car inevitably drifted to a stop. He could tell Resa had been upset but she hadn't said much. She'd put the car in Park and pulled the keys out of the ignition.

"Do you want to save your keys?" she had asked, holding them out to him.

"Sure. Why not," he'd responded. He had slipped the car key in the visor of the car but took the key ring. with his house key and his Granddad's key and dejectedly put it in his front jeans pocket.

It had been hard for Tim to leave so many of his belongings behind again—like his guns but especially his car. He had to leave his car! And bits and pieces of himself all over the southwest. But he still had Mom's ring and Dad's watch. He liked the comforting feel of them against his skin, letting him know they were still with him. He would never leave them. As they had trudged slowly away Tim had looked back only once, giving a tiny wave to his car.

He had walked more slowly than he might have done as his legs were longer than Resa's, but it had been comfortable keeping his stride equal to hers. Hiking was something Tim generally liked. He didn't like walking in the hot desert heat, but it had been a good day for a hike. The temperature was probably in the high 60s, spring flowers were beginning to bloom, birds were chirping, and Max was running along with, ahead of, and behind them sniffing things. If Maine weren't so far away this hiking could be fun. They had walked without talking, listening to nature, the dog rustling in the bushes and panting, and their boots softly thumping on the road. It was restful, this silence. Tim had thought he could walk for hours like this.

And then they had heard the 4-wheeler and met GW.

Tim stretched and woke up, his tent bright with sunlight streaming through his unzipped screen door, trying to remember where he was. Oh, in GW's backyard! Last night he didn't think he would ever fall asleep, but he obviously had. He wondered what time it was. He pulled his arm out from the sleeping bag and looked at his watch. 10:30. Wow! That was late! Apparently Max had run off somewhere as he was no longer sleeping in the tent. Resa must have let him out.

Tim lay comfortably on his back and thought about GW. He seemed ok, but it was so weird seeing someone else who he didn't know. Days and weeks of no one, and then Max and Resa, and now this Gary Walter guy. All of a sudden Resa didn't seem to be a stranger anymore and GW was. And GW was really friendly.

Who was a stranger anyway? Yesterday he'd found it odd that he'd spent the afternoon driving and walking with Resa, who for all practical purposes was a stranger, something his parents had always told him never to do. He wondered how long it was before someone was not considered a stranger. Resa didn't feel like a person to beware of anymore, at least not a creepy person. He decided just spending time with someone didn't take them out of the Beware-of-this-Person mode. But what did? The length of time you knew them? If you were introduced by someone who was family or friend? If you went to school with them? He almost asked Resa what she thought about this, but decided maybe he'd wait until they truly weren't strangers anymore. He wondered when that would be—maybe in a couple of weeks? He guessed he'd know when she wasn't one anymore.

Tim listened for noises from Resa's tent or the house. As he lay silently listening, he looked at his watch again. He was still getting used to wearing a watch. His cell phone was his clock and alarm before. He was glad Mrs. Roiland, his third-grade teacher, and his parents had taught him to read time from a regular clock or he'd be stuck. He remembered back in ninth grade some kid complaining that the teacher had a regular clock on the wall, and he couldn't tell time without a digital clock. The teacher just said this was math class, and he'd learn. Tim wondered if Mrs. Roiland was still alive. Or that kid. He couldn't even remember his name now. That was sad.

Yesterday when GW had shown them around, he'd wanted them to sleep in the house and had shown them the bedrooms where they could stay. Tim's room would have been the son's room. GW's son had died relatively recently. He thought he understood how Gary Walter felt. The grief of loss was like a raw painful hole dug into your heart which didn't heal and was always there. Tim didn't know if he wanted the pain to go away, because if the pain was no longer there, would that mean he didn't care anymore? That he'd forgotten his parents? He shook his head and grabbed fresh clothes from his pack, dressed, combed his hair, and crawled out of the tent to start the new day.

When the smell of frying pork wafted out the open kitchen window Tim realized he was starving. He found the back door leading to the kitchen by following the sound of voices and the smell of pork and coffee. Max was sitting outside the screen door (GW had a 'no dogs allowed in the kitchen' policy) and jumped up to welcome Tim as he approached. He felt a little nervous and stood in the doorway as he looked at Resa talking quietly to GW. She didn't seem scared so Tim relaxed a little. Resa noticed him first and smiled as she saw him standing at the kitchen door. He pushed Max away as he opened the screen door.

"I'm glad you slept well. You didn't even move when I let Max out of the tent. I imagine you're hungry. GW has your breakfast almost ready. Just has to fry up the eggs."

"Hey there, my boy! Glad to see you this mornin!" GW's voice was a little loud, but welcoming. "How many eggs? I assume at least three?"

"Thank you, Sir. That'd be nice if it's not too much trouble." Tim wasn't sure if he should agree to three eggs. He felt he could eat twice that but he was learning to eat a lot less than he really wanted to.

"Now remember, it's not "Sir." I'm GW. And three eggs is no trouble at all! I wish I'd made bread yesterday, but I didn't know you was comin. I'll be makin some later since you're here now. These crackers will have to do. And I know you'll have a couple of slices of this Virginia cured ham. A young man has to eat! I don't have real orange juice but I have some of that orange flavored powdered stuff to put in water. It's not too bad." GW turned the gas stove on to heat the pan.

Tim was soon eating his eggs (he noticed there were four), half a sleeve of saltine crackers, and ham. The ham was a bit salty, but it all tasted so good. Fresh cooked food was better than good; it was extraordinary. He cut a small piece of ham for Max and when GW and Resa weren't looking, tucked it in his pocket. He went back to concentrating on his breakfast and wished he could lick the plate to get the last of the flavor. He was only brought back to the conversation in the room by Resa's question.

"So what do you think, Tim?"

Tim looked up blankly. "I'm sorry. I wasn't paying attention." Embarrassing.

Resa smiled. "That's ok. GW asked if we'd stay and help with a few chores before we head out again. Three people can get the work done a lot faster than one and we can repay his kindness for letting us stay. What do you think?"

"Yeah, sure." Tim was pleased she'd asked him. That was cool. And he had no problem staying a few days if the food was this good. And GW said he'd be baking bread? Tim would definitely stay for fresh bread!

GW beamed. "Great! Let's get started on the garden. I have a large garden to get in. We'll finish preparin the soil and then we'll get in the seeds. You ever plant a garden, Tim?" Without waiting for an answer, he went on. "Well, you'll learn a lot about it here. Lots of work to do outside."

GW glanced at Tim's plate. "Looks like you're finished. Wash your things and put 'em in the drying rack, then meet us outside. Oh, and make sure you wear your hat. You'll need it."

The screen door slammed as GW and Resa walked outdoors. Tim walked over to the sink but before dunking his plate in the hot water, he glanced out the window to make sure they weren't looking, then grinned and licked his plate. As he left the kitchen he slipped the piece of ham to Max, who, Tim was pleased to notice, had waited for him. Probably just because Tim was close to the smell of food. Tim filled Max's water bowl, gave him some kibble, and headed out to the garden.

The day was warm and they worked hard. This was going to take more than one day to get all the work done. On GW's list was to finish breaking up the soil with a small garden tractor, put in seeds and fertilizer, and run the irrigation system. Tim asked GW why he had water when no one else seemed to. GW told him several years ago that he'd had all his electricity including the well and pump run through his solar power system. He used the pump and the water sparingly though so he warned Resa and Tim to use as little water as possible.

Tim liked the smell of the freshly turned over earth and how the dry seeds slipped through his fingers. He looked across at the rest of the garden they hadn't planted yet. It seemed to go on forever. Whew! How was one old man going to eat all these vegetables? He pulled off his hat and wiped the sweat from his forehead. That bread had better be good. He was definitely earning it!

Lunch was at noon. Canned salmon and crackers and canned applesauce. Then back outside and more work. GW seemed to be happy they were there, but Tim thought he was a little bossy considering they didn't have to stay and help. Oh well. GW wasn't a young man and if he was going to be there by himself for the rest of his life, he'd need help getting things ready. Tim didn't really mind, but he was hoping the gardening would be over soon. It was hard work and a little boring now that he'd been doing it all day. Tim thought supper time would never arrive. GW had left the garden early to prepare it and said he'd call them when it was ready. They finally heard GW's voice yell out, "Come and get it!"

GW told them if they wanted to they could shower before supper which Tim thought was wonderful. He needed to get the dirt and stink off before he'd feel comfortable being around anyone. GW put a kitchen timer in Tim's hand and told him he had five minutes to shower. "Can't waste water. My son used to love long hot showers and I finally had to put him on a timer. Wells run dry and we can't have a well run dry just because someone wants to stand under hot water all morning. Nope. Justin didn't like it, but too bad."

Tim took his five-minute shower. "Fastest shower I ever took," he said quietly to Resa as he handed her the timer.

He and Resa felt comfortable enough with GW by the end of the day that in the evening they moved into the house. They helped GW clean up after supper and sat and talked with him til bedtime. Which was apparently 10. On the dot. Tim was given Justin's room and he was finally able to be alone. He sighed as he closed the door and just sat on the bed, shoulders slumped and feeling thoroughly tired. He looked around the room. It looked like a guy's room, painted a pale blue, with sports posters and a .22 rifle hung on the wall. It was a nice room, but it seemed a little odd to have the dead son's room. He reminded himself to not think about Justin being dead. Or anyone being dead. He slowly stood up and unpacked a few things, then crawled under clean sheets, and fell asleep much faster than he had the previous night.

The next few days they worked outside all day. GW somehow thought they'd promised they'd help get the whole garden planted. Tim had thought they'd said they'd only stay a day, but it didn't seem GW agreed. It was almost like he expected them to stay forever.

No more sleeping til 10:30! Tim was awakened in the morning at 6:30 by GW. "We're wasting daylight! Let's get up and rolling!"

Breakfast at 7:30, work in the garden, lunch at noon, back in the garden at 1:00 and work til 5:00. Supper was at 6:00. The food was definitely good and the fresh bread was fantastic even without butter, but they worked hard for it. A good thing about GW was he didn't mind answering questions. Tim liked asking questions about things he didn't know, and he had lots of questions, like how long before the plants would come up, how was GW going to water them, how did the toilets work without city water, and all kinds of questions about the ATVs. He loved riding on the ATVs. He'd ridden them before but only on a track where you paid by the hour. Here he could ride any time of day...well, when it involved coming and going to the garden with supplies and back to the barn. GW was strict about not riding them for fun. Had to save gas. He had a truck but only used it for emergencies as it was a gas hog. Still, Tim enjoyed riding them.

Putting in the garden was nearing completion, and Tim heard Resa mention several times to GW they'd be heading out soon, to get home to her kids.

But GW had just one more thing they needed to do–digging a pit for an outhouse. He didn't want to waste his water on the toilet. They'd been using the used dishwater for flushing to save water. No need for flushing with an outhouse. Yuck! Tim had never used an outhouse before. GW had built the small wooden building before they'd got there, but he needed help putting it in place over the pit.

So they helped dig a pit about five feet deep and then got the little house put properly above the hole. That was hard work and they needed the tractor and rope and Tim was glad when it was done. GW was very pleased when the toilet paper was in its place.

Resa said she'd wanted to leave the next day, but she wasn't feeling very well. Tim wasn't feeling his best either and was glad they'd put off continuing their journey. For the last several days he'd felt fine during the day but had been nauseous in the morning and really tired in the evenings, more so than he'd ever been before. He wondered if it was the hard work, but he didn't think he should be this tired and sick. Not from hard work.

The next day GW wanted his shed roof repaired and they helped with the repairs. Resa and Tim struggled with the work as they continued to feel sick. Tim felt like he was in a fog and his head ached especially in the mornings. They gamely pushed through and by mid-morning they felt better. GW started talking about repairing a fence next. Every day there was a new chore to be done and soon they'd been there almost two weeks. Tim was getting the feeling they'd never be allowed to leave.

GW was treating Tim more like his kid, Justin, telling him when to go to bed, when to get up, how to do chores, like he couldn't think on his own, which was irritating. He'd even started calling him Justin, just occasionally, but more than was comfortable. Tim would correct him and GW would apologize. Tim just wanted to get out of there. And Resa did too.

Leaving was going to be an issue though as neither he nor Resa seemed to have any energy at the end of the day and were too sick and tired to push to go in the mornings. Tim knew Resa had to be sick if she wasn't getting back on the road. This had been going on now for over a week—feeling sick and groggy and headachy until early afternoon. GW seemed to be feeling unwell too. They couldn't understand it. Resa said maybe they'd caught a flu bug somehow.

There was another thing which wasn't right. GW always showed up when they were talking by themselves. If he saw them talking, he'd wander up to them. Tim figured he was lonely and wanted them to be his family and they'd do everything together. But they weren't his family. The guy was getting weirder and weirder. Tim had to talk to Resa on his own.

Chapter 8

March - Arizona

"Resa! Resa, WAKE UP!"

Resa struggled to claw her way out of the fog that had seeped and settled into her brain.

"RESA!" Tim whispered more insistently, his words coming out like a hiss.

She blinked her eyes, confused and groggy. Darkness still surrounded them as she pried her eyelids open and tried to focus on the face of the person shaking her shoulders.

"Whaaat? What's going on?" she slurred and mumbled. She felt heavy, so very heavy.

"Resa, something's wrong! I think we're being poisoned! We gotta get out of here. Max woke up whining like he was in pain. I tried to make him feel better and I was petting his belly, and then he threw up. All over the bedroom floor. He's a little better now, but he's acting really sleepy and he can't walk right, like he's drunk. I don't know what's wrong but all I can think of is I didn't like my supper so I gave Max most of it. And now I don't feel as tired and sick as I have been. But Max is sick. Something's wrong," he repeated.

Resa squinted as she tried to follow Tim's longer than normal speech. She was having a hard time concentrating.

"You know how we've been feeling so horrible when we get up in the morning, and we're better by afternoon. I think GW is putting something in our food at supper. I think he's drugging us to keep us from leaving. We gotta get out of here."

A dim alarm sounded in Resa's muddled brain as Tim was talking. Food...feeling sick...Max...Wait.

"Wait, what?!" Resa felt adrenaline kick in to pull her out of the stupor which had wrapped itself around her body.

"Ssh! Don't let GW hear you!!" Tim whispered urgently, fear permeating his voice. "I think there's something in the food," Tim repeated slowly. "You know how he talks all the time about his wife and his kid and how he could've helped them with those plants he grows in his garden? Like if they would'a had more of his home-grown meds, they'd still be alive. And he has all those homemade spices in his cupboard he uses when he cooks? I think it's making us sick."

Resa's eyes were wide as she stared at Tim. She was now dreadfully aware of every word he was saying and, even more terrifyingly, she had a horrible feeling he was right. Tim's eyes were panicked and darting to the closed door as he tried to get her into a seated position. Could it be true? They'd been at GW's for, well, she wasn't even sure how long anymore. She remembered the first couple of days clearly when it seemed like he always had one more thing for them to do. But then when they started to feel sick, they had decided not to travel until they felt better. At first, she'd been terrified it was K-Pox. She'd had nightmares about dying painfully and never seeing her family again.

She thought of the extreme grogginess in the mornings, but assumed it was because she was sleeping restlessly and pushing her body to the limit during the day. It had never occurred to her that something else was going on. But what Tim was saying made sense. They usually made their own breakfast, then they ate packaged food for lunch because they didn't want to trek back to the house in the middle of the day.

But dinner...GW always left early and had it waiting for them when they got back to the house. He said he liked making a home cooked meal. They ate together and then went early to bed as they were all too tired to keep their eyes open afterwards. Last night she was so exhausted she'd barely eaten and gone to bed without even assisting with clean up, hoping extra sleep would help her body get back on track. But maybe that wasn't it at all...

"OhmygoodnessTim! He's been holding us captive by keeping us weak and sick."

Every night GW talked all through dinner without Resa and Tim getting a word in. At first it was endearing to hear him talk so much about his wife, Debra, and how he missed her. But after the third night when he told the same stories over again, it had started to sound a bit more frenzied. He would talk about how the hospitals and the doctors had been no help for Debra's cancer and they'd made her even more sick with all those chemicals.

Resa had just thought it was the ramblings of a sad old man, torn apart by grief, but he had started to talk more about the herb garden growing miracle cures and he even started mixing up Tim's name with Justin's.

"We've gotta get out of here! Where's your backpack?" Tim insisted. He rustled through the blankets, clothes, and shoes at the end of her bed. Some nights Resa just slept in her clothes, kicking her boots off at the last minute before her head hit the pillow.

"Wait Tim. Wait." she whispered, fully sitting up and holding her aching head.

Tim looked at her as if she were standing in the middle of a railroad track and a train was coming.

"We need to slow down just a second and think." Resa rubbed her hands across her face, trying to get her brain to start clicking together. The headache which was there most mornings now throbbed dully at the base of her skull and pulsed in her left eye.

"We need a plan. We need supplies. We need to know how to get out of here and we need to make sure GW won't follow us and somehow force us to come back," she whispered.

Tim stopped rustling around the room and turned to face her.

"You're right. You're right. Yeah. We definitely need food and water. But how the heck are we going to carry all those supplies when we feel like this?" Tim stopped and looked at Resa.

"The 4-WHEELER!" they whispered together.

"He has two of them, so we wouldn't be leaving him totally stranded if we took one," Tim added.

"We could load it with some supplies and load up our backpacks later when we have to start hiking," Resa whispered as the threads of the plan started forming a picture in her foggy head.

"I was going to take it out anyway to carry the fence posts we're replacing," Tim said, "I can get an extra gas can and maybe even mess with the other one so it won't start right away." Tim and Resa froze as they heard the house creak and moan with the wind.

"GW might be waking up soon. Let's try to sneak as many supplies as we can today, and we'll leave tonight. Tim, we're going to have to pretend like everything's ok so GW doesn't suspect anything. Can you do that?" Resa whispered quickly to Tim as she listened for any signs of movement from the other bedroom.

Tim stood a little taller and simply said, "We have to if we're gonna get out of here."

Resa nodded in reply. "You better go then. I'll get up once I'm sure my head won't fall off and roll away."

"I'm gonna go check on Max and then see what I can pack." Tim quietly turned the knob of Resa's door and peeked out into the hallway.

The door made a small creak as he shut it behind him and Resa froze, listening for any sounds that might have disturbed GW down the hall. Thankfully, she only heard the rise and fall of his snoring.

Resa tried to think about supplies they might need but her thoughts felt like they were floating through mud in her brain. Resa shook her head, anger and the motivation to flee burning away the effects of whatever was in her system.

Ignoring her headache and the waves of dizziness, Resa started to grab everything belonging to her and stuffed it into her backpack. She couldn't believe she hadn't reacted more intensely to GW's ramblings the past few days, week? Or two?? Holy crap! How long had they been here? The days had drifted by. She'd been so very tired though. She was barely able to move her arms and legs down the short hallway every night to make it to bed. Then the next day they'd wake up and do it all over again. No wonder she'd had no energy to be alarmed by what GW had been saying.

"The doctors all had the sign of evil on them. I could tell by the way their eyes looked," GW said one evening after he talked about Debra and their vacations. Resa was pretty sure she could repeat every story verbatim at this point. GW's eyes would grow distant as he talked about the small town with the flower covered gazebo and the world's largest flower pot. There's where Debra collapsed and when they'd found out she had stage four pancreatic cancer.

Just a few nights ago, his verbal tirade had led down an even more bizarre path describing her treatment and the back garden at the cabin. GW's eyes had shimmered brightly in the lantern light.

"They knew. They knew she was special. They wanted her power. I could see it in the way they whispered when they thought I wasn't looking. Justin and I were going to break her out of there, but we were too late. They killed her. Sure as shootin they murdered her." Tears had run down GW's face and his face twisted with grief and anger. After that, GW said he and Justin didn't trust anyone so they made the special garden here with God's own herbs, pulled from the mountain itself. GW said when Justin fell off the roof last year and his leg had been mangled, they knew the herbs would draw on divine power to heal him.

"But those demon doctors must have tainted my garden because my son, our baby, the last piece of my beautiful Debra, turned red with fever. His body shook until his teeth chattered and he died in my arms." GW had paused, and then his voice boomed, "You see? They killed him too. I burnt the garden to the ground and expunged their poison from my doorstep. Now they can't touch the new plot because God sent me angels to tend it." He smiled at Resa when he said the last part about the angels.

Even through her haze, Resa should've seen the danger. She just thought GW was being dramatic. Magic and demon doctors! Resa wondered if it was grief that drove GW to madness. Grief so strong it snapped the threads that tethered his reality to the present. She shuddered. If she found her entire family dead, would she end up like GW?

Tears slid down Resa's cheeks as she searched for a missing shirt. Hot fury bubbled up inside her. How could she have been so blind? How did a 17 year-old kid spot danger before she did?

She was supposed to be the mom! Resa sighed, closed her eyes and took a deep breath. She hadn't been looking for danger. She was too focused on the future instead of what was right in front of her. As painful as it was, she had to pay attention to the 'now,' instead of the 'what will be.' Their survival depended on it.

Resa spotted the shirt and grabbed it along with her wool hiking socks. They really needed to be washed, but there was no time. She stuffed everything in her backpack, double checked to make sure her gun and box of ammo were in the side compartment and folded the blankets on her bed. She would grab her toothbrush after dinner along with the small bottles of soap and shampoo she'd been using. Maybe she could take a bar of soap from the cupboard. She started to make a mental list of what she could grab and hide throughout the day. She only had a small window of time before GW was up.

Hands on her hips, she looked around for anything she had missed and realized if she forgot something, it didn't matter. Leaving things behind was how this new life worked. Satisfied, Resa shoved her backpack in the closet and opened the door to the hallway. She could hear faint snoring down the hall, but there was more rustling too. Resa heard Tim shuffling around in his room. She'd better hurry. Resa crept as fast and as quietly as she could through the small living room and into the kitchen. Her headache had lessened but was still throwing off her balance and she had to grab onto the couch as she went by. GW kept small plastic grocery bags under the sink. She grabbed a couple, walked quietly out to the shelves in the garage, and began filling the bags with canned goods, jerky, granola, tortillas, oatmeal packs, dried fruit, cups of mac and cheese, and instant potatoes. GW had told them he'd been checking his neighbors' houses for a while now, so luckily, the shelves were stocked full. Resa had a small twinge of guilt. She felt bad stealing, but they might die if they stayed. She hoped GW wouldn't notice anything was missing until they were gone.

Resa froze as she heard the creak of the door behind her and started to make up a story of how she was packing their lunch for the day. A small, wet nose hit the back of her leg and Resa's shoulders sagged in relief.

"Where you gonna put that bag?" Tim whispered. Resa reached down to pet Max. His tail was wagging, but Tim was right, he did not have his usual energy and spunk.

"I thought I'd hide it outside behind the chicken coop for now. It's somewhat close to where we park the 4-wheelers so we can grab it later. I'll do it when I gather eggs for breakfast."

"Ok, I'm going to load up the fence posts. I can't disable the other 4-wheeler right now cause GW will take one out today. I'll fill up the gas cans though."

GW had been stockpiling gas from neighbors and cars along the road. He said the truck he owned probably wouldn't even start anymore, so he only used gas for the ATVs. Resa walked out to the chicken coop to hide the bag behind some old crates and wire. The chickens clucked their disapproval, but she shushed them.

"This is not a safe place for us! You'll be ok though ladies." Resa had grown fond of this chore in the morning. She would miss fresh eggs.

Resa quickly walked back into the house and started making breakfast on the propane powered stove. When Tim came inside, she whispered, "We'll have to leave after GW's asleep tonight. Maybe we can push the 4-wheeler down the driveway and on the road for a while so it doesn't wake him up. Hopefully we'll be long gone before he even notices." She handed him a plate of scrambled eggs and a piece of toast and took what was left over for herself.

"He was telling me he got about 60 miles to a tank of gas, maybe we can even get more. And then if we have the extra gas can…"

Tim stopped talking as they heard GW's door open down the hallway. Tim shoveled the rest of his eggs into his mouth, handed Resa his plate, grabbed the toast to eat on his way outside, and whistled for Max to follow him. She put extra toast on a plate next to the eggs she gathered for GW. He would make his own breakfast before he joined them. She hurried to follow Tim outside.

81

Resa was positive GW was medicating himself with herbs from the garden too. He used to get up early to wake them up. But the last few days he barely got up before Tim and Resa headed out for the day and his verbal rants in the evening had gotten longer. Resa had thought it was because he was getting older and maybe not in the best of health. In any other situation she'd feel more compassion for him, but all she was feeling was betrayed. She had her own family to take care of, Tim and Max included!

The day seemed to fly by at times and creep along at others. GW came out when they were digging the holes for the fence posts and kept up a steady stream of chatter about fences and free roaming chickens and the predators he was protecting them from. Isn't that ironic, Resa thought, he saw himself as the chicken savior too.

Lunch was canned ham, packs of dried pineapple, and chips. At least they knew those items couldn't be tampered with. Her headache finally disappeared, and she had been drinking so much water she had to excuse herself multiple times. She wanted all the poison out of her system. She also wanted to make sure she was fully hydrated before going back to hiking where water might be scarce.

"Well, I better get back and whip up something for dinner," GW said when the sun started to sink in the sky. It was late afternoon and they only had a few more holes to dig before they called it a day.

"We'll see you back at the house!" Resa said as brightly as she could muster, feeling her anger rise. She saw Tim steal a side glance at her, then refocus all his effort on digging. To his credit, he hadn't shown any signs something was wrong. He'd taken Max for a small walk after lunch, mumbling something about needing to stretch. She hoped her performance had been just as convincing. After GW rode away, she and Tim stopped digging when they were sure they were alone.

"I think we should go in the middle of the night, like around 2:30, cause it's dark and GW will still be sound asleep by then," Tim suggested quickly.

"That would be good," Resa agreed, "We can both sleep a couple of hours to get our energy up."

"We better get back," Tim said, looking at the afternoon sun slinking down the sky. He stacked the last two posts against the fence and Resa jumped in the back of the 4 wheeler. They didn't say a word on the drive to the house, both of them knowing their plan had to go smoothly.

At dinner, Resa made a big show of her head and stomach hurting, playing off the exhaustion from the night before. GW was deep into telling a story and didn't ask questions when she washed the uneaten food off her plate and retired to her room. Tim had said he would make himself throw up when he took Max out for his walk. Hopefully he would get rid of the tainted food before it had a chance to digest. Resa just hoped he didn't get caught up in GW's ramblings and take too long to get out the door. She took a shower, feeling disappointed they would have to leave indoor plumbing behind, then jumped out, dressed, and grabbed more supplies from the cabinet under the sink.

Resa tucked everything into the dirty clothes she was carrying and peeked into the hall. Coast was clear. Back in her room she pulled out her backpack and packed up any remaining items. Her heart was racing, but she knew she needed to sleep. She heard the front door open and Max's paws on the front porch. Good. Tim was taking Max for his nightly walk, just like always. She dressed in the clothes she'd wear in the early morning and crawled into bed. She heard GW rummaging around the kitchen for the snack he always ate before bed and then pad down the hall to his room. At least it was lights out early around here. Resa set the alarm on her watch for 2:30 am and closed her eyes.

After what had only seemed like a few minutes, Resa shot up in bed, her breath coming in rapid bursts and the alarm on her watch buzzing frantically. Go time. She quickly pushed the button to silent and held her breath as she sat still for a moment, listening to the sounds of the house around her. Loud snoring, like a buzz saw, floated down the hallway. GW was still sleeping...for now.

She had agreed to meet Tim outside and hoped he was up and ready. She didn't want to risk having to wake him and Max. Resa grabbed the full backpack from the floor so she could sling it on her back and picked up her boots to carry until she got outside. As slowly and quietly as she dared, she opened the door and glanced down the hallway. Even though Resa was certain her heartbeat was pounding loud enough to be heard, GW's snoring continued uninterrupted. She tiptoed through the living room and paused to listen by the kitchen door. Satisfied GW was still asleep, Resa stepped out into the night.

She was relieved to see Tim standing next to the ATV with Max. The 4-wheeler was stocked with water, a gas can, the helmets Resa insisted they take, and Tim's backpack, leaving only a little space for her to load her pack.

"Oh wait!" Resa's head snapped up. She almost forgot the bag she'd hidden. She snuck past the sleeping hens and hurriedly added it to the pile.

"I disconnected the battery on the other ATV," Tim whispered. "I was going to deflate the tires, but it seems like it might take too long so I went for the battery instead."

"Ok. Let's hope that's good enough," Resa whispered back.

"Let's get the hell outta here," Tim said and shifted the gears to neutral. He moved to the side and held onto the steering wheel.

Together they started pushing the ATV towards Highway 160…towards escape…and on towards home.

Chapter 9

April - Arizona to Colorado

Tim was glad he'd asked GW so many questions about the ATV. The knowledge helped with planning. Sixty to 80 miles on a full tank of gas. With an extra 5 gallons in the gas can maybe 120 to 160 miles total. But the machine was overloaded with two adults, two full hiking packs, topped up containers of water, and extra gas. So probably closer to 120 miles than 160. Whatever it was, it was further away from GW. He felt sorry for GW, but not *that* sorry.

During their stay, Tim and Resa had told GW about their planned route to Resa's home. Now that they were escaping, they discussed if they should make new plans in case GW followed them. They decided to stick to their original route. Any other road was so far out of their way it would add miles to their trip, and Resa didn't want to add any extra mileage. If GW was going to chase them, they'd deal with it then.

They'd been driving for several hours, Max sitting upright on the seat between them. Every now and then Tim would turn off the engine and they'd take off their helmets to listen for another ATV engine. If they heard GW coming, they would hide. It was the best they could do. Just ride until the gas ran out and hide if they needed to. They didn't want to shoot him. Just get away from him. Tim shook his head. This whole situation was like something out of a movie. In a movie there'd be a scary guy carrying a gun trying to kill them. GW wasn't going to try to kill them. Was he? Tim wished he hadn't thought of it. Now he was going to worry about a crazy, gun-toting man coming after them.

They had no idea how fast they were going as this was an older model ATV and didn't come with a speedometer or odometer. He didn't think he was driving too fast, but any speed seemed unsafe when you didn't have the body of a car protecting you. Driving too fast could cause them to wreck or at the very least would use more miles to the gallon. They needed every mile they could get. Tim wished he could tell how far they'd gone and how much further they could count on traveling. Too bad they wouldn't find filled-up gas cans left conveniently along their route. Now that'd be cool! And water. And especially cooked food. He sighed and kept driving along the moon-lit road.

About 30 minutes later Tim again stopped the ATV. He hated stopping but knew they needed to check for GW's engine sounds, and also to warm up. It was so cold. The early morning temperatures lately had been just above freezing. Tim wasn't used to this temperature. He'd thought Resa was being overly cautious yesterday when she'd told him to layer as much clothing on as he could. He'd hiked with his dad in cold weather before, but it hadn't been like this. Of course when they were hiking they hadn't been going 30 miles an hour on an ATV on an icy spring morning. They'd usually been in a tent in protected valleys or canyons in the summer. And they would've been sleeping this early in the morning. Not running away from a crazy man!

He and Resa ran up and down the road a little to get their muscles warmed up, Max bounding along beside them. They were still feeling slightly groggy and headachy from GW's drugs, but just being away from GW made them feel better. They listened carefully for any noise in the still air. The skittering of lizards or maybe kangaroo rats had at first startled them, but Tim was able to identify the sounds from previous camping trips. They also heard the yips and barks of coyotes. Max perked up his ears and turned his head in the direction of the barks but didn't seem inclined to go. Tim figured Max had probably heard coyotes while living at the store so wasn't particularly curious. He was glad. He didn't want to put Max on a leash every time they stopped to keep him from joining his pack of wild cousins.

Not hearing any suspicious human noises, the three of them settled themselves back on the ATV and continued on. Tim reflected they'd been on a major highway for hours and had not seen or heard anyone. No one. There were no lights anywhere except the stars and the moon. He and his dad would have loved to stargaze with these dark skies. He sighed.

As the sun rose the eastern sky turned orange, shot through with brilliant shades of blue. He squinted as he drove into the colorful sunrise. They were on the east side of Kayenta and now using the last of their gas supply. They drove through the small town hoping no one would jump out at them. Either no one was there, or they weren't bothering with people traveling through.

Neither Tim nor Resa knew what lay ahead. They knew there'd be more mountains and a lot of hiking if they couldn't find another vehicle. Tim was grateful the ATV had gotten them this far. When he got frustrated about how slowly they were going he reminded himself how much faster the ATV was than walking. But what wouldn't he give for a car and a tank full of gas.

They stopped again for a sound check and Resa suggested eating breakfast since they'd stopped. While dipping crackers into peanut butter they heard a motorized vehicle coming from the west. They looked at each other wide-eyed. GW shouldn't have been up this early. Maybe it wasn't him.

Resa said, "We need to hide. Fast."

They looked around for somewhere to take cover. Once GW (if that's who it was) came over the ridge, the road was so flat he'd be able to spot them from miles away. All they could see was flat desert country covered with small bushes and large rock outcroppings. In the distance were mountains but they didn't have time to get there. The best chance was a large rock formation off the road to the right about 100 yards, if they could get to it in time. They threw their belongings on the ATV and listened. They still heard the drone of the other vehicle so knew their ATV wouldn't be heard by the other driver. They quickly drove to the east side of the rock and hid everything from the view of the traveler.

"I'll cover up our tire tracks!" Tim ripped branches off a bush, ran back to the road and began sweeping their tracks away. Walking backwards he tripped over a bush and cursed. His feet were dragging in the sand and he tripped over rocks and bushes as he tried to hurry. This was like one of those nightmares where someone is coming to get you and you can't move fast enough to get away. He stood up again and listened. He could hear the high-pitched sound of the engine getting closer. He was relieved when he finally made it back to Resa. She'd been busy grabbing brush and covering the 4-wheeler. She'd put Max's leash on him and had tied him closely to it.

Resa gave Tim a handful of branches. "Here. Stick these in your clothes to break up your silhouette."

She was busy putting branches in her waist band, pockets, and hair. Tim did the same. They were closely watching the western horizon so they saw the ATV as soon as it appeared on the top of the low ridge several miles away. They sat down, trying to make themselves small and hoped they wouldn't be seen. They didn't know what would happen if GW saw them, but he'd been so weird lately they didn't want to find out. Tim had optimistically thought maybe GW would be ok about their going, but obviously not. Or why would he have chased them this far? To get back his ATV and his stuff? Or did he think they were his family and he wanted them back?

The machine got closer and louder and their hearts pounded harder. They stayed hidden and still. They wanted no movement to attract his eye. This meant they couldn't see him, but they could hear the ATV as it moved past. They peered out again. It was GW. They recognized his plaid jacket and cowboy hat. And he had his rifle with him. The vehicle drove slowly past. Just when they felt they could breathe again, the 4-wheeler stopped. They held their breaths. Resa quietly peered around the rock.

Resa whispered, "He's stopped and I think he's eating. We have to be really quiet. That means this guy too," she said, nodding her head at Max.

Tim noticed she didn't say Max's name because when he thought you were talking about him, he'd get excited and start prancing about. Tim glanced at Max. Of course he knew he was being talked about and his tail thumped happily on the ground.

"Sssh!" Tim stroked Max's back. Max lay his head on Tim's lap and closed his eyes. Tim smiled. All this tension and Max decided this was a good time to take a nap. Goofy dog. It's just as well he wasn't a watch dog at heart. He'd have been barking up a storm right now. They sat quietly and every now and then Resa would peek out at GW. She whispered to Tim that GW wasn't looking behind him at all, mostly looking ahead at the endless highway east and the looming mountains ahead.

"Maybe he'll quit here and go home," Tim whispered hopefully.

Resa shrugged and whispered back, "We can hope. I guess we're stuck here for a while though."

They'd scooted to the shady western side of their rock. Tim wished he could sit in the sun as it was still chilly and he was glad of Max's warmth.

After what seemed ages, though it was only 15 minutes by his watch, they heard the ATV start again. They hoped GW would turn around and go home, but no, he continued going east and disappeared over the next rise.

"Damn! Go home!" Tim wanted to swear more but not in front of Resa. He said lots of curse words in his head even though it wasn't as satisfying as cursing aloud. But this was not the time.

"Ugh. I'm going to stand up. I'm stiff." At Resa's worried look Tim said, "Don't worry. I'm staying in the shadow. He won't see me."

Max jumped up and started to bound away but was caught short by the leash.

"Stay here Max. Good boy. We're just moving around a bit. Gotta stay quiet though." Tim pulled Max close and ruffled the fur on his neck. He looked up and saw Resa watching them. He looked down quickly. It was the kind of look his mom had when she smiled at him. It made him sad but also made him feel less alone.

About half an hour later they heard the ATV coming back and hid again. They watched as GW disappeared over the western ridge and signed in relief.

"How long before we leave?" Tim asked.

"Let's give it an hour or so. I hate waiting that long, but sound travels so far here. We need to be sure."

The breakfast they'd started hours ago ended up being late lunch instead. Tim didn't like skipping any meal, but he figured he'd better get used to it. One of the good things about staying at GW's, besides sleeping in a real bed, was the three meals a day. But he'd rather skip a meal here and there if the alternative was being held there forever.

Around noon they decided they'd head out, and somewhere between Kayenta and Four Corners they ran out of gas. Again.

They sighed as they got off the ATV and unloaded their gear. This was going to be the first real hiking they'd have to do. Tim helped Resa get her backpack settled properly and then put on his pack. He was still adjusting the straps when he looked up and saw Resa striding down the road.

"Hey, wait up! Don't start out so fast. You'll be tired too soon." He took long steps to catch up. "We'll be lucky if we walk two miles an hour so you should go slower! You'll hurt yourself if you walk too fast. Besides, you're still breaking in your new boots."

Resa scowled. "I just want to get moving. I'm so sick of being slowed down and we just spent most of the day behind a rock!"

"Yeah, well, we won't get too far if you sprain an ankle or hurt your feet." Tim didn't want to be rude, but she was walking too fast and they couldn't keep up that pace for long.

She sighed frustratedly and slowed down. They walked silently side by side, their boots quietly hitting the pavement. Tim kept his pace slower than he had when hiking with his father. Resa was more like his mom—shorter legs, shorter stride. He settled into a moderate pace and looked down at Max, now unrestrained by the leash. Max was having the time of his life. He loped ahead, would stop and find things to smell and pee on, and they'd pass him. Then

Max would look up and run to catch up, tail wagging and tongue lolling out. Then it would start all over again.

When they were on the ATV they'd seen signs for Four Corners, and now that they were walking it seemed like ages between the signs. At two to three miles per hour each mileage sign was a reminder of how long it took to get anywhere. Tim glanced at Resa. He could imagine how she felt, wanting to get home to her family. He'd feel the same if he were going home. But he wasn't. He was going in the opposite direction. A part of him wanted to run back home, to be where his family had been. But he'd been through it a million times already and he'd made his decision. Go with Resa as far as Laurel and then head to Maine. At least this time he wasn't using birds for direction. He'd have to tell Resa about that sometime.

One of the things Tim liked about hiking was the quiet. He could actually hear nature. When he walked he could hear his breathing, boots on the trail, clothes and pack brushing on things. When he stopped and was still, he could hear all the noises he often missed: wind blowing in the trees or in this case, across the desert. He stopped to listen. Nothing except the wind. He was still getting used to the silence. No planes overhead. No cars whirring by.

Resa turned and looked at him.

"Sorry! Just stopped to listen. I like listening to things when I hike. Though there's not much here to listen to."

She stopped, cocked her head and listened. "You're right. Not much." She smiled briefly and started hiking again. Tim thought she picked up her pace, as if she were trying to make up for those few seconds they'd paused. He shrugged and caught up.

They were walking through the Navajo Nation Indian Reservation and could see the rock formations in Monument Valley. Tim loved looking at the rock monuments. He imagined what the formations could be. Perhaps a giant's castle which was destroyed by the wind god who tore the castle apart piece by piece shrieking as it cruelly whipped the castle into sand and small rocks. Or maybe it was a giant ant hill where billions of ants built their home and they lay in wait for animals to climb up. Then the ants would drag the animal into their burrow to eat. He liked the giant story better. He didn't much like ants.

As they approached Four Corners they saw motels, restaurants, casinos, gas stations, and other buildings. The closer they got, the more they slowed down.

"What if people are here?" Tim looked at Resa.

"I guess we'll find out," she said and shrugged. "We have no choice but to stop somewhere. My feet and legs are sore, and we need a place to stop for the night. Maybe we'll find someplace that looks ok. I hate to admit it, but I'm exhausted."

Tim looked at her. She did look tired. They found a hotel just off the main road and chose a room where a cart had been left outside the open door, as if the cleaning crew had just walked away. The room had two queen-sized beds and a view of the swimming pool. A swimming pool with water! They looked through the window at the pool with relief and put down their packs. Max trotted over to the shallow end of the pool. Tim laughed as Max splashed in then began to lap up the water thirstily.

Speaking quietly, Resa said, "I'm going to take off my boots and sit for a bit. We can wait a while to see if anyone else is here. If no one is, it wouldn't hurt to go swimming. And soak my feet!"

They sat in the two padded chairs at the little table in front of the window and waited silently, listening intently for any human noise. A wet, smelly Max had tried to join them, but Tim put his leash on and tied him in the doorway. Tim looked around. This was a fairly new hotel and would have been nice when things were normal. A light coating of sand covered everything including the cleaning cart outside, but otherwise the room was clean. They'd tried the water faucets but no water. The pool glittered in the late afternoon sun beckoning to them.

"Don't you think we should swim before the sun goes down?" Tim asked. "It's gonna get cold tonight." He was tired of waiting. They'd heard nothing but the wind blowing against the building.

"You're right. If someone were here I guess we'd have heard them by now. I'm willing to chance it."

They took turns in the bathroom where they changed into shorts and t-shirts and grabbed hotel towels. Before they got in the pool Tim found the skimming net and skimmed the pool for bugs and other floating debris, and Resa filled their water containers and added the purifier tablets. The pool was chlorinated, but they had no idea what could live in old pool water.

They walked barefooted to the shallow end and stepped into the pool. The water was cold but as they got used to it, it felt good to wash away the sand of the day and to soak their aching feet. Tim tried to get Max to swim to him, but he stayed in the shallow end where his paws stayed on solid ground. Tim wondered if they could find hotels like this all the way across the U.S. With swimming pools! Awesome! The sun slowly dipped below the horizon and the wind turned cold. Resa got out and Max followed her, but Tim stayed. Only when his teeth were chattering did he decide it was time to call it quits. He climbed out, grabbed his towel and water container, and went back to the room to dry out and warm up.

They had supper at their tiny table enjoying their first evening without GW. Tim felt better than he had in a while and hoped the dull headaches he'd been having would soon stop. Maybe it was too early for all the drugs GW had given them to be out of their systems, but he did feel better. And every day now would be an improvement.

It was a little odd to be sleeping in the same room as Resa, but Tim figured they'd get used to having close quarters if they were going to hike across the country. And neither of them had mentioned having separate rooms. Tim didn't want to be separated as two people would be better for defense, and in horror movies, once two people separated, they almost always got killed. He mentally shook himself. Why did he always think of scary movies? It shouldn't be scary as they both had guns and Max was there (sleeping on the floor as he was still wet), but just because he had a gun, that didn't mean he wanted to use it.

They got an early start the next morning after checking the hotel for snacks. They found a few candy bars behind the hotel's admission desk and stuffed them away for later in the day. They also grabbed a couple of complimentary toothbrushes and tiny sample tubes of toothpaste and soaps and lotions. They didn't want to use the toothbrushes they'd used at GWs as they might be drug contaminated. Besides, it just felt good to get rid of anything connected to him.

Tim started off at his normal hiking-with-Dad pace, his long legs striding comfortably, Max running a little ahead. He looked down and saw Resa had quickly caught up and started to pass him. He realized that he needed to slow down as Resa was going to walk as fast as he did or faster. He slowed his pace and Resa soon fell into step with him.

"Is this a comfortable pace for you?" he asked.

Resa took a deep breath in and blew it out before answering. "Yes and no. It's the speed I should go, but I really just want to run! After having the cars and the ATV, this is just so painfully slow. I know I have to pace myself, but it's so frustrating!"

They didn't stop for lunch; just rested and ate when they needed to. The day finally ended, but no motels this time so they pitched their tents on the side of the road. They were concerned about water and checked their map. Tomorrow they'd get to a small town along a river where they hoped to get water. Lack of water was going to be a real threat on this trip, especially as the temperatures got hotter.

The next day Tim noticed Resa wince as she put her arms through the straps of her pack, and gingerly put on her boots. He was sore too, but not like she was. He wanted to lighten her pack, but knew she wouldn't let him. Besides, he'd already packed as much as he could comfortably carry. Max seemed to be doing ok. Resa had suggested Tim check his paws to see if they were getting sore. So far so good. He was glad she'd mentioned it as he wouldn't have known. He had a lot to learn about dogs.

They were relieved when they reached the small town of Dennehotso and found a motel again, with a swimming pool, which was good for their water supply, swimming, and soaking tired, sore feet. Max climbed onto the bed and snuggled up to Tim. Tim smiled, but he didn't think his mom would have approved.

After a few more long tiring days they finally made it to Colorado. A new state! They pitched camp along the road and went through their evening routine—resting, eating, then bed. When Resa crawled into her tent Tim continued to sit at the glowing campfire. When they'd started their trek, Tim had kept the pages of a road atlas for the states they'd be traveling through. He pulled the pages out and separated the map of Arizona from the others. He looked at it for a long time, gently touching his hometown. He held the map over the flame and watched as it caught fire. Dropping the burning page, he watched it curl and smoke.

"Goodbye Arizona. Goodbye Mom and Dad. Goodbye Granddad. I love you," he said softly. The page crumpled into ash. Tim disappeared into the darkness of his tent.

The next days blended one into another. They were tired and sore and Resa was limping. They'd cut the toes off her boots with Tim's hunting knife. It may not have been the best thing to do, but she needed relief. The boots she had chosen had turned out to be too small, but they only realized that when her feet were swollen after full days of hiking. Tim had been shocked to see her toenails turning black and was afraid they were going to come off. He'd heard it could happen, but he'd never seen it. It must really hurt! Her slower pace frustrated her. She wanted nothing to slow her down. They'd look for bigger boots in Cortez, but they had to get there first.

The steep upward incline of the highway and the higher altitude made them tire more quickly. Tim could hardly wait til they got back to sea level again and flat roads. They watched the mileage signs for Cortez drop behind them agonizingly slowly.

They finally reached the *Welcome to Cortez* sign. Now they could stop and rest. Resa was looking so tired and had been limping even more the last few days. And Tim wasn't feeling much better. He was tired, his feet were sore, and his shoulders ached. As the buildings drew closer together, they walked more watchfully, staying out of sight when they could. Tim got that *creepy people are watching us* feeling again, and he looked forward to finding a place to rest and be out of sight.

Cortez was a beautiful town and if they were on vacation with their families this would be a great place Tim thought. They found a decent room in a hotel off the main road and planned to stay for a few days to get back into shape. While Resa rested her feet, Tim did some scouting and shopping. First on their list—new boots for Resa. He found the Hiking and More store and brought back several sizes of boots for her to try. They waited a few days until her feet lost some of their soreness and swelling before deciding which ones she'd take. He also brought back books on hiking (which she had asked for), and a book on raising dogs for himself. She read her books with interest and sent him back to the hiking store with a list of supplies. He brought back hiking socks, a headlamp, fuel for their camp stove, and refills of items they'd used up.

After a few days, Resa was ready to get back on the road. Tim thought they should stay longer to let her feet heal more, but Resa said they'd rest longer in Durango which wasn't far. She had told him about this nice old couple who'd given her a car and permission to use their house. The house was totally off the main road, and would add miles to their trip and her feet were already toast. But Resa was determined.

Chapter 10

May - Colorado

On the outskirts of town, they passed signs advertising ziplines and adventure tours.

Resa grimaced and said, "We've had plenty of adventure tours, thank you very much."

Her back, well EVERYTHING, was killing her from carrying the weight of the backpack for 10-plus hours a day. Her legs were weak, her hands were swollen, and her toenails felt like someone had set fire to her nail beds. Also, despite the hiking gaffer tape she had layered on the back of her feet, the blisters on her heels throbbed constantly.

At night Resa treated her damaged skin using alcohol swabs and antibacterial gel. She knew it was important to prevent infection, but once the blisters started there'd been no time to heal. She remembered thinking she'd walk until her legs shattered beneath her. At the time she thought she was being dramatic, but now she wondered if it might become reality.

At an abandoned auto repair shop, Resa laid out her US map next to the handwritten map Isla had given her. When she compared the maps, she nearly wept with relief. The house was miraculously along their route. Well, close enough.

"We just need to make it a little further," Resa muttered, pushing the pain to the back of her mind to focus on the maps. It had begun to sink in that her journey home might take months like she had originally feared. No planes or trains or cars would take her across the country. Only her feet. And frustratingly, she had pushed herself too far and needed a proper rest before she could keep going. So Isla and Alec's vacation house in Durango was it. This was their reprieve.

They had been following the same road for more days than she could count. The date on her watch told her it was May, and she couldn't believe it. She wished there was some way to let her family know she was trying! Sometimes the frustration from being silent burned like hot coals in her chest. It was why she propelled her body past its breaking point. But recently she couldn't seem to push any harder.

They'd just passed a Best Western and debated whether to stop there or push through the rest of the afternoon. Isla's map showed them turning off 160 and traveling along route 210, then on a few back roads until they got to the house. Her other map didn't show the roads Isla had written down, which made Resa a little nervous.

"Does it look close by?" Tim asked.

"Maybe 3 miles off 160? So that's pretty good." Resa replied. "It still means a couple hours walking."

"I think Max is good and I can go longer," Tim looked at her hesitantly. "Can you?"

"I have to," Resa said. She knew her pain was showing. She couldn't hide how she hobbled on her sore and screaming feet. Tim hadn't been able to mask his concern when she yelped in pain after putting on her backpack yesterday. He'd offered to take more in his pack, but she'd refused. She had gotten used to the weight again after they'd started walking a bit, but the first jolt of pain had taken her breath away. Strangely, her pack felt lighter today. He'd been up early this morning and she wondered if he'd snuck a few things out. She was too tired to protest.

She refolded the maps and put the hand-drawn one in her pocket for easy reference. One foot in front of the other. They trudged on, passing dry cleaners, cell phone stores, and kitchen countertop showrooms. Issues like wanting a bigger house or getting mad when a charger cord wouldn't reach the couch seemed like memories from a past life now, Resa thought. When they saw the blue sign for County Road 210, they took a break and sat outside an abandoned bakery. Planter pots were overgrown and sagging from the weight of volunteer weeds and decaying flowers. Resa's headache and overwhelming fatigue made her sick to her stomach. Her voice trembled slightly as she spoke.

"Just down 210 here, a few backroads, and we're there."

Tim gazed down the road as if he could see the house in the distance. They were too exhausted for conversation. Even Max looked drained. He plopped down when they had stopped, and limped up when it was time to go.

As the sun sank lower in the sky, the road turned and stretched ahead of them. Rocky embankments rose up and rippled out to towering buttes in the distance. Rusty mailboxes marked the turnoffs to houses tucked away from the road. She hoped they wouldn't run out of daylight. While they walked Resa grasped at threads of memories to calm her. But the throbbing in her head felt like it was scrambling her thoughts and reached all the way down her spine to shake her screaming nerve endings. She checked the map again. Please let it be close.

"Should be just around this curve," Resa said, her voice sounding thin and hollow.

They turned down a muddy driveway, her feet unsteady on the slick rocks when a log cabin finally appeared. Resa felt like she'd found a small piece of heaven in the middle of this ongoing nightmare. She looked at Tim and saw relief breaking through the lines of exhaustion etched on his face.

"Thank goodness there's only a few stairs," Resa said, climbing up the last step, groaning as she peeled off her backpack and dropped it onto the porch. A keypad lock on the metal front door was the only thing preventing them from entering their sanctuary.

"We'll just have to smash it or something. Or break a window," Tim said, looking around for a heavy object.

The padlock was the type with numbers and three letters under each number. Resa's desperation seeped into the tears forming in her eyes. Her brain slowly turned, something tickling at the back of her memory. What code word would they have used to keep out unwanted guests, but...something Isla had told her...Wait! ISLA!

"Don't forget our names as the code to get in!" Resa shouted. Tim stopped his search at the end of the porch to stare at her. He probably thought she'd finally lost it.

"Remember their names," Resa tried to explain. She limped forward to search for the numbers next to the correct letters. Her fingers were clumsy with fatigue but she finally put in: I-S-L-A = 4-7-5-2.

Resa took a deep breath and pressed enter. CLICK! The lock released and the door popped open. She stepped eagerly into the tidy living room, feeling completely overwhelmed by emotions. She stumbled past the rustic furnishings, collapsed on the couch, and let the tears fall. They had made it.

Resa woke slowly into the world. Light streamed through the windows and gave her a moment's comfort before reality bled in. They had been resting at the house for over a week and Resa's nightmares had mostly quieted. Not being in pain also helped with her sleep. She'd dreamt of soft green fields instead of the barbed wire cage that had no door. The morning after they'd arrived, they'd found clippers to cut down her toenails and relieve the pressure of the bruising and swelling. It had been incredibly painful, but worth it. Now she could walk without limping. The bruises on her shoulders and back were almost healed too. Along with the supplies in the cupboards, Resa was almost certain this house had been the shelter that had saved her life, at least so far. Now that she felt mostly recovered, Tim and Resa had talked last night and decided this would be the morning they'd leave.

Resa dressed quickly, taking time to carefully tape and wrap her feet. The blisters that hadn't split were almost healed and she didn't want to aggravate them. Pagosa Springs was 60 miles away, so it should take them maybe three days to get there and rest again if they needed to.

Resa made the bed, feeling badly that she couldn't wash the sheets or towels.

"Well, hello Max!" Resa said as their furry friend came bounding in to greet her. It appeared his feet were better too. She'd laughed when Tim had first put the walking booties on Max because he'd looked deeply offended, but he was used to them now. They kept his paws from getting blistered and infected too.

"Morning Tim!" Resa called out.

She heard him shuffling and thumping around the living room. They'd loaded their packs the night before so they'd be ready to go. They grabbed more batteries for their flashlights and a rope from the garage.

"I double checked we have everything packed," Tim told her as she walked down the hallway.

"I prefer this way of leaving someone's house rather than pushing a 4-wheeler in the middle of the freezing night," Resa said grinning.

"Definitely!" Tim smiled back.

Tim was actually a pretty handsome kid, Resa thought. All these days of just trying to survive made you forget to actually LOOK at the people you were with. She wondered what Meg would think when she introduced them. They ate their breakfast out on the porch and packed as much water as they could carry. Resa hated leaving the security of this place, but it was time. They made sure the front door was firmly locked and walked down the steps to head back to the highway.

"Admit it, I almost beat you last round," Resa said teasingly to Tim as she looked longingly at the Coffee Grind sign in downtown Pagosa Springs later that week. She'd love a latte right about now.

"No way! I spotted things all the way up to M before we stopped!" Tim protested. It was a game they played to pass the time. There was no music to listen to and no podcasts to entertain them. So before they stopped for a break, they tried to find as many items beginning with the letters of the alphabet as they could. C for clouds was easy, but they almost never found anything with X or Z.

Resa scratched Max behind the ears when suddenly, his whole body tensed. Resa sat up, listening for the sound of an engine or something that signaled danger, but she didn't hear anything.

"Max, what is it?" Tim whispered as he looked in the same direction as Max was staring. In an instant all three of them were on their feet. What had appeared to be a shadow under the awning of a barber shop transformed into a person.

"Hey!" the shadow called out as it walked across the road to meet them. "HEY!"

Even though Max was wagging his tail slowly, Resa and Tim took a step back. Apparently Max didn't think the thin, tangled haired, waving woman was much of a threat, but they hadn't spoken to anyone in weeks! And they'd learned their lesson. Trust no one.

The woman stopped about ten feet from where they were standing and looked them up and down. Resa had been wrong about her age. This was not a grown woman. In fact, she couldn't have been more than 16 years old.

"Hey," she said again, "Where'd you guys come from? Did you drive a car?"

"We're walking," Resa answered. "We don't want any trouble."

"How long have you been here? I've been coming back and forth to the store to get stuff. It seems like most of the town is gone, but I don't care. There's NO WAY I was gonna let Nana die alone." Then she mumbled to no one in particular, "Don't give a damn that my mom and her stupid boyfriend left without me. They're probably dead anyway."

Resa snuck a look at Tim who appeared dumbstruck. She watched the girl blink back tears and then let out a strangled yelp as Max walked towards her. Resa took a step forward.

"Max won't hurt you. And neither will we. We're just passing through," Resa said calmly, then asked, "Who is dying?"

"My Nana. She's not really my grandma, but she's the only person in the world who cares about me and I don't think she's gonna make it much longer." She took a breath. "Wait. You're not staying? You literally JUST got here." She looked over at Tim.

"Yeah. Well, no. I mean, we're just passing through." Tim's brow creased as he looked somewhat curious and confused all at once.

"Well, we have food and water. You can stay with us. Nana won't mind. It's gonna be dark and you gotta sleep somewhere, right?" The girl raised her eyebrows and looked hopefully between Resa and Tim.

"Oh! Well. That's very generous. Hang on a minute." Resa stepped back and drew Tim with her.

"What do you think?" she whispered. "She seems kinda nervous and all over the place... But if her Nana really is dying, I'd hate for her to be alone to face that. Of course, this could be a trap."

"She doesn't look dangerous. She looks kinda lost actually," Tim said, glancing back at the girl who was letting Max sniff her hand. She laughed as he licked her palm.

"I think she's lonely. And it will be getting dark soon," Resa said.

He shrugged. "I dunno. She's probably alright, but we got some mace at the last store if we need it. And we can always decide to sleep outside if we're not sure."

"And we can eat our own food to be safe," Resa added..

They wanted to be cautious, but Resa looked at the young girl running zig zags across the pavement as Max chased her and couldn't help but feel empathetic. This disease had destroyed life in so many different ways, but they didn't have to let it destroy compassion.

"Ok. We stick together and stay alert," Resa said quietly. Tim nodded in response.

"Soo, hey there!" Resa realized she had no idea what this girl's name was. "Thank you for asking us to stay. We'd like to, if it's still ok."

"But Max comes too," Tim added.

The girl ran over to stand in front of them.

"Yeah? Great! And of course your dog can come. I parked over there. I'll drive us back."

"You have a car?" Tim asked, surprised.

"It's Nana's car. I only use it to get groceries or whatever. All the gas stations are closed, but I still have almost a full tank of gas and Nana figured it was safer than walking by myself."

"How far is it to your house?" Resa asked as they followed her across the road.

"Just a couple of minutes away."

At least a short drive didn't get them too far off the path if they needed to make a break for it. If she had learned anything so far, it was to have a backup plan... or two.

The girl stopped at a blue Honda CR-V to open up the back hatch.

"You can throw your stuff in here if you want," she said.

"We didn't officially introduce ourselves. I'm Resa and this is Tim. What's your name?" Resa asked as she and Tim loaded their packs in the trunk.

"Amber Sierra Nevada Clarke." She rolled her eyes and slammed the door, "My mom thought it would be funny to name me after her favorite beer. But Nana calls me Sierra because she says I'm beautiful, just like the mountains. You can call me Sierra too."

Resa and Tim got in as Sierra started the car. The brakes squealed slightly as she navigated out of the parking lot. After walking for so many days, it felt like they were flying down the road. Soon they were turning into a residential area. The houses sat close together, a maze of porches and stone pillars framed by front yards striped with scraggly grass and clay. Trees stood tall with green and brown pine needles covering the ground around them. Sierra pulled into the gravel driveway of a small log and stone house with a wooden porch. A satellite dish jutted out from the corner of the roof.

"I'll tell Nana you're here," Sierra said, opening her door and bounding up the stairs. The clack of the screen door carried back to where Tim and Resa stood in the yard. They grabbed their backpacks and took a deep breath before they slowly followed her.

"Hopefully there's not a gang of terrorists with machine guns in there," Tim whispered.

"Fingers crossed," Resa whispered back.

Inside the front door, mud caked boots were set neatly beneath a wooden bench. Above, there was a mirror in which Resa saw a wild-haired woman staring back at her. Resa's face was rough and reddened in spots. Her hair stubbornly refused to stay under her hat and her face looked drawn. A small hand painted sign hung on the corner of the mirror and said, *Today is your day! Your mountain is waiting. So...get on your way! - Dr. Seuss.* Resa smiled. She had loved reading those books to the kids when they were little.

Resa could hear quiet voices drifting towards them from further inside the house. Thankfully she only heard Sierra and another woman's voice coming from the dimly lit room at the end of the entryway. They set their packs by the front door, but left their shoes on, just in case.

"Sierra?" Resa called out as she took a few steps.

"In here!"

As Resa's eyes adjusted, she could make out a living room next to a kitchen with white-washed cabinets. Resa found Sierra in the living room sitting next to a hospital bed. The bed was close to the lit fireplace. She was holding the hand of a broad-shouldered, gray-haired woman propped up by pillows and covered in quilts despite the warmth from the fire.

"Nana, this is Resa and Tim," Sierra said quietly. Max had wandered over and wagged his tail so it hit the foot of the bed with a thump.

"...and Max," she added, smiling.

Nana looked up at them and smiled pleasantly.

"Nice to meet ya."

Resa wasn't prepared for the strong gravelly voice that greeted them. Nana's face was weathered from years of sun and mountain air. Her brown eyes were bright, but her lips were tinged with shades of blue, the skin on her cheeks sagged, and under the covers her chest seemed like it was caving in on itself. Resa realized Sierra had been telling the truth. Nana would not be with them much longer.

"Thank you for letting us stay," Resa said.

"Grateful you're here," Nana took in a few shallow breaths. "Sierra shouldn't be here all alone takin care of me like this. She's got her whole life to live. She ain't dyin like me."

"I'm not leaving you. Ever." Sierra tucked her feet underneath her.

"I understand exactly what you mean," Tim muttered.

"Bedrooms are down the hall. Sierra, show 'em the bathroom and tell 'em about the generator." Nana closed her eyes as Sierra unfolded herself from the chair and motioned for Tim and Resa to follow her.

"There's Nana's room and my room. You guys can use them. We haven't slept there in months. I sleep with Nana to keep the fire going and keep her propped up so she can breathe." Sierra pointed to the bathroom. "We have a generator, but only run it for an hour at a time. It uses water from the well so you can take a shower. Towels are in the closet. It's cold and you gotta be fast, but it works. I make Nana coffee too. It's her favorite."

Resa's eyebrows went up. "You make hot coffee?"

"Yeah, there's plenty if you want some," Sierra answered. She walked down the hallway but stopped and turned back to face them.

"She doesn't have K-Pox or anything. She got lung cancer a year ago, but the treatments didn't work. Then all this pandemic crap and we couldn't get her meds. So I've been taking care of her the best I can. She said it's just her time to go." Tears filled Sierra's eyes and spilled over. She wiped at her nose and cheeks with the back of her hand.

"She won't even let me have a funeral. Said to cover her with a sheet when it happens, she doesn't need a fuss. But I wanna do right by her like she's done with me."

Tim took a step forward so fast, Sierra startled and almost tripped. He caught her by the elbow and steadied her.

"Don't worry," he said with determination. "She won't die alone and she won't be covered only by an old sheet. We'll find a proper way to bury her, I promise."

Sierra's face softened and she nodded at him.

"If you need anything, we're out here." Sierra turned and walked away. They could hear the chair creak as she took up her spot next to Nana.

"We can't leave her alone," Tim said to Resa, his back still turned to her.

"We won't."

Over the next few days, Tim and Resa settled into the house. There were no red flags this time, only sadness and waiting. Sierra rarely left Nana's side. Resa took her place when Nana was sleeping so Sierra could slip out for short walks and stretch her legs. They even had the chance to celebrate Tim's 18th birthday with some Hostess cupcakes they'd found in a Quick Mart storeroom, and the expiration date was still good. It was a welcome distraction.

They'd been talking to Sierra about the future and traveling with them. Even though she seemed uncertain and didn't want to talk about Nana's death, she was listening. Tim burned off energy by looking for new supplies in town. Sierra went along to try on hiking boots and to find a new jacket. She and Tim came home giggling after they'd gone into the abandoned bowling alley and Tim had hit a strike.

"Tim told me about his eighteenth birthday plans to go bowling with his folks and how he'd never gotten to go. So we figured we might as well check it out," Sierra explained. "He even did a cartwheel in celebration! His legs flailed everywhere, it was the funniest thing I ever saw!"

Resa's heart swelled to catch a glimpse of them simply being teenagers and having fun.

"That strike was your parents telling you they're still with you, Tim. Life is always worth livin cause you never know what miracle is just down the road," Nana told him. Tim ducked his head and smiled.

Sometimes Resa heard Nana's gruff whisper rise and fall in the living room. She knew Nana was telling Sierra to live her life, even if it meant leaving behind the home she'd always known. At night they'd all sit together, and Nana would talk about growing up in the mountains, visiting the hot springs before they became a tourist trap, and how a little Sierra had shown up on her doorstep after she missed the bus on the first day of kindergarten and couldn't find her way home.

Over the past day or so, Resa noticed Nana was sleeping more and more. Tim had been working in the backyard, the sound of his shovel sometimes echoing in the wind. It was bittersweet, Resa thought, that she and Tim had come into town at the exact moment where they could share this heavy burden with Sierra.

The last day Nana was with them was on a Thursday. Resa was in the kitchen making coffee when she heard Sierra say, "Nana, I'm not ready for you to go."

Resa walked in and gently set Nana's mug on the side table, then sat next to Sierra on the couch. Sierra lay her head on the pillow next to Nana and held her hand. Resa heard Max whimpering at the back door and was relieved when she saw Tim walk in.

Nana's body quieted and her breaths became almost imperceptible beneath the log cabin quilt. Tim leaned against the wall and lowered his head. After Resa's parents died she hadn't seen much point in talking to someone who never answered back. Even so, she knew Nana was a Christian woman, so she sent out wishes into the universe for a smooth journey to wherever Nana might be headed.

They were still, listening to Nana's breaths grow shorter and further apart. Strange, Resa thought, they were frozen in the land of the living while Nana's breaths drew her closer and closer to the realm of the spirits. Nana took one last breath, breathed out, and like the wisps of smoke rising from the coffee mug, she was gone.

"Goodbye Nana," Sierra whispered and started to weep in sobbing waves. Resa wrapped her arms around her and rocked slightly back and forth. Resa glanced up and held Tim's eyes as tears streamed down their faces, acknowledging this intense moment of sorrow that now forever shaped a piece of their journey. The three of them stayed suspended in time until Sierra's tears lessened.

"She was a good lady," Resa said, handing Sierra some tissues.

"The best," Sierra replied, blowing her runny nose. "I guess I have to get a sheet to cover her." She burst into tears again.

"No!" Tim said from beside them, making them both jump. "I mean, no," he said more gently. "I know you said she didn't want a fuss, but I made a place for her to rest...when you're ready I can help you take her there."

Sierra's grateful nod gave way to another round of tears. Grief was a heavy, barbed burden to carry. As the afternoon slowly faded into early evening, Resa watched Sierra take a candle from the mantel.

"Tim," Sierra said quietly, "I'm ready now. I'd like to bury her in this quilt that she loved."

Tim nodded and stepped over to the bed. Resa helped them wrap Nana in the quilt and Tim lifted her into his arms. Her body looked petite and frail. When they went down the back steps, Resa saw the pile of earth in the back corner of the yard. There were large stones sitting next to a deep hole.

Tim lay Nana on top of a sheet he had already laid out on the ground. Resa noticed he'd spread a thick layer of grass and pine needles along the bottom of the hole. A fitting final resting bed for this kind and generous woman.

Sierra stood next to Nana and lit the candle. "This candle is for the light Alice Jean Howard brought to this world. Her light will never be extinguished and will live in those who loved her. May she rest in peace."

"May she rest in peace," Tim and Resa said together.

"If you both grab the sides of the sheet, we can lower her down." Tim explained, "If her feet go this way then she'll face the mountains and the sun will rise over her every morning."

They all started to cry. They grabbed the sheet and together lowered Nana onto her soft resting place. Resa and Sierra each took a handful of earth to toss on the quilt and Tim told them he would take care of the rest.

"Thank you," Sierra said to Resa and Tim before blowing out the candle. She lowered it slowly into the grave and let it go when she could reach no further. The candle made a small thump as it hit the earth. Sierra stood slowly, turned away, and walked around to the front of the house. The wind carried the sound of her footsteps on the front porch, the creak of the rocking chair as Sierra collapsed into it, and the sounds of grief as her heart broke into a million pieces.

Chapter 11

May - Kansas

A car! Tim couldn't believe it. He was actually driving a car! And even better, they didn't have to hike out of the mountains! Hiking downhill was the pits and being saved from all the pain and jarring of joints and toes was wonderful! The miles slipped by and he enjoyed every single minute of the quickly passing distance. He would look up a slope and think "Didn't have to hike up that!" and see a particularly steep downward curve and smile. "Didn't have to walk down that!" When they had passed the first 15 miles from where they'd started in the morning, he'd said, "Don't have to camp there!" He and Resa grinned as the car cruised along. The absolute luxury of a car.

He felt slightly guilty being happy. Nana had just died. He was sad. He really was. But her death had been expected, and Nana herself had been pleased about their future adventures with Sierra. So he had mixed feelings. But he did understand how Sierra was feeling.

If he had anything to complain about it was, unfortunately, Sierra in the back seat. Whine whine whine about everything. "Can't you turn on the air conditioning? It's hot!" (No. It uses up too much gas.) "Stop! I have to throw up!: (Again? You just did that!) "I have to pee!" (Seriously?! You couldn't have done that when we stopped for you to puke?)

Tim tried to cut her some slack due to her Nana, but you didn't see him complain all the time, and his parents were gone too. Spending these last weeks with Sierra and her Nana gave him a feeling of being part of a family again, but if this whininess was what having a sister was like, he wasn't sure he wanted one. He liked her better back at Nana's. She was cute and could be fun, like when they went to the bowling alley to celebrate his 18th birthday. He hadn't expected anyone to do anything for him.

Tim liked having a young person to talk to. He and Sierra talked about missing their friends and technology and music and not being in school anymore and a bunch of other things that Resa didn't care about as much as they did. Sierra could be pretty funny and had a lot of crazy stories about stuff she'd done. She'd gotten into way more trouble than he had in school. His mom would've killed him if he'd done half the stuff she had. He respected that Sierra was so good to her Nana and Nana wasn't even a blood relative. But Nana had mostly raised her since her mom had apparently been pretty terrible. Tim thought about his parents and knew how lucky he had been. He wished they were here with him now so he could tell them how much he appreciated them. He glanced at Resa and decided she was probably a pretty good mom. Just look at her trying to get home. And Sierra's mom just up and left with some drug addict boyfriend. Just left her! Some people shouldn't have kids. Seriously.

Ever since he turned 18, Tim wasn't sure how to feel about being an adult. He was now legally a grownup but that didn't really make him feel like one. Before K-Pox he had planned to save up money and get his own place with some friends while he went to college. He was so excited about moving out of his parents' house. Well, he'd moved out. But this wasn't exactly what he'd foreseen. And on this trek a person's age wasn't that important. Maybe it will be later, but right now it wasn't the big deal he had thought it would be. It was a little disappointing, but he was glad there had been a party. Made the birthday a little special.

They'd left that morning from the mountains of western Colorado and had dropped down to the plains of eastern Colorado and Kansas in a matter of hours. It was amazing how quickly the land changed. He liked the plains better than the mountains. In the mountains he worried every time they drove around a turn wondering if there'd be another car coming their way. Or perhaps a blockade with criminals stopping traffic. It was always nerve wracking, always tense. When they hit the plains, he relaxed somewhat as they could see all around for miles. Still Tim continually scanned the horizon for other vehicles or human activity. He liked seeing so far, but he knew if there were people out there, they could see and hear them coming as well. He could tell by Resa's and Sierra's alert looks they were watching as well. Back before Tim and Resa had run into GW they'd talked about what to do if they met someone and had decided to stay cool and friendly but have guns ready if needed. The policy remained the same now. Sierra chose to carry mace; she didn't like guns. Tim was ok with that.

He glanced down at the gas gauge. He sighed. It was dropping close to the empty mark. Resa looked over at him and nodded.

"We'll be walking again soon," she said.

"At least we drove out of those mountains. Walking into them was the pits and hiking out would have been a real pain! And we'll be on flat ground." Tim looked around. He'd never been this far east before.

Sierra was sitting back looking with interest out of the window with her hand on Max's back. She leaned forward. "Are we gonna be out of the car soon? Driving through those mountains made me so sick. I've never been so car sick before. I feel awful!"

Resa said, "I think we might have less than an hour and we'll be hiking again. The weather's nice today. That'll help."

The car thermometer registered 75 degrees outside, and the sun was shining brightly as big puffy white clouds cast shadows across the plains. A variety of plants were growing as far as they could see. Nothing had been planted this spring and fields were full of all kinds of plants growing helter skelter and all mixed up. Tim wondered what they were. Probably mostly weeds since they always did best, but Tim could recognize corn starting to show above other knee-high plants.

"It sure is flat. And green." He liked the greenness of the fields better than the desert climate he'd grown up in. More like the Maine he imagined moving to, only there were fewer trees here. More trees would be good.

Sierra agreed. "It's so weird. You can see all the way to the horizon. And there's nothing out here. I mean what do people do for fun?" She looked around again. Suddenly she got a big smile on her face. "I bet you could race cars really fast on this road! It goes on forEVer and it's sooo flat!"

"Yeah! That'd be fun!" Tim grinned back and glanced sideways at Resa.

"Umm...NO thanks," Resa said, but smiled. "We'll get more miles driving slower."

Tim and Sierra looked at each other in the rear-view mirror and rolled their eyes.

"Such a mom thing to say," Tim said smiling.

Resa chuckled. "Yep! That's what Moms do. Say sensible and safe Mom things."

The car ran out of gas. They had known it would happen, yet when it finally coasted quietly to a full stop, they groaned and sat silently for a few minutes. Resa said quietly, "Well, we might as well have a snack before we start walking."

They dejectedly climbed out of the car and rummaged through their packs for something to eat. Max bounced around and was the only one happy about the situation. He loved this life of always moving. So many new smells! So many things to pee on. And his people were always around!

It was a quick and silent lunch as they looked at the miles stretching endlessly ahead. The wind blew steadily as they resignedly put on hats and sunscreen and helped each other shoulder their packs.

Tim and Resa had worked with Sierra back at Nana's to get her used to hiking with her weighted pack. Nana had enjoyed watching Sierra try on new boots and arrange the hiking gear and hike around the neighborhood. Nana had mentioned numerous times she was pleased Sierra would be going with Tim and Resa. She'd been so worried about what would happen to Sierra after she died.

Before she passed away she'd told Tim privately she wanted him to be a proper gentleman and watch over her two ladies. He hadn't known what to say so he'd just nodded. Tim felt the responsibility of Nana's charge—to watch over the two ladies and make sure they were taken care of. And to be a proper gentleman, whatever that was. He wondered if he'd be expected to carry out any violence or bad stuff. He could do it, but he hoped they'd not bump into any violent situations. He didn't want to shoot anyone.

Tim glanced back at Sierra. They'd been walking about 20 minutes and he wondered if her backpack practicing had been worth it. He'd been pulling ahead so slowed down and fell in with Resa and Sierra. He wondered how long she'd be able to walk before having to stop. It had taken a while for him and Resa to get their backs and feet toughened up, and Sierra was just beginning. Tim sighed. Here we go again. They'd have to slow their pace as Sierra dealt with sore feet and an aching back. It was going to take forever to get to Laurel. And then to Maine.

As if she could hear his doubts, Sierra said, "I'm gonna get sick. Someone get my pack off!" She turned her back to Tim and he quickly pulled it off. He and Resa looked the other way as Sierra wretched up her lunch.

"I need some water." Sierra got out her water bottle and rinsed her mouth, then greedily gulped her water.

"Hey," Tim said quickly. "We have to conserve water. You can't just drink so much all at once! You'll use it all up and where're we gonna get more?" He waved his arms around at the flat landscape. He didn't mean to sound annoyed, but really, couldn't she figure it out herself. Sierra made a face at him and started to respond.

Resa quickly said, "It's ok, we know this is all new to you and motion sickness can last for a while. Maybe next time you could just rinse your mouth with water and drink just a little." She gave Tim a pointed look and then turned back to Sierra, "You're still learning. No worries. You ready to go or do you need more time?"

Sierra said she was ready, and they started back down the road.

Throughout the afternoon Tim continually had to slow down his stride. When he and Resa had first started hiking he'd taken smaller steps for her, and he'd gotten used to that. But she had gotten faster and they had walked well together. Now their pace was slower than ever with Sierra. If it wasn't her slow walking, she had to stop and throw up. What was wrong with her? She kept saying she was still car sick. Really? They'd been out of the car for hours.

The longer they walked, the more he wanted to get ahead of them. It was like being in the hallways during class break; students moved so leisurely he'd wanted to push through everyone and run. He'd actually tried it in elementary school and had gotten a quick trip to the office for his efforts. He had suggested a fast lane and a slow lane for the halls, but they hadn't taken him up on it. He sighed. He knew Resa and Sierra couldn't help that they had shorter legs and couldn't walk as fast but it didn't mean it wasn't frustrating. He glanced down at Max. At least Max could keep up, especially with his little booties. Max was wearing booties for half a day and the other half without until his paw pads got tougher again. It had taken him a few days to get used to them but now he pranced along just fine.

They walked until the sun was low in the sky and they saw a farmhouse and outbuildings surrounded by a windbreak of trees.

"This might be a good place to stop for the night." Resa looked at Tim. "What do you think?"

"This early? We got more daylight."

"It could be awhile before we see another house, and I hate to pass this one and not have another option. I don't want to end up in the dark, looking for a place to camp. And if there are people here, we'll be moving on anyway."

While Tim didn't wish death on anyone, he found himself hoping no one was alive in the houses they passed. He was ashamed of his thoughts but it was the truth. People could turn out to be like GW or worse.

"I guess. Let's check it out."

Sierra looked worried. "Are we just gonna walk up and go inside? What if there's," she hesitated, "gross, creepy people in there. Do you think there are zombies?"

Tim rolled his eyes. "There are no zombies!"

"Just because YOU haven't seen them doesn't mean there aren't any," Sierra snapped back, "And besides, what if there aren't zombies but there are mean creepy people. You don't know THAT, do you?" She tipped her head with attitude and put her hands on her hips.

"Ok. No need to fight. Now sssh! Let's walk up quietly," Resa said in a low tone.

Tim and Sierra knew enough to be quiet and walked with Resa up the gravel driveway. They stood at the edge of the windbreak and waited and listened. At first all they could hear was the wind blowing across the plain and through the shelter of the trees, but as they listened they heard clucking noises.

"Chickens?" Tim asked.

"Sounds like it," Resa responded.

"Do you think anyone is here?" Sierra looked nervously around. "I don't hear anyone but maybe they're hiding and waiting to jump out at us."

Tim wondered the same thing. He felt he had to show he wasn't afraid so he waded through the overgrown lawn to the front door. He'd noticed no one had walked through and pushed down the grass. If no one left the house, maybe no one was in there. He got to the front door with Resa and Sierra close behind and they all saw the K-Pox sign.

"We can't go in." He nodded at the sign. "K-Pox."

Resa and Sierra sighed.

"So now where are we going to stay? I'm tired and want to take off my pack." Sierra looked around her and groaned. "This is horrible!"

Resa looked at the barn. "We could try there. It'll be out of the wind."

Sierra looked at the barn with disgust but followed Tim and Resa. The barn turned out to be better than they'd hoped. It smelled slightly of manure, but no animals had been here recently so Tim didn't think it smelled too bad. He glanced at Sierra to see what she was thinking. She had wrinkled up her nose and he hoped she wouldn't start complaining. Or puking. As they dropped their packs, a chicken flew out of the straw clucking madly. They all jumped and gasped, then laughed.

"Hey, we could have chicken for dinner!" Tim said enthusiastically.

"Are you willing to kill it?" asked Resa. "I'll cook it if you kill it and clean it."

"You can't kill that little chicken!" Sierra scowled at Tim. "I won't let you!"

"You won't let me?" Tim didn't really want to kill the chicken but her telling him he couldn't do it irritated him.

Resa stepped in. "Ok, you two," she said with exasperation, "No chicken for dinner, but maybe there's eggs. Let's look around and see what we can find."

Tim and Sierra moved to opposite ends of the barn to explore. Exploring their surroundings put Tim in a better mood. Between them they found six eggs for dinner. They also found fresh hay bales to break up and use under their sleeping bags. In his search outside Tim found an old-fashioned water pump. He showed the pump to Resa.

"My grandparents had one of these," she commented. "You pump the handle and it pumps water up from a well." She started pumping, the handle making loud metallic scraping, screeching noises as she moved the handle up and down.

"Can I try?" Tim asked. It looked kind of fun.

"Sure." Resa moved aside.

As Tim pumped he heard a gurgling sound and then they saw water spurting out of the mouth of the pump.

"Look! Water!" Tim exclaimed. "That is so cool!" Max, tail wagging, lapped up the water as it splashed on the ground.

Sierra watched the water flow as Tim continued to pump. She reached out and put her hand under the flowing water, then wiped her face. "It's cold! Can we drink it?" she asked Resa.

"If we boil it first. Just in case."

"But then it'll be hot water and not nice cold water." Sierra complained.

"Well, if it's contaminated, it'll make you throw up even more than you have been, so let's not risk it."

Evening came quickly as they busily settled into their first night on the road. They cleared a wide area in the barn so the small campfire flickered cozily far away from the hay. There was water for drinking and washing, eggs for supper, hay for sleeping on, and a place out of the wind. Tim thought things could definitely be worse. He preferred the motels they'd stayed in, but maybe there'd be more ahead. He liked sleeping in a bed.

He smelled the fresh sweet smell of hay as he twisted himself around to get comfortable on top of his sleeping bag. He was having trouble falling asleep. Too many things on his mind. He thought back to Nana's funeral. He wished he could've had a funeral and dug a grave for his parents and Granddad. He should have done that. He had wanted to, but they'd made him promise he wouldn't. They'd made him *promise*! It wasn't fair they got sick and died and he couldn't be with them. He had wanted to be there. To get one more hug. To say I love you. It wasn't fair Sierra was able to be with her Nana and he couldn't be with his family. It wasn't fair! It wasn't!

Tim sat up. He wanted to run and scream and cry but he couldn't, not this close to where they were sleeping. He quickly got up and went outside. Max uncurled himself from his warm bed in the hay and joined Tim. As soon as he was away from the quiet sleepers and in the open, Tim broke into a run, back down the driveway and out onto the road. He ran as though he were being chased, as though he could outrun grief and loneliness. He ran long steady strides to make up for all the little short steps he'd had to take these last months. He ran to escape the fact he'd never see his parents again or his friends or have any of his old life. To ease the tension in his chest and the misery in his brain. To give his muscles and bones a chance to be open at full strength and speed, pounding smoothly on the pavement, to have his lungs ache and to keep breathing with deep even breaths. And as he ran tears streamed down his cheeks. Panting and out of breath, muscles aching, he finally stopped running and threw himself down in the grass and cried like he hadn't cried since his parents died, great noisy gulping sobs. When he had no more tears left to shed, he sniffed and wiped his nose on his sleeve and reached over to hold Max.

Tim smiled wanly at Max. "Sorry, little buddy." He breathed a shuddering sigh. "I'm a mess, huh? I just miss Mom and Dad and Granddad so much. And they aren't coming back and I'm going further and further away from them every day. It makes me so sad." He looked into Max's searching brown eyes. "You're wondering what's wrong with me, aren't you. I'm so glad I have you. You're the best dog in the whole world, aren't you?" He hugged Max and sighed. "Well, I'll be ok. We'll be ok. Let's go back before anyone sees we're gone." Tim brushed his clothes off as he stood up and jogged back to the barn, Max following close beside.

The next day started out like so many of the days had before, at least for Tim and Resa. This was all fairly new to Sierra though and she was still getting sick. She couldn't possibly still be car sick. She didn't have K-Pox but what the heck did she have? Puking sickness.

Flu? Disgusting. And all the food she puked up was totally wasted. Not to mention the water. Tim hoped she'd stop pretty soon. He also hoped he wouldn't catch whatever it was.

After stopping for a short lunch and to give Sierra another break, she said, as she was helped back into her pack, "I really miss hamburgers."

"I really miss McDonald's fries," Tim said hungrily.

"I miss ice cream," Resa added, "With hot fudge and whipped cream. I have a game we could play. How about if we say the things we miss but going in alphabetical order. Like...I miss fresh crunchy apples for A and I miss whatever begins with B. What do you think? Wanna play?"

Tim thought it'd be ok. It was kind of boring just walking across the flat plains. "Ok, was A your turn or was that an example?"

"No, that can be my turn. Why don't you go next and then Sierra."

"I miss..." Tim thought about what he missed that started with B. All the B words just flew out of his mind. A butterfly flittered past. Butterflies! No, he can't miss butterflies. They're right there. "Oh! I miss butter! Butter on popcorn!"

Sierra was ready with her choice. "I miss chocolate, actually all kinds of candy, but mostly chocolate."

"I miss downtown, going shopping or meeting friends downtown. We have, well we had, a nice downtown with little boutiques and everything," Resa reminisced.

They trudged on quietly. "Are you going to take your turn?" Sierra asked impatiently. "You have E."

"I know. I'm thinking," Tim snapped back.

"There's no time limit," Resa quickly chimed in. "Take your time. It's hard to think of things sometimes. But we have all day, so no rush."

"Dog food. Dog food in cans or bags for Max." He looked down at Max jogging along beside him.

Just as Tim finished speaking, Sierra jumped in. "Resa already said a D word. You have to do an E word. My E word is Elephants."

"Elephants?" Tim questioned. "You can't miss elephants. You don't have elephants. Anyway, that's supposed to be my letter. I just messed up. Let me think. All I can think of now is elephants since you said that. This isn't easy. That's it! That's my word. Easy. I miss things being easy! Better word than elephants."

"I miss them on TV!" Sierra stuck out her tongue.

Tim glanced at Resa. He could tell Resa wanted to fuss at them both. Sierra apparently had seen Resa's look as well, and the disagreement stopped.

They continued to walk and add things they missed. Tim liked the game. It gave them something to think and talk about. F for the friends who Sierra got into trouble with. G for gardenias in Resa's garden, H for Halloween and trick or treating when Tim was a kid. Talking about their missed items gave each person time to think of their next letter but they also learned more about each other.

They continued through the letter Z and then were tired they stopped talking and walked quietly until camp time.

The following days went on and on boringly monotonous. They played the alphabet game about once a day, changing the topic of the words: animals, foods, songs. Dull, but better than not talking at all. The only heart racing moment was when they heard a vehicle in the distance and they'd hidden in the tall brush. They cautiously peeked out as it passed them and they saw a car heading west. They stayed down until it was out of sight. But other than that, each day slid slowly into the next.

Resa was very caring of Sierra, making sure they stopped often for breaks and early for the evenings. At first it bothered Tim, but when he remembered he really had no deadline and no rush to get anywhere and if Resa, who did have a place to go and people to see, wasn't worried, then why should he be. He relaxed and began to hike more leisurely and appreciatively through country he'd never seen before and may never see again. Before this cross country hike he'd only paid attention to the outdoors when he was camping with his dad. Now he had all day to notice things. He noticed the wide variety of plants and insects in a land which seemed at first to have no variation, how the sounds of the birds differ throughout the day, how clouds look as they scud across the sky and their shadows move silently below them. He enjoyed the company of Max and Resa and even Sierra. Overall things weren't too bad.

Tim liked walking in the afternoon when the sun was behind them and their shadows lengthened into giants. He breathed in deeply as he thought of the quiet evening supper they'd have and sleeping under the huge wide sky covered in stars. Then, as he looked into the distance, he thought he saw movement. Were those people moving? He looked at Resa and saw she had noticed also and had stopped walking. Then they saw people moving towards them. It was too late to hide.

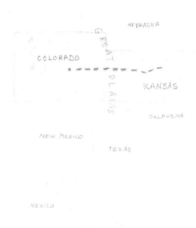

Chapter 12

June - Kansas

No way those shadows were real. Could the sun and heat be playing tricks with their minds? Resa and Tim looked at each other and then back to the figures as if they were seeing a mirage. How could those be people? But step by step, the group in the distance got closer and were definitely living, breathing human beings...with rifles.

"Who are those people?" she heard Sierra whisper behind her.

Max crouched down, walking slowly with his ears and tail lowered, sniffing at the wind. Resa wasn't sure if they should hold up their hands in surrender or pull out their own guns and get ready for a showdown. Her hands trembled.

"What do you think? Tim whispered to her. "I'm gonna unholster my gun."

"I don't want them to start shooting if they think we're dangerous," Resa whispered back. "Maybe I'll call out so they know we don't mean any harm."

"I guess. I'm gonna keep my finger on the safety though just in case," Tim replied.

Resa took in a shuddering breath and called out.

"Hello there!"

"Are you crazy?" Sierra said, grabbing Resa's sleeve. "They could be psychotic murderers!"

"Well it's too late to run. They've already seen us. And I'd rather pass by peacefully, instead of giving them an excuse to shoot us in the back."

They weren't shooting, but they hadn't answered back yet either.

"Resa," Sierra said faintly, "my heart is racing. I'm too hot. The road is moving. I think I'm going to pass out." Sierra started to pant for breath.

"Oh good grief Sierra! This is NOT the time to throw up! Take some deep breaths and get it together," Tim hissed at her over his shoulder.

Resa knew Sierra had never hiked before and she had chalked up Sierra's complaining to her inexperience and her grief over losing Nana. But she kept getting sick and saying she was dizzy and tired all the time. Resa hoped they weren't dealing with heat exhaustion or something worse. They had no medicine for fevers and would run out of water quickly if they couldn't keep going. But she was trying not to worry about that at the moment. She needed to keep her eyes on the three men and two women moving towards them. Max let out a couple of short barks and a low growl.

Tim reached down to steady Max. "Good boy," he murmured.

"Reeeesa...ocean...my ears...black circles..." Sierra's voice trembled as she whispered urgently.

"What?!" Resa was alarmed now. She turned, sacrificing her view of the group. Out of the corner of her eye, she saw the man in front raise his hand in a silent, and what Resa hoped, peaceful wave.

Sierra stumbled and then collapsed backward. Resa and Tim grabbed her and lowered her gently to the ground.

"Sierra!" Resa knelt next to her. Thankfully, Sierra's backpack kept her elevated. Resa could hear hurried footsteps, Max barking, Tim trying to quiet him, and then low mumbling all around her. Sierra's face was ashen and her hands were cold and clammy.

"Better turn her on her side so she won't choke if she vomits," a voice said next to Resa.

She turned and looked into the slightly annoyed face of the woman who had been walking towards them a moment ago. Resa released the chest strap from Sierra's pack so she could angle her body sideways. The woman took out a thermos of water and handed it to Resa.

"Splash a little on her face and see if she wakes a bit."

"Thank...thank you," Resa stuttered and took the thermos.

"My name's Liz," the woman said. "We might be able to help. Wait here."

Liz stood up and walked back to the group, now animatedly whispering off to the side. Max intently watched as they gestured at Sierra.

Waiting was not going to be a problem, Resa thought, as she looked at Sierra's sweaty face and closed eyes. She poured water into her hand and let it run onto Sierra's forehead. Sierra's eyes fluttered and she let out a small groan.

"Sierra, wake up."

"Why'd she pass out?" Tim kneeled on her other side looking concerned. "What do you think THEY want?" Tim jutted his chin towards the group.

"I have no idea what is going on with her. But unless this water is poisoned, maybe they're not dangerous after all. They said they might help us." Resa said.

Sierra blinked her eyes and opened them wide when she saw Resa and Tim hovering over her.

"Wha...What happened? Why is everything so quiet?"

"You passed out, Honey. It's ok. See if you can sit up and drink some water."

Resa didn't think the water was poisoned but gave Sierra water out of her own supply instead. The group quietly watched them. They each wore a side holster with a pistol and carried a rifle or shotgun along with small backpacks. Resa watched one of the men

124

pull out a walkie talkie and mutter a few words into it. They must be staying close by, Resa thought; they weren't carrying camping supplies with them. Sierra groggily sipped from the water bottle.

Liz walked back over and squatted down.

"I don't think you're going to be doing more walking today."

"She's been throwing up pretty often, but I think she's just been car sick or maybe has heat exhaustion." Resa furrowed her eyebrows. "It's not K-Pox, she'd have been dead by now."

Liz nodded, "Yeah, our scouts have been following you."

Next to Tim, Max's ears perked up. There was a muffled sound of a motor in the distance.

"Scouts? You've been watching us?" Resa's voice got a little higher with each question. They'd been followed? What was going on? Maybe she was wrong about them being murderers. Maybe they liked to hunt people for fun.

The woman nodded again. "We protect our own. It seemed like you were passing through and we were watching to make sure. But we can't very well leave you out here with the girl in the shape she's in. Seems like we don't have much choice but to take you back with us."

The motor sound grew louder and soon a truck drove past them and headed down the road they had just come from. Resa and Tim watched with their mouths open.

"We were going to wait til you'd passed by before we took your car, but we'll put gas in it so you can follow us instead. Our town isn't much interested in welcoming strangers, but the girl can recover and you can keep traveling once she's back on her feet," Liz explained.

As they waited, Resa was thankful it was only partly sunny today. June was turning out to be warmer than she'd expected.

Twenty, maybe 30 minutes went by until they heard engines rumbling in the distance again. When the truck and car pulled up, Resa looked at Sierra and pointed.

"Look Sierra. There's your Nana's car." The driver jumped out and brought the keys over to Tim.

"Follow us. The doctor will be waiting," the driver said impatiently and walked away.

A doctor?! Resa looked at Tim, surprised.

"I'll sit in the back with Sierra," Resa said. Tim grabbed their packs and loaded them into the trunk. It was so strange to be back in Nana's car, but Sierra snuggled right in.

"Smells like home," she murmured as she laid her head on Resa's shoulder.

As they followed the truck, Resa and Tim wondered what they might be headed into. The truck pulled off onto a smaller paved road and soon they were driving past houses plastered with K-Pox signs. Resa's eyes widened with fear.

But then she realized there were a lot of signs, like A LOT. They were stuck on almost every available flat surface. It was a ploy. Those signs would keep people away from a place that wanted to remain hidden. Fear kept people out.

"That's cold," Sierra protested. Resa watched as a brusque lady grumbled and held a stethoscope on Sierra's back. Resa couldn't believe she was sitting in a doctor's office. Well, judging from the padded table Sierra was sitting on, this used to be a physical therapy office or something, but it had been converted to an all-purpose medical station. The woman now looking in Sierra's ears was the doctor they had been told about.

"Your mom here says you haven't been feeling well," Dr Walker said once she was finished.

"I'm not..." Resa tried to explain, but the doctor shushed her.

"Yeah, I guess. I've had a headache off and on and felt tired. But that was just from walking and getting carsick and throwing up," Sierra responded.

"Do you have a regular period?"

"Um, yeah." Sierra looked embarrassed.

"Are you sexually active?"

"Well, I don't think that's any of your..."

"*Are* you?" the doctor interrupted.

126

"Yes," Sierra mumbled.

"When's the last time you had your period?"

"What? I don't...." Sierra looked back and forth between Dr. Walker and Resa with confusion.

"We should check. It's one thing not to take care of your own life, but it's quite another to drag an innocent baby through that too."

"Now, wait just a minute. She is doing the best she can to take care of herself. She's been through a lot, we all have," Resa interjected.

"Yes, I'm sure. All these young women living in sin..."

"Do you have any pregnancy tests here?" Resa interrupted. She wasn't sure where Dr. Walker was going with the start of her speech, but she felt a fierce need to protect Sierra from it.

"We have some extras we use for families in unique circumstances. Babies are blessings *after* couples are married and..."

"Yes, well. This is certainly a unique circumstance and as you said, the quicker we know what's going on with her, the quicker we can move along," Resa said. Liz had told them the town was not interested in having them stay, but after hearing the doctor talk, Resa didn't want to remain any longer than they had to either.

"She'll have to take it first thing in the morning to make sure it's accurate. Don't need to go through another test in a couple days, just to confirm something you'll know in a few months anyway," Dr. Walker said sternly.

Sierra was looking at Resa with large, worried eyes. "I...pregnant? I'm not...right?" she whispered.

Resa squeezed Sierra's hand.

"If you are, then we'll know tomorrow and we'll figure things out. Either way, it will be ok," Resa told her.

Dr Walker grunted, but Resa kept her eyes firmly on Sierra's face and gave her a resolute nod. Resa had a sinking feeling she knew what the test was going to say. The headaches, the moodiness, the constant throwing up, the fatigue, the dizziness. The thought had crossed her mind, but she had dismissed it. She was so young! Even younger than Meg.

"It WILL be ok," Resa said again.

"You'll both stay in the Jansen house for the night," Dr. Walker told them as she pulled Gatorade and coconut water out of the cupboard. "Drink these and someone will bring you food soon."

"What's the Jansen house?" Resa asked.

"Betsy Jansen. She and I live there with her sister, Barb. They're widows. You'll meet them in the morning. The young man who came with you can stay in the bunkhouse."

Resa had questions, but she thought she'd had enough of Dr. Walker's explanations for the moment.

"Ok. Thank you for your hospitality," Resa said instead.

No use getting on Dr. Walker's bad side. She was helping them, begrudgingly perhaps, but still helping. Dr. Walker mumbled and walked out the door. Resa and Sierra sat in silence for a minute or two before tears started rolling down Sierra's cheeks.

"It will be alright," Resa said gently. She sat next to her on the table and put her arm around Sierra's shoulder as she cried.

"Do you want to talk about it?" Resa wasn't sure how much to pry or what Sierra wanted to share, but she wanted her to feel safe.

"Braydan wasn't even my boyfriend," Sierra sniffled, "We just hung out sometimes."

"Yeah?" Resa asked gently, "How did you guys meet?"

"I've known him all my life. Knew him, I guess. He's gone."

Resa felt so sad for her, "Did he have K-Pox?"

"No. His family left town when everything started to get bad. I never met his parents. Nana knew about him. She asked me if my mom had explained stuff to me. I told her my mom had been bringing home boyfriends since before I could talk. And we used protection!" Sierra sighed. "Well, most of the time...I mean we weren't together *that* much!" Sierra cried out, visibly frustrated. "He was usually off at his ski competitions or hanging with his 'popular' friends. He only noticed me because we had science together last year," Sierra blew her nose with the tissue Resa handed her.

"Sometimes we ditched school and we'd vape or whatever and hang. We'd get back before anyone knew we were missing." Sierra opened the Gatorade the doctor had left her, "it just didn't seem like that big a deal. He wasn't my first. I didn't figure he'd be my last." Sierra started crying again.

Resa knew there wasn't a whole lot she could say to make her feel better, so she just rubbed her back.

"When his family left town, he sent me a text that said, 'See ya round.' I mean that's not love. I wasn't IN love with him either. I don't know." Sierra sighed again. "He was nice to me at least. That's more than how some of my mom's boyfriends treated her...or me." Sierra's eyes drifted off into the distance.

Resa felt angry for Sierra. She was too young to bear any of this. A hard life even before K-Pox, losing her Nana, and now being pregnant. Maybe pregnant. They heard the door open from outside and the heavy clomp of Tim's footsteps along with hurried paws racing across the floor.

"Max!" Sierra called out.

Resa looked up to see Tim lumbering in behind the ball of fur jumping up on Sierra's legs.

"Hey," Tim said, putting his hands in his pockets and rocking back and forth on the soles of his feet. "How ya feeling?"

"I've been better," Sierra said honestly as she sipped the Gatorade.

"What's going on out there?" Resa asked.

"Remember how we said they didn't seem friendly?" Tim asked. Resa nodded. "Well, it's definitely confirmed. Pretty sure they told me no less than five times that they'll help us get on our way." Tim rolled his eyes. "And then they kept saying they'd pray for me and for all the sin which led me here and kept asking me if I had accepted Jesus. And that was just the teenagers I met! I didn't even talk to the adults and I don't think I want to!" Tim exclaimed, running his hand through his hair.

A knock at the door silenced them. A man in his early sixties came in carrying a tray laden with steaming bowls and covered plates.

Resa's mouth immediately began to water. She had forgotten they hadn't eaten in hours. He set the tray down on a small table.

"Hello. I'm Mr. Joseph Quinn, Bethel's town mayor. The doc tells me this young girl will be taking a test in the morning and then we'll see how to get you on your way." The mayor looked at Tim and said, "While the women are busy in the morning, we have a few men who volunteered to show you some things that might help along your journey. How to cover your tracks, make sure your car runs smoothly, things like that," Without waiting for a response he continued, "I'll let you eat. We have evening chapel and then I'll come back over to walk you to your quarters for the night."

He then launched into a long prayer over the food, leaving all three of them with their mouths hanging slightly open. Resa recovered first and bowed her head, giving Tim and Sierra a look to do the same.

"Amen," Joseph said when he was finished. He mumbled something about how they'd better learn to pray if they were going to survive in this world. The door banged shut behind him.

"Well, that was...interesting," Resa whispered, standing up and scooting her chair over to the table.

"See what I'm sayin!" Tim hissed. "We gotta get out of here."

While they ate, Resa asked Sierra if it was ok to tell Tim what was going on. Then she relayed everything the doctor had said. To his credit, Tim didn't criticize and only asked what this would mean for traveling later.

"If she is pregnant, we'll just have to be more careful about keeping hydrated and pay attention to swelling in her legs and feet. That will tell us if she's overdoing it. Then we'll have to rest a little more. But since we've already been walking so much, we should be able to keep going. Slow and steady is still moving forward."

"I'm so sorry to hold you back," Sierra broke into a fresh set of tears, "I can't believe this is happening."

"We'll just do what we have to do. We're not leaving anyone behind," Tim said firmly.

Sierra gave him a watery smile.

"I wonder how long this chapel of theirs is," Resa said as she stretched and yawned, "A good night's sleep will help us all feel better."

They heard the faint echoes of clapping and singing, rising and falling in the distance. After eating, Sierra lay on the padded table while Tim leaned back in his chair with his legs stretched out in front of him. Resa rested her head on the wall beside her, all of them dozing off until the door banged open and startled them awake. The mayor was back.

"This way," he said abruptly, waving his hand for them to gather their things and follow him. The stars were glittering in a pitch-black night. Mr. Quinn said he would take Tim to a house across the street. Resa and Sierra were shown to a two story house not far from the medical clinic. Dr. Walker waited on the porch and showed them the outhouse in the backyard and a working water pump in the kitchen if they needed to wash up.

"Don't drink from it though, the drinking water is stored in the refrigerator It may not be cold, but it keeps bugs out."

They were directed to a bedroom at the front of the house that looked like it had once been an office. Resa and Sierra could barely nod and say thank you before they tumbled into the twin beds. Resa heard Sierra's slow, even breaths as she laid her own head on her pillow and drifted off to sleep.

"Mornin ladies, it's test time." Dr. Walker knocked on the door and strode in as the first rays of morning light streamed in the front windows.

"Sierra honey, do you want me to come with you outside?" Resa yawned, her eyes were still heavy and her throat crackly from sleep.

"Yes." Sierra slowly rolled over and started to stretch on the side of her bed where Dr. Walker stood impatiently.

"Actually, I brought a chamber pot so you can just do it here." Dr. Walker showed Sierra the test and explained how it worked before giving Resa a meaningful glance and then strode back out again. Resa felt like a kid being admonished by a strict parent.

"Wow. She's intense," Sierra said, shaking her head slowly at Resa.

"Yeaaah," Resa replied, "Let's get this done before she comes back and gives us more instructions...and stern looks!" Resa turned her back to give Sierra some privacy.

They placed the stick on the nightstand and set the timer on Resa's watch for two minutes.

"You know, I remember waiting like this before I knew I was pregnant with Meg," Resa told Sierra.

"Were you scared?" Sierra asked quietly.

"Yes, actually," Resa answered. "Sam and I were very young. We'd just gotten married and had discussed having kids, but not so soon. Nature has a way of giving you answers to questions you don't always ask."

"Yeah," Sierra nodded, glancing nervously at the test.

"Sierra, from what you've said, I know your mom didn't always give you what you needed."

Sierra snorted, "That's a nice way of saying it."

"But it doesn't mean you won't know how to give this baby, if there is one, love and attention. You had a wonderful Nana who showed you everything you need to know. And you have Tim and me now too. You are not in this alone."

Sierra nodded as she nervously bit her bottom lip. They both jumped as the timer beeped. Sierra's eyes were wide.

"You look!" she said to Resa. "Tell me what it says."

Resa walked over to the table and saw there would now be an extra member of their traveling family.

"It's a plus, meaning you are definitely pregnant," Resa said and handed the test and the instructions over to Sierra.

Sierra's body began to shake as she started to weep again. The door opened.

"Your friend is waiting for the news outside," Dr. Walker said as she poked her head in through the doorway. "As the father, he deserves to know sooner rather than later."

"What?" Sierra said, confused. "Tim is not the father! Ew! He's like my brother!"

Resa couldn't help but smile at Sierra's reaction and, catching Resa's eye, Sierra started to smile through her tears. Pretty soon they were both carried away by fits of laughter, dampened only by Dr. Walker's serious frown.

"I brought you some prenatal vitamins," she retorted, placing a bottle on the bed next to Sierra. "We can only spare one, but if you keep up your praying, God will help you find more along the way. Once you get dressed, Betsy and Barb have breakfast made in the kitchen."

"Thank you for your kindness," Resa managed to say with a semi-straight face as Dr. Walker grumbled and walked out of the room. Sierra and Resa started giggling all over again until they felt breathless.

"Do you want me to tell Tim?" Resa asked.

"I can do it. I'm gonna have to get used to talking about it soon enough." Sierra said.

Resa could see a slow change taking over Sierra as she stood and squared her shoulders. Resa was already amazed by Sierra's courage. Resa felt her eyes water again, not with sadness, but with something more like pride.

At breakfast, Betsy and Barb were quite the fountains of information. Betsy explained she was happy to share her home with other women in town. They had lost their husbands to K-Pox the past spring and Barb had moved in shortly after. Both of them had grown up here. In fact, Betsy said with a satisfied smile on her face, their family had been one of the original founding church members when the pastor decided to leave the bigger city and start a more 'respectful place.'

"Don't get us wrong," Barb explained, "it's not that we're trying to be unfriendly. It's just we only have enough resources for the people of this town. That's why our scouts direct others away."

"We had a big meeting when K-Pox was done taking people to meet our maker, and they figured out what we'd need to support the survivors and families we have left. Calculated it down to the last tomato plants and seeds we have." Betsy smiled serenely at Resa and Sierra. "Poor choices could kill us all, you understand."

Over the next few days, Sierra rested and recovered her energy as much as she could. Resa and Tim kept to themselves and avoided the invitations they received to come to gatherings. Despite all the comments about them 'moving along quickly,' the townspeople kept their word about teaching them new skills. And they made sure Nana's gas tank was full when they were ready to go.

Their last night in Bethel, Resa and Sierra sat in the rocking chairs on the front porch of the women's house.

"You know, some of these boys are so weird," Sierra whispered to Resa.

"Why's that?"

"They stare at me like they're hungry, you know what I mean? Like they're starved for attention, but then if I smile or something, the girls all give me looks like I've just stripped naked in the middle of town."

Resa laughed out loud.

"Well, I think there's something to be said about having rules and guidelines, but when things become too rigid, when people can't figure things out on their own or truly express who they are, people suffer."

"Yeah, Nana always said it was better to let trees grow just how God made them, even if the branches went this way or that way. They're all just looking for the light and the sky."

"You know, Sierra, that's a perfect way to think about trees...and people."

"I was thinking," Sierra said softly, "I would've been pregnant when Nana was alive. She would have been with me and little peanut."

Resa smiled. "Always the ever-changing flow of the universe, one life finding its end as another one finds its beginning."

134

"I heard some of the things they say here. When Nana talked about God she never talked about such strict judgment. It was never about using God as a sword. Only love."

"She was a smart lady."

"I think Nana was right. The Bible is about messages of love and to treat people kindly. I can't wait to leave here. I will never raise my 'lil pumpkin in a place where it won't be cherished. Nana said my mama was always so focused on what was wrong, but never celebrated the beauty of what was right in front of her," Sierra sighed, "This baby will never know that pain. Not like I did."

Resa was amazed by the amount of life this young girl had lived in only 16 years.

"You are going to be a great mom," Resa told Sierra.

Sierra turned and smiled.

"Well it takes one to know one," she said back.

The next morning they packed up the car as the sun rose over the horizon.

"Go with God," Dr. Walker told Resa as she nodded her goodbye. No hugs would happen here. "Remember if you just have enough faith, pray hard enough, and try to stay on the right path, God might hear your voice."

Resa wasn't sure how to respond, so she gave an awkward thumbs up and walked to the car with Tim and Sierra. Even though the town had been generous in many ways, the disapproving attitudes and begrudging civility made every act of kindness seem forced and insincere. The trio joked that the extra water and gas were not consideration as much as added assurance they would not be coming back.

At last the only sounds were car doors slamming and the hum of the tires on the pavement. Road signs cast boxy shadows as the highway stretched like a ribbon out in front of them.

Chapter 13

July - Kansas

Nana's car finally ran out of gas and they were back on the road again. Tim packed some of Sierra's kit now but didn't mind as she shouldn't carry as much. Her pack was lighter, but she was determined not to let Tim and Resa tote all her things. He respected her for that.

Tim smiled as he looked at Max, his wagging tail just visible in the undergrowth. Tim refocused his gaze on those never ending, low rolling hills of central Kansas. He figured as slowly as they walked, they'd probably reach Laurel by his 40th birthday. He glanced at Resa. If she was in her 40s now, she'd be over 60 when they reached Laurel. Wow! Could she walk another 20 years? He chuckled. Well, maybe not 20 years, but no time soon, that's for sure.

"What are you laughing about?" Sierra asked suspiciously.

"I was just thinking about something stupid. And not about you. Relax." Tim thought that Sierra could be a little self-centered at times. To change the subject he said, "I wonder how long it'll take to get through Kansas? I think it goes on forever."

"Yeah, I dunno," Resa replied tiredly. "One step at a time though. One step at a time."

Max popped out of the ditch and trotted beside Tim. He reached down and stroked Max's head. Tim started thinking about setting up camp this evening. He liked stopping at night. They'd sit around and talk a while before going to sleep. He hadn't bothered pitching his tent lately. He liked to lie on top of his sleeping bag, Max sleeping closely at his side. He'd look at the stars and listen to the night noises. He never realized how noisy insects could be, chirring away all night. Occasionally they'd hear a cow moo, coyotes yipping, and birds hooting or tweeting. Once they heard a gunshot from far off and hoped the shooter would stay far off. He felt at peace with the black sky and the glittering stars overhead, brighter now without human light pollution. Just looking up into the vast universe made him feel so small, so insignificant, and somehow that made him feel better about life in general. He wasn't sure why, but it did.

Tim remembered a TV show from science class where a scientist said people were made of stardust. Tim liked the idea–being made of stardust.

"Hey, Sierra, did you know we were made of stardust?" he asked.

"Stardust? Really? Resa, are we made of stardust?"

"There used to be a TV show with a scientist named Carl Sagan. He said we were all made of star stuff. Minerals, like the calcium in our teeth and the iron in our blood, once used to be in the stars so I guess it's the same as stardust. Nice thought, isn't it, everything being connected like that."

"Star dust." Sierra kept walking then said thoughtfully, "What do you think about Star for the baby's name? That'd be awesome, wouldn't it? Baby Star. I like it. I'm gonna make a list of all the names I like so I need paper and a pencil. Next time we go in a house, let's get some. Ok?"

"Sure, if you carry it," Tim responded.

"Yeah, of course." She turned and asked Tim to pull off her pack.

"Why are you stopping? You have to pee again?" Tim tried not to look annoyed as he pulled off the pack.

"No, I'm not going to pee again! I'm getting out my dictionary to look for baby names."

"Baby names in a dictionary? That's weird. Where'd you get a dictionary and why are you carrying it?"

"It isn't weird! I like dictionaries. There's cool words in there. And I brought it from Nana's." She squatted down and pulled out a pocket size dictionary. "There's lots of words in here and some of them would be awesome names." Sierra turned her back to Tim again so he could help put her pack back on. As they continued walking she opened the dictionary and looked through it. "Oh, things I miss beginning with F! Fashion!"

"Hey, I want the dictionary when it's my turn! It's hard to think of things off the top of my head. Resa, if we're playing again, it's your turn."

"Ok. I'm on G? Let me think." After a few minutes, she said, "Google. I miss Google. I miss looking things up. Like we could've looked up Carl Sagan and star stuff, and we could look up recipes using wild plants and first aid and everything. I miss Google."

"Yeah, that's a good one. I wish we had computers again. H. What do I miss with H?" He looked at Sierra and said quickly, "Give me time to think. You had a couple of days to think of something. And a dictionary."

They saw a house in the distance and slowed down. Resa and Tim had developed a system of approaching a house. First they looked at it from a distance for signs of life, like grass trampled down around the door. If the house looked deserted they'd quietly walk to the front door. If there was a K-Pox sign posted or they smelled rotting flesh, they left. When a house appeared empty and didn't stink, they'd knock on the door, call out, and wait for an answer. They were careful when they entered, taking their time, being aware of their surroundings. So far, they'd been lucky. No one had shot at them. Yet.

When in the house they'd search for replacement things, mostly food, toilet paper, and other supplies. Tim thought it was fun to go through people's belongings. Some houses were so neat and clean it looked like his Grandma had lived there. Other places were so trashy, he couldn't believe people had lived in such filth. Bugs and gross things crawling around on old food or living under the piled-up trash! Max, on the other hand, loved trash! So much to smell! In the dirty houses they grabbed only sealed cans and left as quickly as possible.

This particular house looked ok so they went in cautiously. Max, nose to the floor, sniffed his way around. Tim felt safer with Max checking things out. If there was someone there Max would find them. Tim went to the bedrooms while Resa looked for food. Sierra followed Resa and sat at the kitchen table. Tim liked finding new clothes so he didn't have to wash the ones he was wearing. He hated washing clothes in creeks; he'd rather get clean ones from someone's closet. He found shirts, shorts, socks and underwear and went back to the kitchen to show off his haul.

"New clothes!"

"You're going to wear some dead person's clothes? Gross!" Sierra looked up in disgust.

"They might not be dead. And even if they are, they're not here and they don't need them. AND they're clean! So I don't have to wash my dirty ones."

Sierra wrinkled her nose. "Well, you do stink, so I guess clean clothes wouldn't hurt. Maybe I should get some too."

Resa found the pantry partially stocked. She grabbed cans of fruit cocktail, tuna, and sweetened condensed milk.

"Are we staying here tonight?" Sierra asked.

"I don't know. What do you guys think? We haven't walked too long today so we could go on, but it's up to you," Resa answered.

Tim and Resa both looked at Sierra. "Don't look at me! I'm not gonna make the decision. I'm only pregnant, not the boss of everyone. Where's the can opener?" She searched noisily through kitchen drawers.

Tim said, "I can go on for a while yet. We can stay here to eat and then walk more til evening. What do you think?"

"Sounds good to me. It's too bad cans and jars are so heavy," Resa said looking at the cabinet filled with items they'd leave behind.

"Found the can opener! I'm having tuna!" Sierra called out. "Resa, is there mayo in the pantry? I'd love some mayo!"

Resa opened a new jar of mayonnaise and the fresh smell of tuna wafted to Tim. Now he wanted tuna. He opened three cans, scooped one into a bowl for Max, grabbed a fork, then sat at the kitchen table with Sierra to eat tuna, mayo and crackers. Resa joined them with chickpeas, water chestnuts, and a jar of pickled beets. Tim shook his head at Max. Crazy dog was eating his food so fast he'd be done before Tim finished his first bite.

"Resa, shouldn't I eat vegetables? For the baby? I don't really like vegetables but there's green beans and corn." She indicated the pantry with a nod of her head.

"You should definitely try to have a balanced diet. Since you don't mind the taste, condensed milk is nutritious and has lots of vitamins. Oh! Vitamins! We have the ones from Dr. Walker, but we should look for more."

"And paper and a pen! I want to write down baby names!" Sierra had finished her lunch and jumped up to search for the paper and pen. "I'll eat some corn in a minute. I wanna see if I can find a notebook." She wandered into the den. "Hey, these people had lots of books!" she exclaimed. "I don't think I've ever seen so many books in a person's house before. It's like a library!"

Resa smiled as she put aside a few cans of beans and corn to take but they were too heavy to carry more. They'd have to make do with what they'd find along the way.

Sierra went through the shelves making comments as she found books of interest. "Wouldn't it be awesome to have this many books? I'm gonna have lots of books someday." After another few minutes she called out, "Hey, look at this book! It's called Bartlett's Familiar Quotations." She held up a thick, heavy volume. "It's got all these famous things people wrote." She sat cross-legged on the couch and started reading. Soon she was back in the kitchen.

"Hey, listen to this! This is us. 'Death and sorrow will be the companions of our journey; hardship our garment; constancy and valor our only shield. We must be united, we must be undaunted, we must be inflexible.'"

She looked up at Resa and Tim. "That's us, isn't it? We are companions and we've had sorrow and death, but we are staying united on our journey. Some guy named Winston Churchill said it. This is a cool book. I wish I could take it but it's way too heavy."

Resa commented, "It should be an easy book to find whenever you start building your library."

"I'm gonna tear that page out so I can have it. I like the companions thing. And there's good baby names in that saying. Constance, Journey, and Valor. Cool, huh? Do you think Valor is a girl's name or a boy's name. Or either? I'm gonna keep the pages of quotes that I like since I can't keep whole books."

Tim wasn't sure what Sierra liked about books, but she could like them as long as he didn't have to carry them.

They spent several restful hours during which time Sierra found several pens, and a small notepad.

"Well, this is kinda little, but I'll get a bigger one later. At least I can write down baby names." Sierra tore off the top sheet. "The people who lived here were gonna buy mushrooms and shallots. Whatever a shallot is."

She said the name Star as she wrote it down carefully at the top of her new list. She nodded in satisfaction. "Star. It's a good name for a little girl, isn't it?"

"Yeah, I think so," Tim nodded.

"I like it too," Resa agreed.

Sierra then added Constance, Journey, Valor, and Alice Jean, Nana's name. She smiled as she packed her paper and pen.

Tim thought this trip was like one long scavenger hunt—with dead things lying everywhere. In some fields they saw the carcasses of cows and horses. One farm was so foul they'd walked as quickly as they could, noses covered. Tim had tried to breathe through his mouth thinking it would help but tasted the smell of rotting flesh instead. Disgusting! They were relieved when they'd finally walked out of the smells' range. He figured the animals that liked K-Pox best were vultures. They were often seen, circling high in the sky before floating down to their next meal.

Death was a part of this whole stinking adventure. Death was the reason he'd left Arizona. He thought about his parents every day and missed them more than he could express. Some days he fought the impulse to run home to see if his parents hadn't died after all, but he knew he wouldn't. He knew they were gone. There was no one to go home to and here at least he had good people to travel with. Companions, as Sierra had said.

Walking across the plains in July was difficult. The sun beat down and the road ahead had those wavy, looks like water, heat mirages. The pavement was so hot it was sticky on the soles of their boots, so they walked on the shoulder instead. Tim noticed plants from the ditches and fields were slowly taking over the roads. On older roads weeds were growing out of the cracks, some almost as tall as he was. Seemed like it wouldn't be too long and roads would disappear. Weird. Walking in the brush was better on their feet but wading through tall weeds was annoying as they disturbed the bugs. Tim didn't mind most insects except grasshoppers. Grasshoppers were big and he could never tell where they'd fly...away from you or in your face or up your pants leg. He didn't like them. He remembered a TV show where people ate insects. Gross!

"Would you eat a bug?" Tim called out. "I mean like if it was one of those bugs that people eat like you see on documentaries."

"Yuck! No way! Don't even talk about it! It makes me want to puke!" was Sierra's immediate response.

Tim laughed. "Everything makes you want to puke!"

"Well, that's true," she replied.

"How about you, Resa? Would you eat a bug?" he asked.

"Well, definitely not my first choice for dinner," Resa answered. "But if it was an extreme situation, I'd do it to survive. Like, if there was nothing else and I was stranded somewhere. But overall, no bugs."

Max had no problem eating bugs and other revolting things. There was the time Max had started rolling on a super decomposed dead animal and Tim quickly pulled him off. Before they could find a pond to wash him off, flies had swarmed all over his fur as it stuck up in matted patches. Crazy stinky dog!

Due to the extreme heat and long days, they walked for shorter stretches. They started shortly after the sun rose, took long rest breaks during the heat of the day, then walked again in the cooler evenings. They set up camp before it got dark, often laying their sleeping bags on the side of the road. Tim hated walking in this heat. He figured the wind was as tired of the heat as he was, as it must have sat down somewhere and refused to blow. He'd often been irritated with the wind constantly blowing, but he missed it now as there was nothing to blow off the sweat. And the sun coming up at 5:30 was irritating. Birds chirping, bugs crawling, and everything awake when he wanted to sleep longer. He'd growl at the sun, "Just wait another hour! It's too early!"

On what seemed like the thousandth day trekking through Kansas he looked up at the sky. No clouds. No wind. No relief. No patience for anything. It wasn't just him. They were all irritable and snapping at each other and they walked long miles silently, dripping sweat soaking their clothes. There were times when he wanted to yell at someone, anyone, but he didn't. He wanted to walk faster, by himself, not think of words for games, and not talk to anyone. Getting angry wouldn't help anything. In the evening they'd hoped for a house to sleep in but didn't find one, so dropped their packs on the side of the road. They were grouchy and trying to stay out of each other's way. He sat down and pushed the hair and sweat from his forehead.

"Would you like me to cut your hair?" Resa asked.

"No. Why?"

Tim wished she didn't notice everything. He'd only brushed the hair off his forehead. He thought if he sniffed, she'd give him a tissue. He didn't need people noticing everything he did. Sierra did the same thing. Commenting on stuff that wasn't her business. He liked his hair getting long. His mom had insisted he keep it short, and he'd always wanted it longer. Besides, shaving every couple of days was enough.

"It just looks like it's getting in your way. I have scissors if you want me to trim it or you could trim it yourself. It wouldn't be as hot."

"Yeah," Sierra looked at him appraisingly. "You'd look less shaggy. You should let Resa cut your hair."

Resa reached for her pack. "It wouldn't take long."

Tim could feel all the frustration of the last few months boiling up. He felt he'd been very patient, with vomiting and teeny tiny steps and listening to a LOT of stupid girl talk and "helpful" comments about him. He did not need to be told when to get a haircut.

"I bet you'd look good with shorter hair," Sierra added.

"I...DON'T...WANT...A...HAIRCUT!" Tim bellowed. "Just leave my hair alone! Stop telling me what to do!"

Resa and Sierra both froze, then Sierra rolled her eyes.

"Well, you don't have to yell."

"I'm not trying to tell you what to do," Resa said quietly. "I just thought it would be helpful, that's all."

"*Helpful*? That's not helpful. I don't *want* a haircut. You're not my mom! I don't have to do what you want, so don't tell me what to do."

Tim could see Resa start to form another sentence and Sierra was going to say something stupid and he didn't want to hear it so he kept on.

"I'm not a kid. You don't have to tell me how to do everything! I'm 18. I don't need you to be my mom. My mom is dead, and I don't need another one. You're always trying to tell me what to do. Like when we took MY car in Arizona and YOU had to be the one to drive it. I wanted to drive my car but NO! YOU had to drive it. You just assumed since I was a kid and you were the grownup you'd get your way. AND THEN the car died and YOU were the last one driving it. Not ME! It was MY car. I should've been the last one driving my car. NOT YOU!" Tim could feel tears welling up and he wanted to punch something but there wasn't anything to hit except air and stupid bugs. "AND I'm so sick and tired of walking so slowly. I'm sick and tired of walking and walking and walking and I don't need the aggravation of people bugging me to get my hair cut. I just don't need it!"

Resa and Sierra just stood there, staring at him, eyes wide, silent. He didn't care. He didn't want them to say anything. He didn't care if he hurt their feelings. He didn't care that it wasn't their fault for being slow and sick or whatever. He was SO sick of caring about other people.

He felt he'd explode if he stayed there and he didn't want to hear them talk or try to explain or argue or apologize or anything. He needed to get away. He picked up his pack and threw it on. "I gotta be by myself. I'm sorry, but...I'm...I'm just outta here."

He turned angrily and stepped back onto the road. He wanted to run but the pack was too heavy so he strode off as fast as he could. He heard Sierra crying and Resa called him to come back. He didn't want to come back. Not now. Maybe tomorrow. Maybe never. He didn't know right now. He just needed space, time alone. He looked down. Max was trotting beside him, looking worried. How did dogs look worried anyway? Tim slowed his pace and reached down to stroke Max's head. "You're my buddy, aren't you? You don't tell me what to do. And you walk as fast as I do. You're a good boy!"

Max panted his agreement, and they continued to walk silently into the darkening evening.

As Tim walked he felt his anger and frustration dissipate and the tension slowly ease in his chest. He told himself he'd had the right to get angry. Well, maybe he hadn't needed to get *that* angry and yell, but he felt better now. And he hadn't been wrong. He'd only said what he felt. He stopped and looked around. It was dark and he was tired. He spread his sleeping bag out. He felt better now, could breathe more easily and wasn't so tight inside. He looked forward to sleeping alone for the first time in months. Another thing he was tired of—there was always someone around. And here there was no one but him and Max. He took off his boots, lay on his back, and looked up at the stars. Again he felt tiny and insignificant and his tininess reminded him that his little puny life didn't really mean that much in the long run, that he should just get on with things and not get so stressed about stuff he couldn't change anyway. Max snuggled up to his side and licked Tim's hand. He reached down and softly scratched behind Max's ears. Tim decided he'd walk a day or two by himself, and when he was ready, he'd wait for the others to catch up and he'd join them again. With his decision made, he fell asleep.

Tim was awakened by Max stirring restlessly. The sky was black overhead but glowing at the horizon. Tim groaned. Sunrise already?! It couldn't be. Then he blinked and looked again. This light was on the southern horizon, not the east. He stood up and tried to figure out what he was seeing. As he stared at the glow, he felt a slight breeze blowing gently from the south. Max raised his head and sniffed the air. Tim sniffed too. It smelled like something, he couldn't place it though. Summer camp? Roasting hot dogs? Then the realization of what it was broke through his sleep-addled brain.

Smoke! It was smoke and the light was from fire! He looked again to be sure. He was right. There was a large fire burning on the prairie and the wind was picking up and blowing the fire north.

He rolled up his sleeping bag as quickly as he could and hurried back down the road he'd so angrily strode hours ago. He had to get back to Resa and Sierra. The fire looked like it was miles away but it might travel fast. He didn't know anything about fires. Why had he walked so far away? Was he going to get back in time to warn them? He wanted to go faster but his leg muscles were screaming. He kept looking over his shoulder at the southern sky. The fire didn't seem to move much but he could smell it. If only it would rain and put the fire out. Please rain! But there hadn't been clouds in the sky for ages. He looked up. The stars were disappearing as the thickening smoke slowly covered them. Tim swore loudly and kept striding west.

When he thought his legs would give out, he saw their camp, almost missing it in the dark. Max ran ahead as Tim called out, "Resa! Sierra! Wake up! There's a fire! We have to move!"

Resa was already up. "Oh Tim! I'm so glad you're here. I woke up and thought I smelled smoke. Sierra, get up! Quickly!"

Sierra groaned in her sleeping bag. "Go away. I don't wanna get up."

Tim said impatiently, "Girl! You gotta get up! There's a fire coming and we gotta move. Wake up!" Tim pointed at the southern sky.

Resa looked at the glow on the horizon and shook Sierra's shoulder urgently. "Sierra! Wake up. Now. We have to go!"

Sierra, eyes widened with confusion, struggled to her feet. Tim helped them quickly roll up their bags and get their packs on. They stood and looked at the fire-lit sky together, scanning the horizon.

Tim said, "The wind's blowing north and the fire is to the southeast of us. If it keeps going that way, we can't go east cause we'll cross its path. We have to go back west to stay away from it." Tim looked at Resa knowing she'd hate the idea of going west.

"You're right." She shook her head in frustration. "We have to go west. Let's look for a river in case the fire comes our way. Alright, let's go!"

They headed back the way they'd traveled just hours earlier, walking as quickly as they could, and trying not to look back at the glowing orange sky. The scent of burning brush became stronger and as the blaze got closer, the road ahead reflected its light. Little flakes of ash drifted lightly around them. The fire appeared to be staying behind them and would hopefully miss them. Tim looked at Sierra. She was struggling to keep up so he slowed his pace.

They walked over a bridge and Tim and Resa looked at each other.

"How deep is the water?" Resa asked.

"Let me check." Tim slid down the bank and splashed into the creek, the cool water coming to just above his knees. "Come on down! It's not deep."

Resa and Sierra slid down and joined Tim on the bank, panting and muscles aching from their forced march.

Sierra looked at Resa. "Now what? Do we stay here? Is the fire coming here?"

"I hope not. We'll just wait here and hope the fire stays away. If it comes this way, we'll stay under the bridge and get in the water if we need to...and hope for the best."

They took off their packs and sat quietly under the bridge catching their breath. Ash thickly fell and the smell of smoke burned in their nostrils. They covered their noses and mouths so they wouldn't breathe in the ash. Tim, filled with nervous energy, climbed up the bank every 10 minutes or so to see where the fire was, Resa anxiously joining him several times. Time passed slowly. Finally they saw the fire had passed and the threat was over.

Feeling safer, Sierra unrolled her sleeping bag in a smooth dry spot and fell asleep. Tim and Resa stepped out from under the bridge to check the fire's progress one more time, when something wet touched their faces. They looked up. Instead of ash, it was the soft drops of rain. Cool welcome rain. With a sense of relief Tim and Resa joined Sierra under the bridge and fell into a deep sleep, rain putting the threat of fire out of their minds.

Baby Names

Star	Adoré	Forest
Constance	Sirius	Atlas
Journey	Sterling	Castor
Valor	Draco	Dakota
Alice Jean	Janus	River
Misty Dawn	Kite	Sky
Echo	Leo	Peace
Hope	Elijan	Frost
Joy	Xavier	Robin
Resa	Rio	Hope
Sarah	Elrond	Mercury
Dazzle	Aaron	Aries
Berry	Ajax	Wander
Daisy	Enki	Rainbow

Chapter 14

August - Missouri and Illinois

It was still raining mid-morning when Resa woke into a world filled with the smell of soggy and acrid earth. It didn't seem like morning. The sky was dark and rain clouds hovered in mounting stacks of gray. Resa stretched her arms as Sierra continued to sleep. Tim and Max were already up and standing on the bank downstream, surveying the world that had drastically changed. Resa stood, shook out her poncho from where she had laid it on the ground and slipped it over her head as she walked out from under the bridge. She wondered how far they'd have to walk to be away from the scorched earth where the fire had touched. She didn't look forward to sleeping on singed grass and grime for the next few days.

"How's it look?" Resa asked Tim, walking towards him.

"Mushy. And the smoldering trees are making it foggy too. Smells like a drenched campfire."

Max was sniffing every scent he could find and his fur was covered in soot from the blackened ground.

"Even though it's drizzling rain, we should eat breakfast then go."

"Yeah, I want to keep moving," Tim replied. "Everything looks weird."

"Eerie," Resa agreed.

She walked back under the bridge and searched in her backpack for breakfast as Sierra yawned.

"I was having a bad dream about burning pies. Then I realized the smell was real," Sierra said, rubbing her eyes. Resa gave Sierra a comforting look.

"We'll make it through."

Sierra got up to join Tim while Resa checked how much water they had left from yesterday. She pulled out the sanitizing tablets and wondered if the stream water would be safe. It started to rain harder, and Tim and Max moved back under the shelter of the bridge with Sierra close behind.

"I guess we'll have to stay longer if it keeps raining like this. What a mess," Resa sat back on her heels and shook her head.

"It's getting slippery out there," Sierra said, lowering herself to the ground.

"Hey Resa," Tim said loudly over Max's barking at branches floating by, "Does the stream look higher to you?"

Resa and Sierra looked down at the graffitied paved incline where the water lapped near their makeshift camp.

"The water is definitely closer. Shoot." Resa said as Sierra looked at her with worried eyes. "There could be flash flooding because the fire burned away everything on the ground that absorbs water or holds it back. We should move." They packed up quickly and made their way up the bank. The ground sucked at their feet until they hit the pavement of the road.

"Ugh! We can't trudge through this muck and crappy weather all day. We'll be exhausted," Tim said.

They stamped their feet to knock off the mud and started to walk. They were already tired from a horrible night's sleep and discouraged by the thought of the long, drizzly day which lay ahead of them.

It rained off and on all morning and there wasn't much talking as they plodded through puddles and around corn stalks blown on the road from the fields. The ponchos they wore covered their backpacks and kept the rain off their heads, but it made it difficult to hear and see around them. They were able to hike for several hours before they stopped for lunch under a lonely tree. It started to drizzle again as soon as they opened their packs.

"We may have to just hang it up for today. This is miserable," Resa mumbled.

Back on the road, Resa tried to picture home to keep herself calm, but she felt cold from the inside out. She usually tried to stay positive, but she was feeling exhausted, frayed, and surly deep down in her bones. Resa knew Meg's 18th birthday was coming and she was going to miss it! Her beautiful and amazing girl. It had been wonderful to be with Tim on his birthday, but bittersweet too. She missed the celebration of Meg transitioning into adulthood. Even in this messed up world, it was a big deal! She wanted to curl up and weep with sorrow. She'd already missed Mitchell's birthday months ago and now Meg. Her favorite son and favorite daughter. The kids always laughed because they knew they were her only son and daughter, but they were two of her favorite people in the whole world. This journey was too much. It was taking sooooo long to get home and she felt her strength being sapped away by the constant challenges. Resa couldn't help but feel wrung out and grumpy after running for their lives and trying like hell to survive. Resa was jolted out of her grumblings when she almost ran into Tim who had suddenly stopped. The road in front of them dipped and was completely covered with rapidly flowing flood water.

"I don't see how we can get around it. The sides are flooded too. Maybe I can test how deep it is," Tim said.

"Wait!" Resa said as he started walking forward. "When roads are washed out like this they can sweep a car off the road. Even a few inches could knock you off your feet and you could get seriously hurt."

"What about the rope from the Durango house? I'll hold onto it and wade in slowly. Then you guys can pull me out if I lose my footing," Tim suggested.

"If you fall we may not be able to hold on to the rope or we might fall too," Resa said and looked behind her. "Here. We can loop it around this road sign."

Ironically, the sign was to warn drivers of a dip in the road.

"Yeah, and then look," Tim said pointing across the water, "There's a sign on the other side too. I'll tie it to that and then you guys can use it for balance when you cross.

"Tie the rope around your waist or something," Sierra said, "and don't be a dummy. Don't go swimming around. Who knows what's lurking at the bottom."

"Check. No swimming. No wrestling crocodiles."

Sierra stuck out her tongue and Tim cracked a smile before tying the rope around his waist. He handed the other end to Resa who secured it around the sign.

"Max, stay," Tim commanded. Max's body tensed as he watched Tim walk until his feet and calves disappeared into the water below.

"My feet are still touching!" Tim called back. "It's only above the knees in this one spot."

"Lucky for him. His knees are higher off the ground than mine," Sierra muttered.

"We'll help each other," Resa said in what she hoped was a reassuring voice. It was taking all the strength she could muster right now. She felt panic rising in her chest.

"It's not super deep," Tim called out when he reached the other side and tied the rope to the sign post. "I'll come back to help." Using the rope that now stretched from one side to the other, Tim sloshed back to grab Max and his pack. He set them both safely on the opposite side of the road then waded back to grab Resa and Sierra's packs. Holding them over his head, he called back for them to follow.

Resa motioned for Sierra to go in front of her and stayed close behind as they cautiously stepped forward. Resa shivered when the chilly water soaked through her shoes and crept up her pant legs. The water came all the way up to Sierra's thighs. Resa's eyes were on Tim's outstretched hands when suddenly, Sierra stumbled and fell sideways into the murky water.

"Sierra!" Tim and Resa yelled together. Sierra flailed her arms as Resa grabbed on to her and Tim splashed back into the water. Together they helped Sierra regain her footing and push up to standing. Sierra coughed and sputtered. She had only been under the water for a few seconds, but she was completely drenched.

"DAAAAAMN IT!!!!" Sierra screamed, crouching down and pounding the water with her fists.

"DAMN IT! DAMN IT! DAMN IT!" She added a few more colorful words as tears ran down her cheeks and she roared into the sky.

"WHY does everything have to be so hard?! Why is life always such a disaster? Why am I in this disgusting water instead of home with Nana?" Sierra's shoulders shook as she gasped for breath and covered her face with her hands as she sobbed. "I can't...I just can't..."

Resa's panic quickly turned to tenderness as she threw her arms around Sierra, hugged her close, and whispered, "It's ok to be frustrated and sad. It's ok to feel angry about things being hard and unfair. It's ok to cry."

That just made Sierra cry harder and blubber incoherent words as Resa held her.

"I'm sorry. I'm just so tired. It's one awful thing after another. I don't think I'm strong enough for this journey," Sierra said, finally raising her face off of Resa's shoulder.

Tim stepped closer to put his arms around them too.

"Hey, like you always say, we're in this together and that makes us all stronger," Tim said softly, "We're a family."

Resa felt her own frustrations from the day slowly fade away. Tim was right, Resa thought, no matter how awful they felt at times and how many challenges they faced, they had each other.

"We pull each other through," Resa told Sierra.

"Like literally this time," Tim smiled. He backed out of the group hug and stepped onto the dry road, reaching out his hand. Resa grinned and put a steadying hand on Sierra's back. Sierra took a deep breath, grabbed Tim's hand, and walked out of the water.

"Well, I guess this brings us to the end of our water therapy session for today," Sierra said, smiling wide with her tear-stained and puffy cheeks.

They all laughed as they realized how pitiful and bedraggled they looked.

Tim waded back one more time to retrieve the rope while Resa surveyed the clouds stacked to the horizon. Midwest weather was crazy. Yesterday was steamy and today the breeze blew chilly tendrils through their soaked clothes. Their shoes squelched as they hiked away.

In the afternoon they found a house where they could rest for the night. Their clothes were still damp and caked with grime after hiking through the flood water and charred landscape, so they did laundry before they explored the cabinets. After they changed and hung their wet clothes to dry, they looked through the rooms.

Tim burst into laughter as he found a waterbed in the basement bedroom. "Hey! I found a waterbed! Come look!" he yelled.

"I've never seen a waterbed!" Sierra called back as she walked down the stairs.

"I'm good," Resa yelled from the living room. "I've had enough water to last me the whole trip."

"I'm gonna try it tonight!" Sierra said, coming back up the stairs with Tim. "It will be like sleeping on a boat! Maybe Baby Safari and I can finally get comfortable." Sierra was trying a different baby name every day to figure out which one she liked.

True to her word, after dinner Sierra tucked herself into her sleeping bag on top of the waterbed while Resa and Tim found other bedrooms upstairs. They all fell asleep to the rumble and growls of the storm brewing in the distance.

The next day brought more rain, but it gave their legs a chance to rest and their clothes time to fully dry. Tim was excited to find Pop-Tarts and Fudge Rounds in the back of the cabinets and said he'd guard them with his life.

The morning after, Resa heard Tim bumping around and calling for Max to go outside. She smiled as she heard Max's toenails click and slide across the floor. The world outside was soft and the sun peeked from behind the drifting clouds. Her emotions still felt heavy, but she was slowly making peace with her frustrations. After breakfast they packed their bags and headed out.

By mid-morning they crossed over a bridge and Resa gasped. She realized in the distance she could make out the Arch glinting in the sunlight. They were in St. Louis! Wow, she thought. The Arch memorial was built to symbolize opening doors to the adventures in the West and now it symbolized being closer to the East.

"Hey guys! Look at the St. Louis Arch. This means we're going to cross the Mississippi River! Do you guys know how to spell Mississippi?"

They smiled as they walked across and sang the m-i-crooked letter-crooked-letter rhyme a few times before their song quieted in the middle of the huge bridge. Water lapped at the cement columns that stretched deep into the river below.

"The river is way bigger than I thought it'd be," Sierra said. "This is the furthest east I've ever been in my whole life!"

"Just wait until tomorrow, you'll be even further!" Resa joked.

"It feels creepy to be out in the open like this," Tim said quietly.

Resa hadn't thought of it, but he was right. They were completely vulnerable targets. There was nowhere to hide. Finally, they stepped off the bridge into Illinois. They walked most of the day until clouds gathered again in the late afternoon.

"Guys," Sierra said, sounding exhausted, "I hate to be a jerk, but me and Baby Wander are feeling pretty tired."

"Maybe she's right," Resa said. "We should find a place and wait it out in case there's another storm coming."

"These annoying storms are messing up our travel plans," Tim said, annoyed.

Shortly after, they found an old motel with locks which weren't hard to open. The three hunkered down and tried to sleep as the storms raged and rolled by in the night. The next morning the sun shone again and the green of the earth stood out against the waves of heat already rising from the road. The air felt heavy.

"We should get Sierra up and get moving. It's going to be a hot one," Tim said.

"Do you want the honors?" Resa gave Tim a side-eye look.

"What's that, Max? You need to go pee?" Tim said as he ran with Max towards the grassy lawn.

"Coward!" Resa yelled jokingly.

Resa went inside to drag a reluctant Sierra out of bed. She was handing her some food when Tim walked back in.

"Gonna be a hot sticky day," Tim told her.

"Too bad we're not in Florida. I bet we could pick fruit off the trees down there. Oh, what I wouldn't give for a big watermelon right now!" Sierra moaned.

"Hey, I think I saw a billboard for a small town in the distance. Maybe they have a store with watermelon candy or something," Tim said, loading up and adjusting his backpack.

Once they were walking again, Resa watched Tim slow down so she and Sierra could catch up. Resa had watched him do that several times now. It was sweet of him. The trio walked in comfortable silence, breaking only for lunch and a nap under a shade tree during the hottest hours of the afternoon. Finally signs pointed towards a drugstore and a gas station.

"There it is!" Sierra called out, "At last!"

Resa was glad to have a break too. She'd been struggling to keep the sweat out of her eyes and the heat had made them all fatigued and weary. They were grateful the store still had magnesium, prenatal vitamins, and watermelon Jolly Ranchers for Sierra.

"Look! They have powdered donuts!" Tim said excitedly as he ripped open the package and bit into one.

"Oh gross! It's moldy! I need water. Gross gross gross!" He quickly spit the chewed donut pieces back into the bag, grabbed his water, and rinsed his mouth. Sierra laughed and Resa tried to hide her smile.

"Oh that was disgusting. It was like eating spider webs!" He shuddered.

They went on looking for supplies, staying away from the packaged pastries. Resa pocketed some more lip balm and sunscreen and saw some runner's Gold Bond friction cream. Maybe it would help with the sore spots in her armpits where her shirt seams rubbed all day. Of course the water was gone, but there were bottles of tea Resa grabbed to have something different to drink.

"I'm getting some nail polish," Sierra said, "We all need a little color sometimes."

As they were walking out the door, they froze as they heard laughing from the gas station across the parking lot.

"Too bad the slushie machine isn't working! I could really go for one of those right now!" a man's voice said.

Resa, Tim, and Sierra backed into the store doorway, but Max barked and blew their chance of sneaking away. Two bearded men waved and walked towards them.

"Shalom my friends! Too bad we can't stand in the freezers for a bit and cool off, right?" bearded man number one said, giving them a wide smile. Though he was smiling, Resa noticed he had a firm grip on the rifle he was carrying.

"When I was a kid, we used to open up the fire hydrants on the street and run through them," Resa said back pleasantly, retaining a tight grasp on her pistol as well.

She noticed Tim had drawn his gun from his holster. Resa felt a small wave of sadness about living in a world now where no one could even say hello without bracing for the worst.

"Ah, you must be a city girl. How are you holding up?" bearded man number two said.

"Not the greatest," Resa answered honestly.

"Understandably so. Everything's flipped upside down. Cities look totally crazy. We went through Atlanta a few months ago and it's like the apocalypse movies. Desolate, trash blowing everywhere, and buildings in disrepair."

"You went through Atlanta?" Tim asked curiously, noticeably relaxing his arm.

"We've been to lots of places."

Bearded man number one made a show of taking his hand off the trigger grip and rested the gun, muzzle down, next to his leg.

"Tell you what, we were going to break for dinner and find somewhere to rest for the night. Do you want to join us and I'll tell y'all about it?"

157

"That's very kind. Give us a minute?" Resa said, motioning to Tim and Sierra to take a few steps back.

Once they were out of earshot, Sierra whispered, "I'm not getting any bad vibes from them."

"I think if they were dangerous, they'd have already taken us out," Tim added.

"That's true," Resa agreed. She looked over to watch the two men wave their arms animatedly at each other and chuckle at what must be a funny story.

"It'd be nice to break early. The humidity has been bothering me today." Sierra massaged her neck and rested her hand on her growing stomach.

"Ok, we all agree. Let's keep our eyes open and our guards up," Tim said.

"Sounds like a good plan." Resa said. She called to the two men, "Did you have a reservation at a nearby restaurant?" Both men laughed and everyone visibly relaxed.

They found outdoor tables at an ice cream stand by the gas station. Dinner was filled with stories and laughter. It was nice to have other adults to talk to, Resa thought. The two men were brothers and they'd been on the road traveling across the country as well.

Robert and James were twins, but Robert said he was older 'by 2 minutes' so he was in charge. James rolled his eyes but laughed. Robert was divorced and said he wouldn't be surprised if his ex-wife made it through K-Pox without a scratch.

"Meaner than a junkyard dog," Robert said, with James launching into a hysterical story about a Thanksgiving turkey being thrown across the room during the only holiday dinner they had all shared.

"I warned you!" James told Robert, nudging him with his elbow. "Twin intuition," he said, tapping the side of his head.

James said he'd choose adventure over marriage any day. Since they were both single, every year the two of them had tackled a new challenge. Skydiving, mountain climbing, and waterfall rappelling were just the short list of things they had done. Originally from Colorado, they had been in Florida for kayaking when the pandemic hit. Their parents still lived outside of Denver with their sisters' families and a gaggle of extended family.

"We talked before all communications went down and they seemed ok. They own a family furniture business and the whole family hunkered down when things got crazy." James explained.

"Good thing it's a big property or there might be murders of biblical proportions with them all living there together! All the commotion is probably good for deterring criminals," Robert joked. Everyone laughed.

"We told them we'd mosey on home after a while. They know we keep each other safe and alive. Our mama's brother lives in West Virginia. So we explored our way up to his house to check on him. He was fine when we got there. Ornery as ever," James said.

"Wait, you've already been through West Virginia?" Tim asked.

James and Robert explained they'd headed north out of Florida and zig zagged through coastal states for a while, then turned west through West Virginia towards home.

"We thought we'd make it for Hanukkah and light the Menorah with the family. A way to honor the new start you know?"

Tim asked about the cities.

"There's pockets of people hiding here and there. It's amazing how quickly nature takes back what it's lost though. There was a whole village of possums in one building! We avoid zoos. We heard people were letting animals out instead of having them die in the enclosures. We actually saw giraffes and elephants wandering outside a theme park in Florida," Robert told them.

This new tidbit made Resa want to avoid cities even more at this point. Now there were wild animals to worry about!

"That was nothing compared to the huge herds of deer and packs of coyotes we saw on the east coast," James interjected.

"Oh! And remember that huge beaver dam we saw in Baltimore! And the black bear that was using it to stretch into the water and catch fish?" Robert shot back.

Resa looked at Tim and Sierra, leaning forward, absorbing all this new information. She smiled at the easy way Robert and James volleyed back and forth in conversation, picking up each other's leads and finishing each other's stories.

"How many people did you run into along the way?" Sierra asked.

"Sometimes we go for weeks at a time without seeing anyone and then sometimes we run into smaller groups." Robert scratched his head. "We started to map things out. We're making copies to give to others. Maybe it will help connect everyone again."

"That's a great idea," Resa said. "It's hard to imagine the world will get back to how it was before, but we have to hope."

"Yeah, we found this newspaper article when we were poking around New York," Robert said, rummaging through his backpack.

"Talk about eerie," James said. "An abandoned Times Square is one strange place. There were communities rebuilding, but we didn't stay long."

"Here it is." Robert handed Resa a crumpled newspaper article. The top read 'The Boston Times, March 9th' and painted a pretty grim picture. Resa felt the blaze of hope dim inside her chest. Tim and Sierra clustered around her to read.

"90% or more of the world's population is gone?!" Tim said.

"People from the same bloodline may be genetically immune," Sierra read aloud.

Maybe her family would be together for Halloween, Resa thought. What a treat that would be! She smiled, but then looked over at Tim who dropped his head and mumbled something about taking Max for a walk. Her smile crumbled. His whole family hadn't made it. Why had he? She was sure he was thinking the same thing.

Robert watched him go, nodding as James got up to walk with Tim down the gravel lined street.

160

"You know, he never wanted kids, but I always thought he'd be a great dad," Robert said.

Robert, Resa, and Sierra swapped stories about interesting food they had found until the guys got back. Tim told them they'd found a motel up the road.

"It looks ok. Better than sleeping on the ground," James said.

"Yes! Real beds again tonight! I'm in!" Sierra stretched out her legs then stood up slowly. Sierra had told Resa she got dizzy sometimes when she got up too fast. Gotta keep her well, Resa thought. Let this baby be a new hope in this strange new world.

Before falling asleep Resa thought about the article and how so much had been destroyed by K-Pox. It was more than she'd imagined. Please, please please, she called out to the universe. Please, please let her family be alive. She felt restless, but exhaustion took over and she fell asleep to the sound of Robert and James's voices in the room next to hers.

The next morning, Resa got up early. Her mind started spinning when the sun rose. She walked outside and saw Robert drinking instant coffee out of a collapsible drinking cup. He'd built a small fire outside to heat it up in a saucepan.

"When we're not in a rush, I like to remember what a normal morning feels like. Want some?" he asked when she walked over to say good morning, "I even found a fancy creamer in the gas station."

"That'd be great."

The warm coffee was strong but tasted amazing. Robert glanced around before speaking again.

"I want to give you a copy of our map with the settlements we've found. It'll come in handy as you head east. But I want to explain the markings." He paused as he pulled a folded map out of his backpack. "There's a settlement in West Virginia that asked us not to give out their location unless we thought the folks headed their way were honest and decent."

"Oh, you mean like…no serial killers and arsonists allowed?" Resa said.

Robert chuckled. "Right."

"Are they…," Resa wasn't sure how to phrase it. "Are they a restrictive community?"

"Tim told James about the place you guys were when Sierra found out she was pregnant."

Resa nodded and said, "You'll understand why I don't want her to be anywhere near a place like that when she has her baby."

"Oh, I understand. Even with a huge portion of the population gone, there's still all sorts of people out there. This place is not like that at all. They call themselves Preppers. Preparing for all possibilities. Just a bunch of regular folks trying to figure it out together." Robert chuckled, "They call their settlement, Outtatown. Before K-Pox, it's where they went when they wanted to get out..of...town. Now it's their home. They seemed pretty supportive and open to new ideas when we were there. Heck, they even sent a team to ask my uncle to come live with them if he wanted." Robert grinned his wide grin.

"He refused, but they said they'd check on him from time to time. Their scouting team takes supplies to people. They just don't want any trouble or people trying to take down what they've built."

"Sounds like a good place for us to make a stop," Resa said. "Thank you for trusting us. We'll keep the map safe."

"I haven't even gotten to the best part," Robert said excitedly. "They have a nurse there." Robert sipped his coffee. "Ann's a real firecracker. She'll be good with Sierra."

"That is incredible! I am so relieved," Resa said.

"I marked Outtatown with a tree, the one with the longer trunk."

Resa opened up the map and saw it was dotted sparsely with trees, flowers, and animal paws.

"The trees are for communities where we stayed a little longer."

"The non-serial killer ones," Resa smiled.

"Right," Robert smiled back, "The flowers were for safe communities, but temporary and the animal paws are places to

162

avoid. They were more interested in themselves or preying on others passing through."

Resa teared up, "This means a lot. I'm really grateful for you and for this moment. Thank you."

Resa pulled out a folded piece of paper from her pocket and handed it to him. "Friends let us stay at their vacation house. I'm sure they wouldn't mind you staying there a night or two if you need it. I wrote down all the details. And," she said flipping the paper over, "I mapped out my house in Laurel in case you ever come back through Pennsylvania and need a spot to land. Hopefully you can meet my family when you come to visit."

"I'll be looking forward to it. Leich L'shalom, Go towards peace, my friend," Robert said, bowing his head over the folded paper.

Resa stood with Robert watching the sun rise slowly over the trees, warming her hands with her coffee mug. She finally started to feel undaunted by the next steps of the journey.

"Here's to the road ahead." She raised her mug and toasted the sun.

Chapter 15

September - Indiana and Kentucky

Robert and James had not seen anyone in Kentucky or Indiana. Tim thought again how empty the country was. The last people they'd seen (before the two brothers) were back in Kansas. No evidence of anyone. Anywhere. He was glad they were keeping track of where they'd bumped into people. Little communities were starting up again all over the U.S., probably even the world. Tim found it interesting that some places were seeking new members and others were hiding. He totally understood the communities swearing Robert and James to secrecy. You never knew who'd come through. The wrong people could totally mess things up.

He glanced at Sierra and her growing belly. What if her baby was one of the only babies born in the new world? That'd be weird, and a little scary.

Tim wondered if he'd ever have a girlfriend. He'd always kinda figured there'd be a girl for him somewhere. He and Sierra weren't right for each other. He knew that. Not because she was pregnant. But she was more like an irritating little sister. He liked her. Just not like *that*. And survival was topmost in his mind right now. Still, he'd always thought he'd get married someday. James had said there were young people at Outtatown. And this community *was* looking for new members. Well, he'd find out; they were headed that way.

They'd decided to head to Outtatown so Sierra would have help with delivering her baby. Tim found himself watching Sierra more now that she was showing. She was a little more clumsy and tired easily. Resa had informed Tim if Sierra delivered early, he'd have to

164

help. He was *not* looking forward to that *at all*. If Outtatown had a nurse, then they needed to hurry and get there.

He was glad the extreme, exhausting heat of summer was over. Hiking in 70 degrees was way better than 90 plus. The evening temperatures were brisk, and they'd started sleeping *in* their sleeping bags again instead of *on* them. When possible they stayed in deserted motels though they weren't always able to sleep in the beds as mice and other creepy, crawly things had often gotten there first. But sometimes the beds were ok, and they slept on real mattresses and had a roof over their heads. Now that they were further east, there were more rivers and ponds to resupply their water bottles. Such a relief.

They started playing word games again. Tim noticed how most of the things they missed were food. They'd just gone through the entire missed food alphabet (Hamburgers, Icecream, Jalapeno peppers, Kettlecorn, Lasagna, Meatballs with spaghetti, Nachos, Oranges, Pizza and so on). Before they started on the next round they agreed they couldn't use food. It made playing harder but at least they didn't think about eating all the time. Tim was always hungry and would've given a lot for a Big Mac, fries, and a Coke. Just thinking about it made his mouth water. It was his turn again. What did he miss with a D.

"Diners! That should count. It isn't food."

"Sure," Resa said.

"No! It's the same as food!" Sierra jumped in.

"Resa said it was ok so it counts. Now you have E."

Sierra scowled but didn't argue. She wasn't happy with the new rule that they couldn't use the dictionary anymore. Tim thought it odd Sierra liked her dictionary so much. She was always looking up words and commenting on them. She was also adding to her list of baby names. She'd found a little journal to replace the notepad she used for baby names.

For once Sierra didn't have her answer ready. "E. I forgot to think of something with E and we can't use food. Aaah! This is harder since we can't use words we already used. The only thing stuck in my mind now is eggplant and that's a food I don't even miss! It just got stuck in my mind. Dumb! I'll have to think longer."

Tim suggested, "Wanna sing a while to take a break? We could sing something together if there's songs we all know. I used to sing in the car with my parents when we went on trips. I'm not a great singer, but it was fun!" Tim tried to think of songs they might all know.

"I like to sing. What song?" Sierra asked.

"What's something we all know or we can learn quickly?" Resa asked.

In a clear steady soprano Sierra started singing a song which had been popular before life changed. Tim joined in with a quiet baritone. After he sang the first verse, he felt more confident, and his voice became louder and more on key. When they arrived at the chorus the second time, Resa joined in with her alto, struggling a little to hit the higher notes. They sounded stronger as they sang the song through several times, learning to harmonize, making comments and laughing on how they could improve. They went through several more pop tunes, trying to remember lyrics and making new ones up if they didn't.

"Do you know the song 'This Land is Your Land'?" Tim asked.

"I've heard it but don't know all the words," Resa said.

"Yeah, same here," added Sierra. "I think I sang it in a school program once. Can you sing it?" she asked Tim.

"It's one of the songs me and my parents used to sing in the car but it's been awhile. I can probably remember all the verses. It just seems like it's a good song to sing right now." Tim started singing. Sierra and Resa listened through the first time and after going through it several more times were able to join in. Then they sang America the Beautiful and every song about America they could think of. For several hours they learned verses and played with harmonies and sang the songs with feeling.

Tim heard these lyrics now in a different way from when he'd sung these songs with his parents. They'd only traveled in the southwest, never in the rest of the U.S. He couldn't believe how these songs touched him. It felt so personal now. They had seen so many of those things–spacious skies and fruited plains, wheat

166

fields waving and dust clouds rolling, shining deserts and definitely ribbons of highway. Very long long ribbons of highway.

"How'd you learn all these songs?" Sierra asked.

"My parents had an album of folk songs, and we learned the words and sang when we went on trips. Singing in the car was kinda a family tradition." Tim looked sadly down the long stretch of road ahead. He missed his parents when he sang, but it helped him feel like they were there with him as well. Sad but happy. He touched his mother's ring still on the chain under his shirt.

"I think I'll have that tradition with my baby too," Sierra said. "If we take trips. I wonder if we'll ever have car trips again. Maybe we'll just take walking vacations everywhere for the rest of forever. Ooh! Or horses and carriages like the old days. But whatever we do, I want Baby Tripp to learn this song. It will always remind me of our travels together." Sierra's eyes filled with tears. "I don't know what I'd have done without you two guys. You saved my life. You really did. I love you both so much!" and she burst into tears.

Tim looked helplessly at Resa who pulled Sierra into her arms and held her close. "We love you too, Sierra," Resa murmured as she rocked her gently.

Tim reached out and awkwardly patted Sierra's shoulder. He didn't know what to say. Finally he mumbled, "Yeah, me too." Then he backed away a step wondering if it was a dumb thing to say. Resa nodded slightly to show approval. He sighed in relief. He never was comfortable in emotional situations.

As Sierra slowly stopped crying, they all slipped their packs off and sat down on the side of the road.

"I'm so sorry! I didn't mean to get all stupid and start bawling right in the middle of the road." She sniffed and dug in her pack for tissue. "If we were on "K" and it was my turn, I'd say I miss Kleenex. And "H." I miss hugs." She attempted a weak laugh.

"Sierra, after everything you've been through this last year, I think a few tears on the side of the road are fine. For all of us! And I can give you all the hugs you want." Resa leaned over and gave Sierra another hug.

"Yeah, me too," Tim said, then wondered if he meant giving Sierra hugs or that she could cry on the side of the road or both. He looked down hoping no one could read his mind. No problem there. Resa was still comforting Sierra, telling her women could be more emotional when pregnant and she and Tim loved having her with them and on and on. They sure did talk a lot. He wanted to get up and do something. Anything. This was uncomfortable. He didn't want to know about pregnancy and emotions and stuff, and he was bored sitting there.

"I'll get some water." Tim got up, went to his pack, and pulled off his water container. "According to our map, there's a creek close by so you can use what water you want. You know, to wash your face or whatever. If you want to. Not that you need to." Tim groaned inside. Sometimes saying the right thing was difficult. He hoped he hadn't insulted her. He hadn't meant to but he never knew. She was more emotional now and could take things the wrong way.

"I'm going to take a walk up ahead to see what's there. Should be a creek. I'll be back in a bit." He picked up two empty bladder type water containers.

When he was out of sight, he broke into a run, Max loping alongside. He loved running. When he got into a rhythm, he felt as though he were almost flying; his feet barely touching the ground. He loved the way running made him feel free and light and fast.

He liked Kentucky. It looked like the type of land he wanted to settle in someday...lots of green. Green grass, green trees, green weeds. It was very restful. He had nothing against the desert, it had its own beauty. But he liked green rolling hills. He thought back to Colorado. The mountains were amazingly beautiful, but he had no desire to settle there. When he was in the mountains, he felt surrounded by them. He couldn't see out, almost claustrophobic. And it was so difficult to get anywhere. Up and down all the time which was hard on your legs. He was so glad they'd had a car to get out of the mountains quickly. If they hadn't had a car, they'd probably still be there, walking up and down. He liked the flat plains of eastern Colorado and Kansas, but it was too flat. He liked the rolling hills of Kentucky better.

Max lapped up water as Tim filled the water containers, he thought back about their crossing the Mississippi River. That was an experience he'd never forget. He'd never seen such a wide river. When they'd crossed the bridge he'd felt so exposed out over the water where anyone could see them. It was different from the plains where they'd been walking in the open. There they might be visible to anyone around, but the people watching were also visible to them. Walking over the river, whole villages of people could be hiding in the buildings watching their progress. Fortunately, if there had been people hiding, they'd stayed hidden.

And then they'd crossed the Ohio River. He didn't realize the Ohio was so wide, almost like the Mississippi. Well, to be honest, he hadn't known anything about the Ohio River so anything he learned was new. It was similar to crossing the Mississippi, being vulnerable out on the long bridge. They'd moved across as quickly as they could and breathed easier when they were back on more secluded highways.

He liked learning all these things about the United States. He'd always liked learning by doing activities and seeing demonstrations. Sierra liked learning through her books, reading whenever she could. He didn't like to learn that way. Reading had always been hard.

Heading to the Outtatown settlement in West Virginia was taking them further south than originally planned. He wondered if they'd ever get to Laurel. Didn't seem like it, but at least they were still heading east.

Tim picked up the full water containers and he and Max headed back to where Resa and Sierra were ready to go again.

A short while later Tim looked over his shoulder at Sierra. She'd dropped behind, reading while she walked. Her pace dropped with her increased level of interest in the book. She'd been picking up books to read when they stopped at deserted homes or stores and would leave behind those she'd finished.

"Hey Sierra! If we're gonna get anywhere in the next year or two, you gotta walk faster. Come on!" Tim called back.

"Oh sorry!" She closed the book and caught up with Tim and Resa. "Nana said she could drop a frying pan next to me and I'd not notice if I was reading. I get so involved I forget where I am."

"I hate reading. I like watching TV better."

Sierra said with enthusiasm, "But when you read, you can be anywhere, with anyone in the whole world without leaving where you are. I love it! And you don't need technology to read a book. Besides, TV is probably gone forever now."

"Aah! I know!" Tim groaned. "I really miss video games and movies and YouTube and apps and everything! Maybe someone someday will get power going again and we could watch videos and play games again. That'd be so cool if that happened!"

The long days slowly came and went. One late afternoon they approached a large, modern house set a short way off the highway. They decided to take a chance on at least one of them finding a pair of shoes and they'd look for warmer clothes as nights were getting cooler. Tim hoped for something good to eat. He bet Sierra would want to find another book. He didn't know what Resa wanted, but she was always practical so was probably thinking about new socks or something. As they got closer to the house, Max started growling. Oh no, Tim thought. Max was off the leash and too far away for Tim to grab his collar. Max slowly moved towards a large tree surrounded by tall weeds, nose and tail down low. They all heard Max snuffling loudly. Tim waded through the weeds to see what Max had found. A swarm of insects and flies buzzed around a deteriorated body. Tim inhaled in shock and yelled, "Max! Come here!"

Tim slipped on Max's leash and backed up about 10 feet. He held his breath against the smell and noticed the decomposing body was dressed in hiking clothes, a backpack close to the body. Insects hummed and crawled over what used to be a human being. There was an empty water canteen leaning against the tree trunk. He thought the body had probably been a man due to the clothes and his size, but he wasn't sure. And he wasn't going to get closer to make sure.

"What is it?" Sierra called out.

"A dead guy," Tim responded quietly, shuddering.

Max tried to get back to his discovery but Tim held the leash tight. He didn't want Max sniffing or licking a dead person. That wouldn't be right.

Sierra took a few steps towards them, tempted to look, but stopped when the breeze blew the smell towards them. "Oh, I'm gonna be sick," she said, turning away and retching into the tall grass.

Resa walked gingerly through the trodden weeds, stood next to Tim, and peered over the weeds at the hiker. Her face was grim and sad. "Poor guy. I wonder if he was out here all alone. He couldn't have died too long ago, maybe a couple of weeks."

They walked quickly but somberly to the house, their happy shopping mood vanished. They wondered about the hiker and why he'd died there. Did he die of K-Pox? Or starvation? Tim could tell animals had carried off body parts. It's not how he wanted to end— eaten by animals and bugs, his bones scattered all over.

They went through the house quickly, without their usual enthusiasm. Tim found a pair of boots that fit. They all found warmer clothes. Sierra found a couple of paperbacks and they grabbed a few canned goods. Everything was found in record time. The dead hiker weighed heavily on their minds, and they just wanted to leave.

"Shouldn't we do something for him?" Sierra asked as they were leaving. "I mean, I know we don't know anything about him and he could've been a terrible person, but it just seems kinda wrong to leave him like that."

Tim glanced at Resa.

"Hang on. Let me get something," she said.

She went back into the house and came back carrying a black scarf. Tim tied the scarf around a low hanging branch over the body and Sierra said a short prayer. It was one thing to know millions and millions of people were dead. It was another thing to see one of those people, someone who had died relatively recently, decomposing under a tree. It wasn't the first time they'd seen dead people, but it had been a while. They didn't like to be reminded they'd escaped an unpleasant death, and death could be anywhere ahead, anytime, just around the corner, ready to take one or all of them.

They walked quietly for the rest of the afternoon. No singing or chatting. Just silent and thoughtful, their boots crunching loudly in the stillness of the upcoming evening. They settled into camp and ate their supper with few words.

The next day clouds gathered ominously. As rain started coming down in big drops, they ducked into a deserted gas station which probably hadn't been used in decades. Weeds were growing all over the tiny, paved lot and up the sides of the building and the door was rotted, but it was a shelter near the road and it was empty. Not knowing how long it would rain or how long they'd be there, they tossed out the old papers, weeds, empty liquor bottles, and scraped down the spider webs. The small room didn't take long to clean up. They settled in, wrapped themselves in their sleeping bags, and soon were drowsy from the drip drip drip of the rain. Getting more sleep was something their bodies always craved. They never minded having a few days rest every now and then. While the rain fell, they slept easily. About three in the afternoon Tim woke up hungry. He went through his pack and opened a can of pork and beans. They were never his favorite when he was living at home, but he liked them now. Lots of protein and energy and were filling. Sierra and Resa woke up as they heard Tim and Max moving about. Max was crunching loudly over his kibble. Tim smiled at him. He sure was a noisy eater!

Sierra and Resa joined Tim and they ate, sitting on their sleeping bags and watching the rain. They were comfortable not talking, and often had long stretches of time when they were peacefully silent. Between dozing and watching the rain and running out quickly to pee, they spent a quiet afternoon. They turned off the lantern early and, too tired to do much else, slipped into a deep sleep.

It was still raining the next morning, a steady rain, not heavy enough to worry about flooding (yet), but enough to stay under cover. As they'd slept most of the day before, they had more energy when they awoke. They did their usual morning activities which included breakfast and cleaning up and brushing teeth.

They sat in the dim rain-filtered light and wondered what to do. Tim pulled out a deck of cards and they decided to play. They started out with rummy and moved on to poker using pebbles for money. On their rest days they played a variety of games. Resa had taught them several types of solitaire. Tim had watched his Mom play solitaire on her Kindle but he'd never played. It hadn't occurred to him that you could play solitaire with real cards. Sierra had learned solitaire games from Nana, and they'd occasionally try a new game. It wasn't an exciting way to spend the day, but it beat walking in the rain. Tim soon tired of cards and watching the rain.

"Hey Sierra, what are you reading?"

"A romance book. I don't think you'd like it."

"What else you got?" he asked.

"The Secret Garden. It's an old book written back in the early 1900s. Nana read it to me when I was in elementary school. I wanna read it again."

"What's it about? Somebody's garden?"

"Sort of. It's about a little girl who's an orphan and goes from India to an old country mansion in England somewhere and she finds a secret garden. I don't remember the details much though so I want to read it again."

"How about if you read it out loud so we could listen? You wanna do that?"

"Yeah! That'd be fun! And you and Resa could take turns reading. Resa, you wanna read too?"

"Sure, I'd like to."

Tim quickly said, "I don't wanna read."

Resa said, "That's ok. We'll only read aloud if we want to."

Tim liked the story. At least it was better than watching rain fall. They decided to continue reading every night. It wasn't as good as TV but better than sitting with his own thoughts, which were getting decidedly boring. Same stupid thoughts day after day. They'd each choose a book, and since Sierra and Resa liked reading aloud, Tim wouldn't have to. Worked for him!

The next morning the rain came down hard, but by early afternoon the downpour turned into drizzle and finally stopped. They decided to move on, even if they only got four or five miles down the road. He hoped the rain would hold off for a few days as they needed to get some mileage behind them. Max was bounding ahead and behind and beside them, tail wagging. He was as happy as the rest of his pack to be traveling again. Tim watched Max wander through the weeds exploring things of interest. As the afternoon waned, the sun began to show through the clouds.

"Oh man! Look at that!" Tim pointed up at a bright perfect rainbow arching across the sky.

"Oh, so beautiful!" Resa exclaimed.

Sierra stopped and gazed upwards. "That's so awesome! Nature makes amazing things. Like rainbows. And flowers. And mountains and trees and clouds and a million things. And babies." She put her hand on her stomach.

They walked slowly and watched as the rainbow gradually disappeared. Tim wished it would have stayed longer. It seemed to be such a hopeful sign.

"Resa? Nana told me God sent a rainbow to show He'd never destroy the earth with water again. He'd do it with fire next time. Do you know that? Do you think K-Pox was the fire?" Sierra looked at Resa questioningly.

"Oh Sierra, I don't know. I don't think so. I think sometimes bad things happen in the world and it's not anyone's fault and it's not the world ending either. It's just things changing, like the universe has always done. But I don't think K-Pox is a version of fire."

Tim asked, "So why would God destroy the world if He made it? Wouldn't He know that people were gonna mess it up and He'd have to destroy it again? Seems like He'd be able to either make us so we wouldn't mess things up or He wouldn't bother to have made us at all."

"He gives us the chance to make up our own minds about how we live," Sierra told him. "So if we mess it up, it's our fault."

"Yeah, but He *knows* we're going to mess it up. Right? Because He knows everything. So why does He make us so we hurt each other and mess up the world with pollution and violence and whatever. It makes no sense. If He can make us, He could have made us perfect. Right?"

"I don't know. I just know I believe God has a plan and we have to have faith and it will be ok. Resa, don't you agree?"

Resa looked out ahead of her and down the road. Then she looked over at Sierra. "To be honest, Sierra, I stopped believing in an all-powerful, all-knowing God a long time ago. There were just too many things that didn't make sense to me. But it doesn't mean I don't respect your beliefs or understand what you're saying. And I still have a lot of my own questions. Tim, the questions you have are the same ones people have been debating for centuries. I think the answers lie in what you put your faith in. And faith depends on the person who you are in your heart. I'm sorry I don't have any concrete answers. I think we're all just trying to figure things out. And this pandemic hasn't made things any easier," she smiled ruefully.

They continued to walk down the road, each wrapped in their thoughts. Just before dusk, they approached a small town and saw a small used car dealership. They slowly approached the building and when they were confident no one was there, went in and started looking for keys. They'd had so many attempts of cars not starting, mostly due to dead batteries, so they didn't hold out much hope. But you never knew. They each grabbed a bunch of keys and tried to start the cars. They thought this would end like every other time with nothing for their troubles, but Tim turned a key and got the sound of an engine slowly trying to turn over. He continued to hold the key and they heard the engine get momentum and then kick in. It was running, a little rough at first, but then more smoothly. They couldn't believe their luck! A running car! Now if it just wouldn't die. They watched the car quietly run, and let it idle for about half an hour or so to recharge the battery and to get the oil flowing again. With an almost full tank of gas, they'd be ready to go tomorrow! Tim slept very little that night. A new car and lots of mileage to cover! If it started again. But if it did, they could actually make it to West Virginia and have a car to go up and down all those mountains!

Baby Names

Aerial/Ariel	Rocky	Sunrise
Angel	Ice	Summer
Briar	Xerox	Sunset
Cassiopeia	Hike	Cheyenne
Cybele	Quest	Safari
Virginia	Trek	Jack
Fawn	Storm	Azure
Grace	Hunter	Trip(p)?
Dawn	Excalibur	Odyssey
Diantha	Griffin	Flame
Alwen	Tim	Brook
Aurora	Fisher	Achilles
Amer	Deuce	Storm or
Indigo	Ace	Stormy

Chapter 16

October - Kentucky

Yes! I'm going to make it home by Christmas! Resa thought as the sound of the tires hummed against the pavement. They had all whooped with joy this morning when the car started again. They had grabbed a portable jump starter box with cables in case they found another car with gas, but a dead battery. It was such a fragile victory but covering miles this way felt amazing. Resa pushed the gas pedal harder. She was getting more and more anxious with every stop. When they were walking it almost seemed like a natural rhythm to stop and check for supplies, rest, then go. But in the car she wanted to fly. The stops felt irritating, like tiny gnat bites.

At the last gas station they'd found new neck pillows and Sierra was dozing in the back with her feet stretched out across the seat. Max was snoozing on the floor and Tim was working on a word search in the front seat. The break from birds chirping, insects buzzing, and the slap of their feet on the road was a welcome change.

Resa finally had the mental space to think. She was going to hug her family for days. She'd been gone for almost eight months! The horrible hurts this stupid, stupid disease had created made Resa's heart pound. Maybe that's why they tried to fill the silence when they walked.

She was sure Sam was doing his best to take care of everyone. Being a parent was hard work and as a mom, she felt like she could never truly let her guard down. She had to be strong for everyone else, even when she felt like she was on fire. Just keep moving forward. Resa rubbed her temple. Family was a complicated, beautiful mess sometimes.

Resa's thoughts wandered as the road whirred under their tires and Tim snoozed quietly in the passenger seat. She and Sam had met by accident. Resa had been walking around the corner when Sam came rushing from the other direction and they collided. Resa smiled a nostalgic smile thinking about how he had been so apologetic and sweet when everything they'd been carrying had crashed to the floor. Of course, that's how things got mixed up too. She ended up with his computer bag and he had hers. Luckily she found his business card stashed in one of the pockets. She had called him the next day and he offered to buy her a coffee to make up for the trouble. They spent the afternoon talking about his job at a computer tech agency and her hopes to work as a museum researcher.

They had both been so young and full of excitement back then, Resa thought. Her parents liked Sam immediately. In fact, they almost seemed relieved. Resa knew it was because she had made a surprising arrival in her parents' lives, years after they'd given up on having children. Her dad had told her once she had been their miracle baby. They worried about her being on her own without other family to rely on. Both of her parents had grown up in coal mining towns. The lasting effects of black lung and health issues cast a dark shadow on the short lives of dwindling family members year after year. Resa was raised to work hard, fight for what was right, and be loving and kind. Her parents were genuinely happy with her successes and quick to sit down with a cup of tea when she needed to talk.

It wasn't too long after she and Sam started dating when Sam had asked her to marry him, and not too long after that she'd found out she was pregnant with Meg. Resa smiled sadly. One of the last pictures she had of her parents was right after Resa and Sam told them the good news. Yet, her parents never got to meet Meg in person. It had been a Sunday afternoon when she got a call from the police. Her parents had been driving home from a movie when their car hit loose gravel and slid off the road. The car rolled down an embankment and killed them both. In an instant, her life had turned upside down. She flailed against a world she no longer recognized.

Sam had been so supportive during those months. He'd understood when she wanted to drive because riding in the passenger seat made her feel helpless and out of control. Together they sorted through and sold the house where she had grown up.

When they were packing, they'd found a box of baby blankets in her mom's closet with a handwritten note which said, *To all the miracle babies in your future*. Resa had wept, feeling like she had lost her parents all over again.

Resa had received a small inheritance, so she'd quit her job and focused on being a mother. Deciding to stay home full-time with Meg had been one of her best decisions. It was fun being one of the 'park moms.' It had been wonderful to know all of Meg's favorite things, like the songs she sang and the special crackers she wanted after naptime.

Resa sighed. She knew her stress and focus on having more children in the years that followed was the start of issues between her and Sam. Being an only child herself, Resa had always longed for a sibling and even though she knew it wasn't her fault, she started to feel like every month was a reminder of how she was failing Meg. Then finally, when Meg was four, they got the news they were expecting again!

Resa remembered they'd gone out for giant ice cream sundaes to celebrate. It felt like this victory had wiped away all the stress of the years before. But their happiness was short lived and the precious baby boy they'd celebrated was gone before she had even met him.

The months and years after that were a blur. Sam threw himself into work and Resa felt distant and alone. Resa knew the pain of loss was a ravine separating her and Sam, and the youth and excitement of their younger days tumbled down the rocky sides into the depths below.

It came as a total shock when she found out she was pregnant with Mitchell. Her new miracle baby. Her ball of energy! He was such a different baby from Meg, but she was so grateful and for a while it seemed like bridges across the ravine could start to mend.

Resa sighed and glanced at Tim and Sierra. Problems of her old life seemed so distant now. No more fights over money or vacations after K-Pox wiped everything out. The last time she and Sam talked was a text from her saying she had arrived safely in California. Would this crisis have forced them to face their chasm of hurt? Did certain things still matter in a world flipped upside down?

A pothole in the road jarred Resa from her wandering thoughts as Tim stretched his arms overhead and he yawned awake. She checked the gas tank and saw the needle had slipped below a quarter of a tank. She had been trying to keep her eye on her speed. They'd all decided 50-55 mph would conserve gas without feeling like they were crawling along like snails.

"Looks like it's time to start looking for another place to stop so we can start walking," she said to Tim.

Signs for lookout points rolled by the side of the road. Forests of trees grew thick and buzzed with unseen life in the dark clustered branches.

Ten minutes ticked by. Then fifteen, with no signs for exits or towns. Sierra stirred in the backseat.

"Are we stopping soon?" she said groggily. "Baby Hike is sitting on my bladder. I wouldn't mind a bathroom break soon."

"We're looking for a good place to pull over because we're running low on gas. We can stop now if you need to," Resa said.

"I always need to," Sierra said.

Resa pulled over on a wide shoulder and they all got out for a minute to stretch their legs. They left the car running in case it wouldn't start again. When they were ready to get back in the car, Max froze. He stared into the thicket of trees and growled low and menacing in his throat. All three of them were surprised and turned to see what danger lay beyond their view. His hackles were raised and his gaze never left the tree line.

A few branches swayed and the shrubbery snapped and rustled. A large black dog emerged. It was followed by several more medium sized dogs in all shapes and colors of russet and golden brown. It was a startling sight. All the dogs were wagging their tails in what seemed like a friendly hello. But Max was not. He kept his head and tail lowered and started to creep slowly towards the black dog. Tim grabbed his collar and pulled him back.

"Max, the last thing we need is a fight," Resa heard Tim say.

Max barked and lunged against Tim's hold. Sierra stepped a little more behind Resa and put her hand on the car door handle.

"They're probably abandoned pets. They don't look vicious," Resa said quietly and walked towards the driver's side door.

Tim put the leash on Max. The dogs in the pack perked up at the sight of the leash and started wagging their tails even more. A few of them whimpered.

"Awww. They're probly lonely. Can they come with us? They'd be extra protection," Sierra said.

"No way," Tim and Resa said together.

"We can barely feed ourselves and Max, let alone a pack of hungry dogs. I know it's sad, but they have to stay behind," Resa said.

"And Max does not want to be friends," Tim added as he pulled on Max's leash.

"Let's get in the car and go," Resa said.

Sierra opened her door slowly, keeping her eyes on the dogs and climbed into the back seat. She shut her door softly behind her. Tim opened his door and was pulling then pushing Max into the car before he sat beside him. Max was standing on Tim's lap, growling through the window as Resa slid into the driver's side and shifted into drive.

They drove away and watched as the pack trotted onto the road. Their tails dropped. The black dog lifted his head and let out a long howl as the sight of them disappeared in the rear view mirror.

They all exchanged sad looks. Tim hugged Max and looked out the rear view window. He whispered, "Goodbye doggies. Sorry you can't come. I hope you find a good home. Take care of each other."

They sat in silence. Max had jumped into the back seat and was still standing alert as he looked out the back window.

"There's a sign for an Adventure Center," Tim said, pointing to a sign advertising mountain biking, riding ATVs, and hiking. "It says it's four miles away. Maybe they have something there."

Resa let out a big sigh. The gas light had come on several miles ago, meaning there was probably about 10 miles left in the tank. She watched the mile markers whoosh past, relaxing her white knuckled grip on the steering wheel. She hadn't noticed the dull ache creeping through her shoulders and forearms until she flexed her hands and turned onto the exit. They drove around a winding road, through a thicket of trees and pulled up to the Adventure Center building with the speedometer reading exactly one mile left in their tank. Resa left the car running.

"Looks like there's a gas tank around back," Tim said. "They probably use it to fill up the ATVs and trucks. I'll check it out."

Tim unfolded himself from the car, whistled to Max, and disappeared behind the log cabin style building. Resa stretched her arms. She didn't want to leave the car but knew it might be inevitable. Sierra said she was going to find a bathroom and Resa smiled as she noticed Sierra had started to sway from side to side, trying to offset the weight of her growing belly. Sierra stopped as she reached the front door.

"Resa?" She called back cautiously, "This door isn't locked."

"I guess that's a good thing?" Resa called back to her.

"No, I mean, it looks like this place has been trashed."

Resa walked up behind Sierra and the two of them peered into the dark interior of the large room beyond. Shelves lay bare and empty. Shredded food packages covered the floor in a hazardous-looking carpet of sticky crumbs, crawling ants, and swarming flies.

"Looks like some animals found a smorgasbord in here," Resa said.

"Too many bugs!" Sierra said, "I'm going over there to pee."

Tim returned, shaking his head sadly. "Bad news. No gas at all. We can check the ATVs but..." He trailed off and looked dejectedly at the empty parking spots where they all wished a new car would magically appear. Then with what seemed like perfect timing, their car choked and died.

"Well, let's not just give up," Resa said, more snippily than she meant. She knew she should feel sad and disappointed, but she felt more irritated and annoyed.

For the next twenty minutes, they checked every possible vehicle they could find, but none of them worked. They had nothing except their own two feet again. They unpacked the car so they'd be ready to go in the morning. They left the keys under the visor just like they did before, and Sierra said a small prayer of gratitude that the car had brought them this far. They set up camp outside as the sun slid behind the mountains.

They made a fire before dinner, but Resa didn't feel like eating much. She brushed her teeth, packed up the items from the car in her backpack, and wrapped herself in her sleeping bag. She slept fitfully, tears held back by a wall of anger bubbling just beneath the surface. Why did everything have to be so hard?

The morning broke with birds chirping cheerfully, but Resa felt dark clouds of emotion swirling around her despite the sun's rays beaming down. They had just finished breakfast and had packed up when they heard Tim yell, "Hey! Look what I found!" He walked over and proudly stood in front of Sierra and Resa, holding the handlebars of three mountain bikes.

"I pumped up the tires. It might be kinda hard to ride with our backpacks, but they have racks we could strap the packs to." He was smiling excitedly.

"Are you serious right now?" Sierra asked him with a slight growl in her voice.

Tim's smile faltered slightly as he looked back and forth from Resa to Sierra. Resa's eyebrows furrowed.

"What?" he said more defensively, "It would be faster than walking and we can figure out the backpacks. What's the problem?"

"What's the problem? What's the PROBLEM?" Sierra's voice rose, causing the cheery calls of the birds to still around them. "The problem IS I don't know how to ride a bike! Even if I did, how the HECK do you expect me to ride a bike and balance this belly AND my backpack without completely rolling down the mountain and killing myself AND Baby Rocky?? Are you crazy?! Are you literally INSANE right now??!!"

Tim's face turned bright red and he yelled, "Well, I thought it was a good idea Sierra! I'm SOOOO sorry. I thought everybody knew how to ride a bike! My parents...my parents who are DEAD by the way, taught me when I was four! Soooo sorry it's not all about YOU and how I can't remember all the details of YOUR life and how YOU don't ride a bike and how you have to pee EVERY DAMN MINUTE and slow us down!" Tim threw the bikes on the ground with a roar of frustration.

Resa stood frozen. The battle smacked her from both sides, but all she could feel was the rising churn of resentment she had been so carefully working to smash down.

Sierra gasped, "Do you think I like having to pee all the time? Do you think I ASKED to be in this condition? Do you think I wanted to be terrified out of my mind? NO!" Sierra started to cry. "And I'm sorry your parents are dead Tim! But no! My parents didn't teach me to ride a DAMN BIKE because my dad abandoned me and my mom was a DRUG ADDICT and she and her creepy abusive boyfriend left the first chance they got and probably died in a ditch somewhere jacked up on crack! It's NOT ALL ABOUT YOU, you selfish jacka...!"

"STOP IT!!! JUST STOP IT!!" Resa's voice echoed off the walls of the building, causing both Tim and Sierra to whip their heads towards her voice.

"JUST STOP!!! Do you two think you are the only ones hurting here?! I live each day not even knowing whether my family, my KIDS are dead or alive. Can either of you imagine what THAT'S like? To live in a place between constant fear and sorrow AND to be strong and comforting and keep SANE because my fear and sorrow does nothing, NOTHING to keep us going! IT'S HORRIFYING!" Resa's voice had risen to a shrill cry now, but she couldn't stop the torrent of words tumbling out of her mouth.

"But it can't be a competition of who has been hurt the most and who gets the most attention. We are all hurting! We have lost almost everything and it is stupid, STUPID to sit here and to spit venom at each other! We are in this WHOLE stupid god-forsaken horrifying mess TOGETHER! There's not a damn thing we can do except keep putting one stupid blistered stupid ridiculous stupid STUPID FOOT IN FRONT OF THE OTHER AND HOPE WE LIVE LONG ENOUGH TO FIGURE IT ALL OUT!!"

Resa was shaking and breathless now. Her last words came out cracked, pained, and bristled with a deep hurt she didn't know how to feel. Tim became very quiet and she could hear Sierra crying silently next to her. She desperately didn't want them to hurt either, but right now she couldn't find her way around her own bruised heart.

"Now!" she said, sucking in a shaky breath, "I'll tell you what I'm going to do. I'm going to SURVIVE! Like we have been doing every minute along this very long journey. I am going to keep looking out for THIS family standing in front of me and I am going to keep fighting. Because what we have is each other and that's a hell of a lot more than 90% of the damn world! AND since the bikes are not going to work out, I am going to pick up this DAMN backpack and march out on that road and we are going to keep it together and find that town Robert and James told us about so we can take care of each other and EVENTUALLY, FINALLY, MERCIFULLY make it HOME!!"

With that, Resa threw her backpack onto her shoulders, spun around on her heels, and marched away. The volcano of anger and hurt was still erupting inside of her, but she breathed easier when she heard the rattle of backpacks being lifted and sounds of footsteps following behind her.

Chapter 17

November - West Virginia

"No! No no no no! No babies! We're in the middle of nowhere!" Tim said, trying not to panic. Sierra couldn't have her baby now! What if something went wrong? How could things *not* go wrong? They should be at Outtatown by now, but they hadn't found it yet. This was horrible!

Tim looked at Resa, sitting on the side of the road with Sierra, looking calm and not freaking out. How could she not be freaked out!? He usually wanted to run when stressed, but right now he felt frozen, like he couldn't move at all.

"Tim, we're going to be alright. Just stay calm. Sierra's cramps don't mean the baby's coming right now, but she does need to rest. Maybe you and Max can find a house close by where we can stay awhile. And if it has a water supply, that'd be great." She nodded reassuringly at him. "If you go now, we'll be fine til you get back. Promise."

Tim decided he'd believe her as it was better than the alternative. He'd definitely rather look for a house than stay here feeling helpless as Sierra winced with pain.

"Ok. I'll go up the road and maybe there's a place close by.

"Good. Find us a house, and we'll be fine." Resa said quietly, "Having a few early labor pains is her body getting ready for the real thing."

Sierra sat awkwardly in the weedy ditch looking scared to death. Part of him wanted to stay and keep her company, but he knew he couldn't help her, so he turned slowly to start his search. The paved road was narrow and twisty and he was soon out of sight. He broke into a slow trot, Max loping beside him. He hoped he wouldn't have to go far. There weren't many houses on the main road and he'd have to explore down side roads for a house close by.

Back in the mountains again. Ugh! So much harder to hike. He thought November in the mountains wasn't as pretty as October had been—now it was just various shades of boring. Most of the leaves had fallen and the shrubs and grasses were a variety of dull

186

golds and browns. The weather had fortunately been clear, but it had gotten cold, especially at night.

Tim walked down every side road he came to. If he didn't find a house with water close by, he returned back. About five hours after he'd left Resa and Sierra he finally saw a small house near the bottom of a valley, set next to a swiftly running stream. Tim walked quietly down the narrow, weed-filled driveway. The house looked deserted and he hoped nobody lived there—or if they did, they wouldn't shoot him. He glanced down at Max, busily exploring the underbrush without any sign he sensed anyone. Tim felt less nervous but remained cautious.

When he got to the door, he knocked and called out, "Hey there! I'm looking for a place to stay. Anyone here?" No answer. He opened the door and went in.

The house was small and a little messy, as though someone had gone through their belongings and had chosen which things to take and left the discards. There was some food in the pantry and the beds looked relatively clean. There was also a fireplace and the stream was close enough to fetch water easily. This would be a good place! Thank goodness! He headed back to Resa and Sierra.

Just as Tim was wondering how much longer it would take to get back, Max lifted his head, wagged his tail, and ran ahead, disappearing around the curve in the road. He heard Max barking and Sierra's voice.

"Resa, Max is here! They're back!"

Tim rounded the curve and saw Sierra hugging Max who was happily wagging his tail and licking her face. Resa saw Tim and her face relaxed and she looked relieved.

"We were getting a little nervous. You ok? No trouble? Did you find a place?"

"Yeah, I'm fine. It took me ages to find a good place though. It's on Valley Dream Road. It's not very close but it's the best I could do. Anyway it has everything we need and it's on a little stream." As Tim told them about the house, Resa packed their belongings.

Sierra sighed. "Tim, how far away is it? My pains stopped but I'm so tired. I don't even want to think about walking anymore."

187

"I don't know how many miles it is. It's not that close, but it's the best I could find," he said, wishing it were closer.

"Well," Resa said, "I know we're exhausted, but let's start walking and see how far we get. If you need to stop, Sierra, we'll stop. If it takes us three days to get there, then it takes us three days. The important thing is you don't have this baby before it's time. Ok?" She looked at Sierra affectionately.

Sierra sighed. "I don't really have a choice, do I? Alright, let's go. Misty Dawn needs me to be careful."

She pushed herself up and one foot after the other, started walking. Tim thought she looked like a little round bundle of coats and scarves waddling ahead of him...not that he'd tell her.

They walked slowly for a few hours that afternoon, and another two or three hours the next day, stopping often to give Sierra long breaks. While Sierra rested, Tim and Max went between them and the house bringing food and fresh water. He'd also made the beds and generally cleaned up. Resa and Sierra reached the house, cold and tired the third day.

The first thing Resa and Sierra saw when they walked in was a fire blazing in the hearth. Resa smiled wide and gave Tim a big hug. "This is amazing! You've done a wonderful job of getting it ready! Thank you so much. It's perfect. And look at the fire! I love it!"

Sierra looked around. "Tim, this is so awesome! I can't believe we get to live here." And she burst into tears.

Tim smiled and shook his head. He could hardly wait to show them the best part of the house. The bathroom!

"So the house has a septic tank so we can use the toilet if we bring water from the stream to flush it. At least it's worked since I've been here. If it doesn't, we can always go outside. We're used to it." He showed Resa and Sierra two buckets filled with water standing beside the toilet ready for flushing.

"Indoor plumbing! You are full of surprises," Resa said.

Sierra said, "Wait to finish the tour! I'm gonna try out the toilet!" and quickly shut the door. She returned with a big grin. "I LOVE LOVE LOVE indoor plumbing! Thank you thank you thank you, Tim! You're my favorite almost big brother ever!"

188

Tim laughed at her enthusiasm. "Yeah, indoor plumbing is the best! Hey, come see your rooms."

Sierra squealed excitedly when she saw her room and immediately went to her bed. She scrambled awkwardly under the covers, turned onto her side, and lay her head on the pillow, her dark hair haloing her face.

"I'm laying right here and not moving for hours and hours. OH! This is wonderful!" She closed her eyes and gave a deep sigh. She peeked at Resa and Tim. "You still here? Good night! Close the door on your way out!"

Tim and Resa laughed and chorused back, "Good night" and quietly closed the door.

"Tim, I can't tell you how much this is going to help Sierra. Thank you. This is just great."

Tim smiled shyly. "Thanks. It was fun. I wanted to surprise you. But there's still some things I wanna show you."

Tim showed Resa the kitchen and pantry. There were some provisions, but not enough to last more than 2 weeks, if they were careful.

The next morning they awakened in their new home. They loved the fireplace and their beds and especially a real toilet! Tim hauled a lot of flushing water but didn't mind. They spent the first few days resting, getting to bed early, and rising late in the mornings. Sierra began to look and feel healthier and the cramping stopped. They all felt better than they had in ages.

As they approached the end of their first week at the house, Tim saw Resa looking in the pantry. He moved to her side and said quietly, "We're running out of food. You want me to go get more, or are we gonna move on? There aren't any stores around here. I can try hunting. We've seen deer and squirrels."

"I don't know. We can't stay here much longer. We need to find Outtatown. She's going to need medical help soon. It's got to be close by, but it's not clear on Robert and James' map. So I'm not exactly sure where they are, but we can't stay here forever."

"How about if I go see if I can find them?" he suggested. "They gotta be near here, and I wouldn't mind hiking some. I'm kinda cramped staying in here all the time."

"Yeah, that might be best. I'll stay here and you can go look." She rubbed her hand across her forehead worriedly. "My best guess, from what Sierra told me, she has another three or four weeks before she's due, so hopefully we'll have time to find them. I really hope Robert and James were right about them being friendly and they take us in." She sighed. "But we don't have a better option." She looked at Tim. "If you're up to it, when do you plan on going?"

"Probly tomorrow and get an early start."

Tim was excited to be doing something again. He was bored sitting around and filling up water pails. He organized his pack for tomorrow's departure, then decided to take a walk. He yelled back into the house, "Max and I are going for a walk!" and started up the driveway. The cold clear air felt wonderful, and he broke into an easy run, Max alongside, tail wagging.

He'd gone about 25 yards when Max stopped and growled low in his throat. Surprised, Tim stopped and looked at Max, then followed his gaze off to the right and back in the woods. Something moved and Max lowered his head and growled louder. Two men came out from the cover of the trees.

Tim cursed under his breath. He'd left his gun in the house and here were two fully armed strangers. He hoped Resa was looking out the window and would get their guns ready in case they needed them.

"Hey! We're friendly! Will your dog bite?" The man who spoke appeared to be in his mid 20's and the other looked about Tim's age.

"Yeah, he bites strangers," Tim responded. Actually Max hadn't ever bitten anyone but they didn't know that.

"OK, we'll stand back here then. Just wanted you to know we've been watching you for a few days and saw your pregnant friend. We thought she might need some help pretty soon." The older one did all the talking and the younger man watched Max warily.

"You've been spying on us? How'd you know we were here?" Tim was disconcerted to know they'd been watched. Again! Creepy!

"You're pretty close to our settlement and we saw the smoke from your fire. We wanted to make sure you were ok before we came down here. We're careful who we talk to. I'm sure you understand."

Tim nodded. "I get it." Then he had a thought. "Hey, you wouldn't happen to be from Outtatown? We met up with Robert and James awhile back, and they said you'd be a good place for us to go to since Sierra's gonna have her baby soon. So that's where we've been heading."

"You know Robert and James? Awesome! If they told you about us, they must trust you, so you're probably ok! By the way, I'm Alexander. This is Noah," with a nod of his head to the young man, "and Emma's our sharpshooter back there in the trees. You won't see her unless she wants you to. And you are?"

"I'm Tim. I'm with Resa and Sierra." Resa joined him carrying her pistol. Tim was glad to know she'd been watching, and he breathed easier now that she was standing beside him.

Max had stopped growling but was still watchful. If Tim was relaxing, he would as well. But he'd wait to see what his people would do.

"Tim? Everything ok?" Resa asked.

"They're from Outtatown!" Tim exclaimed.

The guys raised their hands in greeting and Tim heard Resa take a deep breath of relief.

"Well, that's good news," Resa said with cautious optimism.

Tim wondered what they'd do next. Tim glanced at Resa. She was studying the men, deciding if she could trust them.

"Would you like to come in?" she said with more confidence. "We don't have food to offer, but we have water and a place to sit."

They moved into the house and sat awkwardly in the living room. Resa went down the hall and Tim heard her talking with Sierra in the bedroom. Resa came back with Sierra quietly behind her. She sat close to Resa, eyeing the men suspiciously.

Resa started, "Well, I guess we should tell you a little about us."

She and Tim filled them in briefly about their journey, and then Alexander told them about their community. Outtatown was started about 15 years ago by the Owens family as a weekend getaway.

They'd wanted a self-sustainable wilderness home, with the goal of an off the grid community. Over the years they'd invited a few close friends and family members to join them so there were now seven families living on several hundred wooded acres. The majority of the families moved in full time in the late winter before the pandemic. The rest moved when K-Pox hit.

Tim was ready to pack up and go right then, but Alexander told them he and Noah had to go back first to report in. Other community members would come talk to them as accepting new members was a community decision.

Over the next several days they met Emma, the sharpshooter, and other members including Ann, the nurse/midwife, who James had told them about. They were relieved when they were told they'd passed muster and an ATV was sent to pick them up.

Tim was amazed at the settlement. The houses were fairly far apart, hidden from each other by hills and vegetation, but close enough for safety. Alexander told him all the houses were built differently, from log cabins to a geodesic dome. They used a combination of wind, hydro, and solar power. He and Sierra were very curious about what they used for toilets. They were not disappointed. Some homes still had the chemicals for compost toilets inside but for the most part there were fancy heated outhouses—with sinks and mirrors and heat. Totally awesome!

At the center of the community and closest to the Owens' home was a large pavilion used for meetings and special events with a wide fireplace at one end and picnic tables down the center. Grills were available as well as a wood heated pizza oven. Canvas walls could be raised and lowered as the weather dictated.

There were so many people in one place. Tim didn't realize how much he'd missed seeing people. It was a bit overwhelming at first having so many individuals talking at once and asking and answering questions. The first evening he was relieved when he could go to his room and unpack. As he put his stuff in the dresser, he realized he hadn't put things in drawers since he'd started this journey back in March.

Tim, Resa, and Sierra would stay at different houses as there were no guest quarters. Sierra would live with Ann until the baby was born and Resa would be with the Munroe family. Tim and Noah were the same age so Tim moved in with Noah Grant, his parents Sean and Emily, and his sister, Sarah. He knew right away they'd be ok to stay with. He and Noah got along well from the start. They were both quiet and liked being outside. Noah's younger sister was 16 and a lively, flirty girl. She liked to hang out with the guys until they headed out to hunt or fish; then she stayed comfortably close to home. She said she'd rather garden and grow vegetables but did not like hunting. She and Sierra soon found interests in common and their friendship grew. Tim and Noah could hear them giggle about seemingly anything. When the boys entered or left the room giggles increased so they'd promptly leave.

Tim and Noah enjoyed walking through the cold autumnal woods. Max almost always went along, and he snuffled at scents and bounded after any animal he spotted. If they were going hunting, they'd leave Max with Sierra. Max was not a hunting dog; he was more of a chasing and barking-at-animals dog.

They were comfortable hiking, talking very little while looking for game. Emma often walked quietly with them and was a quick and accurate shot. She and her parents had moved to Outtatown full time about a year ago. She was an independent young woman. When she turned 18, she'd helped build her small log cabin so she could have her own place.

Hearing the squirrels chirring, birds fluttering in the undergrowth, and their quiet footsteps crunching through the leaves brought Tim a peace he hadn't known in months. He began to feel safe. The new friends spent hours in the woods often talking about their changed lives. He wondered when this new life would be the regular normal life. Maybe when they were old, they'd say stuff like, "I remember back in the day I could go to the store...or watch TV...or play video games...or text...or...or..."

One afternoon, shortly after arriving, Tim, Noah, and Emma wandered through the brush, killing time. Tim was curious about how the community had found them.

"Hey, Noah, how'd you find us, and do you accept everyone who comes by? Like Robert and James. They didn't stay but they could have? Have other people come through?"

Noah and Emma exchanged glances.

"Nah, we don't take just anyone. We would've taken Robert and James if they'd wanted to, but they didn't."

Emma's eyes became harder. "Yeah, we don't take everyone. If someone tries to get in and we don't want them, we make sure they know they can't stay."

"Really? How?" Tim asked.

"Fire and manpower," Noah said.

"And woman power," Emma added.

"What do you mean? You stand around with guns?"

"Pretty much," Noah responded. "If someone gets close to us, we already know. We keep a watch out all the time. Like when we found you. We'd watched you for several days and figured you guys were ok."

"So then what?"

Emma said, "If they wander on, we let them go and they never know we're here. Which is what we want. If they find us and try to push in, we push back."

Noah jumped in, "Yeah, only there's a lot more of us. If you were surrounded by a bunch of armed people wearing ski masks and telling you to move on, you move on. At least they have so far."

"You actually had to do that?" Tim asked. "How many times?"

"Three," Emma stated. "We thought there might be a fourth, but those two guys moved on."

"Man, that's so weird. Isn't it scary to do that?" Tim asked.

"Nah. Too many of us packin'. They're the ones scared and you should see them hustle on when they see us! I gotta admit, we look pretty mean!" Noah laughed.

Emma added, "We keep an eye on them for several days to make sure they keep going. No one has turned around yet."

Tim would share this information with Resa and Sierra. They'd like feeling guarded and safe.

The day was chilly and Tim was glad he'd picked up winter clothes somewhere on their travels. He shivered.

"This is the coldest I've ever been," he commented.

"Seriously? Dude, this isn't even cold yet. Wait til January!" Noah responded.

"Yeah. January's the coldest month. But it isn't too bad. Just dress warm," Emma added. "I like it best when there's a little snow on the ground. Everything is so crystal clear. The only sound is you and whatever animals are around."

Tim asked, "Do you like hunting?"

Emma responded, "I started hunting with my dad ages ago. I always liked it. Sometimes people told me it was mean to kill animals, but I just told them hunting your meat is way kinder than raising animals on big meat farms where the animals live in little cages and get sent to slaughterhouses."

"Yeah," Noah said. "Besides, wild animals pretty much always die a violent death or of disease. So shooting them is quicker. If you shoot well."

"Did you hunt before you came out here?" Tim asked Noah.

"Nah. Emma's been teaching me. Me and her like to hunt together. Dad said he'd teach me but I see enough of him at home. I seriously don't need to spend the whole day walking through the woods with him too," he laughed. "Besides, if we stick around the house, our parents find stuff for us to do. If they don't see us, they can't find us to do other work."

Emma said, "Well, if they do need us, they just wait til we return. We don't get out of our work."

Tim wondered if he should stay here. Noah and his family said he could stay with them, but he knew Resa expected him to go to Laurel with her. He could always come back. He liked it here.

"Even if I wanted to stay, I couldn't right now," Tim had explained to Noah. "I've gotta go with Resa. I mean she can't go on her own."

He and Resa planned to stay until after the birth, but no departure date had been set. Sierra hadn't decided yet whether to stay or go, but wanted to do what was best for the baby.

"Nah, she definitely can't go by herself. I wonder if I could go with you guys," Noah wondered aloud.

"That'd be so awesome if you could come with us. Do you think you could?" Tim asked.

"I don't know. I know my parents wouldn't like me leaving. They're still freaked out about K-Pox and us getting it and dying. And not knowing who survived out there in the world. I know they wouldn't be happy if I left." Noah was silent for a while. "And I'd miss my family. I guess I'd have to think about it. You think you'll stay in Laurel?"

"I don't know. My original plan was to go Maine cause I wanted to be in the woods and snow and be on my own. I'd never lived in the cold before. But now, I don't know, man. I've been camping out since April and I'm tired of camping and being on my own. So I don't think I'm doing Maine anymore. I like being in a little town. Outtatown is pretty cool." He shrugged. "I don't know what I'm doing now. Just see what happens, I guess."

"Yeah, that's how I feel. I don't see myself staying here forever, but I can't leave yet. Maybe someday. Like you said, just see what happens."

Tim and Resa decided they'd probably leave in January. Traveling through the icy, windy winter months wouldn't be easy and walking in these mountains would be slow going. But they figured they'd be rested and well-fed when they left. And for the time being, Tim was going to enjoy the settled life they had here.

As the weeks slipped by, Tim realized he'd never been so strong or in the shape he was now. His parents would have loved seeing him filled out and with actual muscles. He considered growing a beard to go with his long hair, but when he didn't shave for a few days, Sierra made comments. "Eww! You look awful! You need to shave!" And rather than listen to her complaints, he'd shave. But he was determined to grow a beard someday. Maybe in January.

As November came to a close, Outtatown planned a big Thanksgiving. The pavilion fireplace was blazing and the side flaps were down holding in the warmth. Tables were laden with turkey, venison, potatoes, sweet potatoes, green beans, gravy, and pies. Tim, who never felt totally full, looked at the tables crammed with food and could hardly wait to dig in. Before they dished up, Dan Owens gave a short Thanksgiving prayer thanking an almighty being for the new life they'd been given here and for their friends and family who were safe and healthy.

Tim, Noah, Emma, Sierra, and Sarah piled their plates full and sat together at a picnic bench. Conversation and laughter flowed from one subject to another: old movies and TV shows, favorite video games, humorous stories from high school, favorite songs, anything they thought of. They went back for seconds and thirds. Tim hadn't felt so stuffed in ages, maybe since last Thanksgiving at his parents' dining room table. Thinking back to their last Thanksgiving made him wish they were here with him now. He missed them. He stopped listening to the chatter and stood up. "Hey, I'm gonna take a walk." He strode away with Max at this side. Emma and Noah watched him walk away.

"I bet he misses his parents," Emma commented.

"Yeah, probably. I'd be lost without mine. Even if they do drive me crazy," Noah said.

When Tim came back, Noah and Emma didn't say anything about his red eyes. If he'd cried, it wasn't their business. They went back to talking and eating and pretended nothing had happened.

Days slipped by, the weather got colder, and the traveling companions knew they'd be separated soon. They had been asked to be a part of the community, and while Tim and Resa knew they'd be leaving, Sierra finally decided to stay. It felt odd to Tim that Sierra would remain here when he and Resa left. They didn't want to leave her, but knew she was in a good place. She couldn't travel safely with a baby in winter. If she was going to go to Laurel, Resa and Tim would have to wait months or even longer before the baby could travel.

Ann liked Sierra's company, enjoyed her youthful energy and humor, and after talking with Resa, had asked Sierra if she'd like to continue living with her.

Sierra confided to Tim, "I like Ann. She's like Nana. She's nice. She doesn't make me feel like I'm in the way or anything. And when you and Resa are gone, she said she'd help with the baby. I'm really nervous about taking care of the baby and I'll need help. But I don't know what I'm gonna do without Resa. I don't even wanna think about it."

"Well, Ann's nice. I mean, she's not Resa, but you like her, so that's good," Tim said.

"Yeah, but I'll really miss Resa. And maybe I'll even miss you too. But only a little." She playfully punched Tim's arm.

"I'll miss you a little too," he smiled. "It'll be weird not having you around. But it's not til after the baby comes. We got time. We're not gone yet!"

As the December days moved closer to Christmas, Sierra's baby decided it was time to be born.

Baby Names

Mariposa	Aerie	Nova
Willow	Alpha	Phoenix
Misty	Bilbo	Violet
Destiny	Caesar	Jordan
Estrella	Mars	Legend
Jada	Orion	Zion
Laila	Cosmos	Comet
Kiri	Dash	Lynx
Serenity	Bjorn	Sage
Lune	Falcon	Rose
Ivy	Hawk	

Chapter 18

December - West Virginia

Dusk was falling as Resa watched the young people talking and laughing under the pavilion. 'Young people.' Good grief she sounded old, she thought. Resa passed by the pavilion, grinning at the loud stories floating through the air. She took a walk every night after dinner. She wasn't used to sitting still and she felt restless. Waking up in this community and not worrying about where they were going to get their next meal still felt surreal. But this was a friendly place where they had been taken care of and been shown compassion. This is what Nana wanted for her girl.

The echoes of the teens' laughter fell into the distance. Resa made her usual circle of paths and walking trails the families had carved out between houses. At first, it had been strange moving into separate houses with different families, but having the space apart from Tim and Sierra was ok. She loved watching them connect with others their age. Even though she missed the closeness of their trio, their connection could never be broken.

200

Resa's boots crunched on the snow and icy wood chips as she thought about the new friends they'd met here. This place was pretty incredible. After the scouts' visit, they were greeted by others before they were welcomed into the community.

Dan and Kathy Owens told them Outtatown started with a one room cabin. Dan's grandparents had built it as a hunting lodge. Dan and his cousin Mark spent their childhood here and when their parents passed away, the family inherited the property and surrounding land. Then Kathy's brother, John Davis, and his wife Angie moved away from the hustle and bustle of big city life. There was a strong belief that getting back to nature helped everyone remember their roots. Sometimes literally! Kathy said some of the trees were hundreds of years old. Resa could almost feel it too, the groundedness.

Thankfully, they were high enough in the mountains and far enough away from most roads that they didn't have many problems with drifters. Dan had told her most people passing by on the outskirts were satisfied with replenishing their supplies and moving along. Kathy said some people seemed kind and generous and others she wouldn't trust at the end of a ten-foot pole. About 70 percent good-ish and 30 percent looking for trouble she said, maybe the same as before the pandemic.

Resa smiled as she thought about the easy camaraderie the family showed at get-togethers. She could tell they had a long history of laughter and shared memories. Dan was quick to tell about the time Mark tried to set up a bear trap, but only managed to snap the teeth onto his pants. And Kathy and Angie were more like sisters than in-laws. Family didn't always come from being blood related.

The connection with Angie was how the town found Ms. Ann. She had been working as a head nurse and midwife at a hospital in Maryland. Ann knew Angie, who was a pediatric dentist. When John and Angie moved away, they kept in touch. Ann didn't have children of her own and had married late to a man Angie described as joy incarnate on earth. Energetic, loud, and loving, Carl had been interested in outdoor living just like Ann. They had hiked parts of the Appalachian trail on their vacations and visited Outtatown several times before he'd unexpectedly passed away. When Ann retired, she was invited to move there. Angie and Ann were a great team for dental and medical care. The community was fortunate. They truly had everything they needed.

When Sierra had been invited to stay in Ann's cozy cabin, it seemed logical that Sierra should have the supervision of a nurse during the final stage of her pregnancy. But it was a perfect spot in more ways than one. Resa watched as Sierra grew closer to this boisterous force of a woman whose vigor for life kept her walking five miles a day before the town was even awake. Sierra had mentioned more than once Nana and Ann would have been good friends.

Resa looked at the dome house as she walked past. The Garcias. Most of the time they were busy working on improvements and running around after the two little kids whose energy Resa wished she could bottle. The youngest was still in diapers and Resa often saw her helping her mom and grandma put out dried seeds for the birds. Resa couldn't imagine raising her kids in a round space like that, especially one where she couldn't make the kids sit in a corner in time out. There weren't any!

Up ahead was Emma's log cabin off to the side of her parents' place. It was good that becoming an adult and having your own place was still valued here. It seemed like Outtatown would've been a wonderful place to live even without the disease.

Resa walked past the turn off for the old mine. Kathy had told her there'd been a small coal mine there back in the 1800s, but it had collapsed and been abandoned shortly afterwards. While exploring, Mark and Dan discovered the entrance was a perfect space for storing extra supplies. They built supports inside the mine and made large, heavy doors to keep animals out. They were also experimenting with underground hydroponic planters in one of the small side tunnels. Who knew!

Beyond the mine, the Davises had a cabin in the woods, and the Grants, where Tim was staying, was further down the path. She usually didn't walk this far before sunset. She'd heard there were other families close by too, including Edward, the uncle Robert and James had mentioned. Uncle Ed had decided to stay in his own house and not come to Outtatown, but someone checked in on him often.

Resa turned back towards the center of town and walked past Mark's house. Mark lived with his 14-year-old son, Ethan, who would wander down to the pavilion when his chores were done. Since it was only the two of them, they had more to do for their garden and supply upkeep. Ann told her Mark had lost his spouse to cancer a few years ago and he and Ethan had moved up here to get away from all reminders.

The trails were designated with little signs, but you had to know where to look for the markers on the trees. It was a security thing, Angie had told her. Keeping the families together but separate just in case something dangerous happened. Resa certainly felt protected here. Just terribly restless. She kept reminding herself it was for the best. As the Munroe house came into view, she smiled at the fact that it reminded her of a Lego mansion. She was surprised when the Munroes explained it was built from tightly bound hay bales, covered in plaster and sealed against moisture, which explained the boxy shape. They said it was incredibly energy efficient and easy to upkeep. They had added on several more rooms when this became their permanent residence. Alexander, their oldest son, was one of the scouts Resa had initially met back at the little house. They'd built him a two-room house of his own on the edge of their property, but he still came over for dinner most nights. The rest of the five kids ranged from seventeen to four and were an ornery, fun-loving crew. They were homeschooled in the mornings by their mom and all had chores. Even the four-year-old fed the chickens. The older ones were helping to build another house for the seventeen-year-old. It was on a different part of the property with room to expand, just like Alexander's.

Lizzy and Charlie Munroe were extremely organized and planful in how they ran their gardens, building sites, and the family for that matter. Resa envied the time they had, watching their children grow and hearing about their days. Being around the children made Resa deeply sad some days. She wished more than anything she could wake up and see Meg and Mitchell's faces staring back at her across the breakfast table.

Resa decided she wasn't feeling calmer yet so she took a side path before she reached the Munroes' driveway. This was a cut-through to Ann's cabin and Resa thought she'd check in on Sierra before heading back. She passed a small smokehouse everyone used to smoke and dry deer meat, wild turkey sausage, and fish. Resa could barely believe Thanksgiving and now Christmas had been several weeks ago. It had been really wonderful to share the literal fruits of their labors and to be a part of a community. The celebrations were bittersweet with stories of hardship and family lost and so many unknowns. She appreciated it when Dan and Kathy said they were grateful for how Sierra's coming baby reminded them that goodness and miracles never ceased, even in the face of tragedy.

The understanding looks around Resa told her they all felt the shared trauma and the bonds of connection to what had happened in the past months. She realized she was not alone in her feelings of loss. It was the first time in a long while she actually felt whole and embraced.

The solar lights along the path to Ann's porch blinked on as Resa walked up the creaking steps to the front door. She knocked and heard the melody of Ann's voice along with footsteps.

"Well, hi there!" Ann boomed as she opened the door. "Out for your nightly romp around the settlement?"

"Sure am. Just thought I'd check on Sierra before I turn in for the night." Resa smiled at Ann's infectious good cheer.

"Come in. Come in. We just finished up the dishes so you came at the perfect time." Ann's eyes twinkled, but Resa could tell there was something else too. Sierra was making her way from the kitchen.

"Hi!" she said, skirting past the armchairs and coffee table. Resa's hips hurt looking at Sierra's heavy belly. Resa remembered those feelings of pregnancy well.

"You're looking great Sierra!" Resa said as she hugged her. Sierra's face was rosy pink, and she looked less tired now than those days when they'd spent all their days hiking.

"Ann says it might be any day now," Sierra said with a slight tremor in her voice. "I'm ready, but not ready, you know?"

"I know exactly what you mean," Resa said. "It always seems like forever to get to the end, but then you still feel unprepared."

Sierra nodded. "Yeah. Ms. Garcia dropped off their bassinet today though, so now I have a place for little Quest to sleep. Want to see?"

Resa followed Sierra down a short hallway. Ann's house had four bedrooms. Ann's was on one side, but on the opposite side there were three rooms Ann used as a medical station, an observation room, and a smaller back bedroom she'd fixed up for Sierra and the baby.

"I tried the name Trek yesterday. It sounds too choppy though. Ann says I may have to wait and then I'll know when I look into their eyes."

"Sounds like a good plan to me," Resa answered. As dusk was falling, Sierra lit an oil lamp in the corner which gave the room more light. The light bounced off Sierra's bed and the rocking chair in the corner. Resa's eyes fell on the baby quilt hung over the side of the bassinet and she smiled at the pile of folded baby clothes and cloth diapers stacked on the dresser. Everyone had been so kind, making sure Sierra had what she needed. Resa imagined the history of love and life woven into these clothes and blankets.

"Well, it's just beautiful," Resa told Sierra.

"Ann said I'd labor in the other room and then move back here so everything would be clean and ready for us to rest." Sierra's eyes showed her worry, but also a glow of a mother's excitement.

Ann cleared her throat at the door, "Sierra, did you say you were going to put on your jammies? I wanted to ask Resa something about the house the Munroes were building."

"Yes! I'll be out in a minute. More than a minute actually, it takes me forever."

"Do you want me to make you some raspberry tea?" Ann asked her.

"Yes please, that sounds really good."

Resa followed Ann back into the kitchen, fairly certain Ann did NOT want to ask her about the Munroe house.

"I think Sierra's time might be getting close," Ann murmured once they were in the clear. "I'm seeing a few signs of pre-labor. I've been talking with her about the birth process and trying to prep her for some of the pain and the uncertainty she'll face. I know she's still going to be afraid, but the worst thing to slow down labor is stress and skyrocketing anxiety."

"How can I help? Should I stay the night?" Resa asked. They had talked about her being there for the birth as Sierra's coach and cheerleader. Resa had packed an overnight bag a week ago, just in case. The rest of the women in town would also be in and out providing help and support.

"That might be best," Ann agreed. "She'll feel better knowing you are close."

"Ok," I'll run home to get my bag and tell Lizzy where I'll be." Resa's voice was a little shaky. She wanted everything to go smoothly, but worried about everything that could go wrong in childbirth. Ann must have sensed her growing concern and put her hand on Resa's arm.

"No reason to fret. Women have been having babies for thousands of years," Ann smiled and nodded her head encouragingly, "and we have the best group of loving, efficient, courageous, strong, and steady women who will be here to help her through it. None of us is in this alone."

Resa felt the truth of Ann's words. She asked her to tell Sierra she'd be back in a jiffy. Then she slipped out the door and covered the small distance to the Monroe's' house in no time. She found Lizzy sitting at the table working on lesson plans for school next week.

"Hi," Resa said, slightly out of breath, "I'm going to stay at Ann's tonight. Ann said it might be getting close." A wave of understanding crossed Lizzy's face.

"Ok. You grab your bag while I get a few things I've set aside."

Resa walked into her bedroom, grabbed her bag, and threw in her toothbrush, toothpaste, hairbrush, and pajamas. She grabbed a book too. She was reading Anne of Green Gables and thought maybe there'd be time to read when Sierra would be resting. Resa took a deep breath before walking back into the kitchen.

"Here are some sheets and blankets I kept from when I was in labor. Since those have gone well, I thought it might give Sierra some comfort and a little bit of luck," Lizzy said, handing Resa a neatly packed reusable bag.

"Thank you so much for all your kindness," Resa said, her voice quivering.

"You give us a shout on the walkie when things start to happen and all of us gals will be there. You'll need support too. We're all family here." Lizzy grabbed one of the walkie talkies and handed it to Resa. Everyone in town had a walkie-talkie and each house had a different channel assigned. This way people could call who they wanted, and no one had to listen to the squawking back and forth all day. It was their very own phone system.

"Take our extra one so you can use it and not have to worry about finding Ann's. You call us anytime. And don't worry," Lizzy said more gently, giving Resa a quick hug. "We'll be over to help when the time comes."

"Thank you. This means a lot," Resa said and headed out the door. On her way back, she radioed the Grants to update Tim.

"Is she ok? Is the baby coming? Tim asked, worry creeping into his voice.

"Everything is just fine," Resa said soothingly. "Just wanted to be there in case. I promise to keep you in the loop, and you can stop by tomorrow if you want."

"Ok. Tell Sierra I'll be thinking about her and baby Odyssey."

Resa laughed, "Odyssey? I think she called him/her Quest today."

Tim laughed, "Well, it does change every day. Tell her to take care of baby Whatsitsface."

"I will. Goodnight Tim."

"Night, Resa."

Ann and Sierra were lounging cozily in the living room, curled up by the fireplace when Resa got back. Sierra was thumbing through one of the birthing books Ann had given her.

"Oh good. Ann said you were going to stay the next few nights just in case," Sierra said, glancing at Resa's bag.

"Yep! I think I'll just hang around a bit. Don't want to miss anything!"

"Don't think you could miss me, even if your eyes were closed. I lumber around here like a baby elephant," Sierra giggled nervously.

Resa sat down and took Sierra's hand.

"We're all here to support you and cheer you on through the entire thing. You are not alone."

Sierra's eyes welled up with tears and started to spill down her cheeks as she nodded.

"The important thing is to relax, rest, and let your body do what it knows how to do. Ok? We're not going anywhere when you need us the most. We're all here for you." Resa told her. She knew Sierra's past hurts had been hard but wanted her to feel secure as this new chapter of her life unfolded.

That night Resa tossed and turned, listening to every creak and groan of the house. She had finally slipped into a restless sleep, when Ann opened the door.

"Resa," she said calmly, "it's time." Then she added, "Take a deep breath before you come out." Ann shut the door with a small click behind her.

Resa intentionally relaxed her shoulders and took a deep breath before both of her feet hit the floor. Ann was right. No stress. Things were going to be fine. Resa threw on a sweatshirt over her jogger pants, took another deep breath, and then walked out into the living room.

As the sun started to dip down into the horizon, Resa stood holding Sierra's hand as Ann gently spoke words of encouragement. The three of them had spent the day walking, resting, and distracting Sierra. The visitors had helped too. Lizzy had spread the word and visitors had shown up quietly all day, bringing small snacks, wood for the fire, and baby blankets they had used for their own babies. Tim had stopped by around lunchtime to check in and tell a few jokes to make Sierra smile. Salena Garcia had brought a handmade embroidered baby carrier she and her mother had been working on since the trio had arrived. It was so comforting that everyone was offering support.

Kathy, Angie, Lizzy, and Emily washed blankets and dishes, keeping the stove hot for water, and offering kind words and empathetic looks when they saw Sierra. They even had some of the guys bring in a bathing tub and filled it with warm water for her to rest in by the fire. Lizzy had made a warm rice compress and when that became irritating, Kathy and Angie filled pillowcases with snow from outside to put on the back of her neck.

During the evening when the pain was difficult to ignore, Sierra told Resa she couldn't do this, wouldn't do this, didn't want to be the same sort of mother hers had been. Ann whispered this was part of the process and all the women stayed close by, telling Sierra she was stronger than she knew.

Resa understood Sierra's fears. Sierra felt she'd never live up to the expectations this responsibility required. But Resa knew love was the most important thing and Sierra would have plenty of that to give. Resa kept reminding Sierra of how far they had come. After all, they'd survived a pandemic, a prairie fire, and almost got caught in a flood. She could do this!

"Ok, Sierra," Ann said, "a couple more pushes." She nodded to the other women who had gathered around Sierra to help support her back, prop her up, hold her other hand, and wipe the sweat off her forehead.

"I can't," Sierra whispered, "I'm so tired."

"Yes, you can, Love," Resa said, resting her forehead against Sierra's head. "You can do great things. Remember those pages you tore out of the books with the quotes for women? Laura Stavoe Harm said, 'We have a secret in our culture, it's not that birth is painful. It's that women are strong.' Remember?" Resa looked at Sierra's face and could see the fire gathering in Sierra's eyes.

Ann said, "Next contraction, you're going to push. Strong and steady."

Resa nodded to Sierra as Sierra's forehead started to furrow, signaling the contraction was starting again.

"And Eleanor Roosevelt, 'You gain strength, courage, and confidence by every experience in which you really stop and look fear in the face.'"

Words started to hum around them. You got this. You are strong. We are all here for you. Sierra clenched her jaw and then roared into her final push. A tiny wail broke through the layers of voices, followed by tearful cheers and relieved laughter.

Ann looked up from the tiny bundle she was holding in her hands, "You have a beautiful baby girl, Sierra."

Resa didn't realize she was crying but wept harder as Ann laid the tiny wriggling body on Sierra's chest. Blankets were draped over her legs and pillows fluffed up behind her. Resa kept one arm around Sierra and was laughing and crying with everyone in the room. They all hugged and told Sierra what a brave and amazing mother she was already.

"Even through suffering, light finds a way to shine," Ann told her, her own eyes shimmering brightly. Sierra smiled through her tears and looked up at Resa.

"I did it," she said.

"Perfection," Resa answered.

Sierra looked down into the eyes of her sleeping newborn girl and murmured, "Hello Journey Alice Jean. May all your days be beautiful."

Chapter 19

January - West Virginia

Tim drove down the driveway of Outtatown and looked in the rear-view mirror. Everyone was waving and Sierra was bawling her eyes out. Noah looked like he wanted to run after them, but his mother put a restraining hand on his arm, which he shrugged off, but stayed beside her. Further back in the woods Tim saw a flash of movement to his left and caught glimpses of Emma. He smiled as he thought of her running lightly across the ground, with bow and quiver. She reminded him of The Lord of the Rings when Aragorn, Legolas, and Gimli were running all the time. She was also strong and lean like an elf. He'd miss her. He'd miss all of them. A lot.

He wasn't sure how he felt about leaving. The community had given him friendship, stability, and a home. It was amazing how quickly he'd gotten used to having a community again. Yet here he was, heading back out into the great unknown. The great scary unknown. He wished Noah was going, but his mom was adamant he wouldn't go now. Maybe next year–if someone was going that way. How likely was it someone would go to Laurel? Not likely at all! He sighed. Oh well. He understood, but it didn't mean he had to like it. His mom would have done the same thing.

He glanced at Resa sitting beside him–eyes sparkling, a slight smile brightening her face. She'd been crying when they left and had hugged Sierra so tightly Tim thought Sierra and Journey might get squished. They'd both cried and hugged and needed a bunch of handkerchiefs. They'd all said goodbye again and again. Then Resa and Sierra hugged and cried some more. Tim thought they'd never leave but finally Resa gave the baby one last hug and kiss and jumped into the passenger seat. "Let's go. Before I start crying all over again."

Tim knew she could hardly wait to get home. Resa had checked their road map almost hourly in the last few days and had determined they could be a good way there in a day or two. The car, given to them by the Outtatown families, was tanked up with gas, and depending on how long the gas lasted and if things went well, they could be out of West Virginia today. Oh please get us out of these mountains. He really did *not* like mountains. And West Virginia had a LOT of mountains.

The road out of the Outtatown settlement was one of those long two-lane gravel roads which seemed to go up and down and sideways more than it went in any one straight direction. Tim and Resa spent the first couple of hours driving slowly through the turns and checking their map. Some roads weren't well marked, and some signs had been torn down. About an hour into their drive, they found they'd taken a wrong turn and had to go back. An hour lost! So frustrating! They initially thought they'd stay off the main roads since they now knew there were more people alive out there than they'd originally thought, and they didn't want to draw attention to themselves. But after getting lost and losing so much time and gas, they changed their minds. Mountainous roads were not good for gas mileage. They finally picked up a four-lane road and drove faster without fear of getting lost.

Tim had been driving all morning but felt he could use a break. "Resa, I'm gonna stop. I think Max is gonna need to go out too." He looked back at Max sleeping on his blanket in the back seat. Hearing his name, he pricked up his ears and his tail moved happily.

"Sounds good. I could stretch my legs." Resa said. Tim could tell she didn't really want to stop so soon, but nature did call, even when you were in a hurry.

Tim decided to stop where they were. Max felt the car slow down and stood up and panted in Tim's ear. Tim reached back and patted Max's soft head. "Crazy dog," Tim murmured. He pulled over on the gravel shoulder. As he did, he wondered why he'd pulled over. Why do that when no one was going to come along and bang into them. They'd seen no traffic in months, except for the two communities where they stopped. But it seemed weird not to pull over. He turned off the car, put on the parking brake, slipped the keys in his pocket, and after putting on coats they got out. Max bounded away to the closest road post to sniff and pee. Tim looked around. To his right the road dropped off at a steep incline and they looked straight into the tops of the trees which had their base many

212

feet below. He peered over. Dang, that's a long way down, he thought. To his left the mountain went almost straight up, with a waterfall frozen into the steep rock. The ice was beautiful but reminded them both they needed to get moving. January in the mountains was windy and freezing COLD!

They decided to eat while they were stopped and pulled their packs out of the trunk. Max was jumping and running up and down the road, happy to be out. After all the weeks of being outside, he wasn't happy being cooped up in the back seat again. Tim laughed at Max running around. He'd found a stick somewhere and brought it to Tim to throw. Tim threw the stick and Max ran up the road. Tim and Resa ran after him, laughing. They had rounded a curve, just out of sight of their car when they heard a motor in the distance. They looked at each other and Max pricked up his ears. Tim looked at Resa with alarm.

"We gotta get back to the car!" Resa exclaimed.

They turned and ran back, but the oncoming vehicle quickly came into view. They heard men yelling and the car speeding up. Tim and Resa ran faster. A shot rang out.

"What the hell!" Tim yelled angrily. As they reached the car another shot rang out, hitting the back of the car. "Grab your stuff! We gotta go down the mountain!"

He and Resa grabbed their packs, jumped over the barricade, and slid down the steep slope, as another shot hit the undergrowth beside them.

"Shit! That was close!" Tim exclaimed.

He glanced quickly at Resa, sliding and scrambling down the mountain as fast as she could, holding onto her pack. Tim's hands were getting scraped and cut as they braced themselves against rocks and trees and bushes and continued their drop to the bottom. Max was doing his best to stay with Tim, his four feet scrabbling to catch a foothold and slipping down with them. They finally landed at the bottom of the ravine and almost into a partially frozen stream, out of breath and scared. They tried not to make any noise, but Tim thought his ragged panting could be heard for miles. They looked up the slope, but rocks and trees blocked their view of the road. They couldn't see the men or their car. Not the car!

Tim and Resa stayed as still as they could. They heard footsteps coming to the edge where they'd jumped over.

"Damn! They took the keys!" they heard a voice call out.

"Hey, bring those keys up here. We need your car!" a second man's voice yelled down. "We won't shoot this time!"

Tim and Resa froze, breathing as quietly as they could. Tim held Max close.

"We know you're down there!" the first voice yelled. "Come on up here or we'll shoot!" A loud gunshot made them jump. Another shot rang out, earth flying up where the bullet hit, closer this time.

"Why'd you shoot at 'em! Now they'll never come up!" Voice Two said angrily. "You're so stupid!"

"Bring us the damn keys!" yelled First Voice. Another gunshot. The shot was high, and bark flew from a nearby tree.

They heard First Voice again. "I'm gonna get those keys!"

Tim and Resa heard someone sliding down the mountain. They looked at each other in alarm.

Tim heard Resa mutter angrily, "I can't believe this is happening!"

They grabbed their packs and ran and fell, scrambling along the edge of the stream. After what seemed like ages they stopped to catch their breath behind a large outcropping of rock. They tried to slow their ragged breathing and listened intently for the sound of footsteps. They didn't hear anything.

Tim whispered to Resa, "I don't hear anyone. But what if he's being really quiet too?"

She shook her head, looking worried. "I don't know. We'll catch our breath and then move on as quietly as we can. Maybe if we walk on the rocks by the stream, it'll be quieter than going through all these leaves. Be careful. There's a lot of ice. We don't want to fall in."

They moved to the shallow, partially frozen stream and walked on the rocks where they could and on the noisier gravel bank when necessary. Max stayed close to Tim. He was glad he didn't have to put Max on the leash. It was hard enough trying to balance on rocks

214

with his pack. He glanced down often to watch Max's ears. If someone was coming up behind, those ears would perk up.

Resa slowed down where the stream bank widened into a grassy flat space. "Let's stop and rest here," she panted. "If we don't hear anything, we probably lost them." She added bitterly, "Besides, they're not going to want to leave their new car behind."

They lowered themselves tiredly down on the bank. Now that they'd stopped moving, they felt the cold and their bruised and torn hands ached from the slide down the mountain. At least being in the valley wasn't as windy, but whatever sunshine there was, it did not get down to them at this time of day.

"We should start a fire if we don't hear them," Tim said. He looked at Resa. She looked tired and worn down. "A small one won't make much smoke." He looked around. The riverbank was wide enough to start a fire and maybe pitch camp.

Resa nodded, "Mm-hmm. We should look for dry wood while there's still light. What if we don't hear them for an hour or so, we start a fire. Max will definitely hear them if they try to sneak up on us. And we'll have our guns ready if they do." She sighed and looked around for the best place to put up their tents.

"I'll look for wood. You wanna unpack something for us to eat?" As he wandered through the brush looking for dry wood and kindling, Resa got out the fire starter kit and enough food for a small meal. Depending on how one looked at it this was either late lunch or early supper. Tim wanted both lunch and supper but figured this would be the last meal of the day. Rationing food again. Ugh!

Evening settled early in the valley and the small fire provided a tiny bit of warmth. Tim was glad they'd grabbed their packs before sliding down the slope. They wouldn't survive without them. They pitched their tents close to the fire. Their sleeping bags were designed for cold weather so while they weren't comfortable it could have been worse. Tim became drowsy as he felt the warmth of his body seep into his sleeping bag and Max snuggled up to his side. He'd gotten used to sleeping in a real bed and didn't relish the idea of camping again. But here they were. In tents. In freezing weather. They had no idea where they were or where the road was.

And their car was gone. Again. It sometimes seemed they'd never get to Laurel. Sort of like that Greek myth person, who was always pushing a boulder uphill and having it fall back down the hill and then pushing it up again. Well, they'd make it, even if they had to walk every step of the way.

Tim and Resa lost track of the next number of days. Looking for a road, they wandered up and down steep mountain slopes covered in rocks, shrubs, and tall thin trees, but found only deer trails. One afternoon, both of them exhausted after another futile attempt to find their way out of the mountain range, Resa's foot slid into a deep crack, and she twisted her ankle. She hit the ground with a loud curse. Tim turned and saw Resa holding her foot and trying not to cry. "Let me stop for a few minutes to rest my ankle," she said between gritted teeth.

They sat quietly for an hour or so then Resa said she was fine, and they could go on. Tim didn't think she was and watched her carefully.

When they started walking she acted like she didn't feel any pain and they pushed on. The next morning Tim noticed she winced when she put her boots on and her ankle was swollen and blue.

"You can't walk on that foot, can you? Tim said. "It looks really painful."

"I'll be fine," she snapped, hiding her ankle so he couldn't see it. "I'll wrap it up tight and the swelling will go down. It's not that bad. We're going to keep going and find our way out of here!"

She tried to hide the pain, but Tim knew she was hurting, and walking and climbing were difficult. He tried to help Resa walk less by having her wait while he climbed to the top of a rise and looked around. If nothing looked fruitful, he'd clamber back down, and they'd decide on another direction. This helped to some degree, but they still hiked every day and her foot kept getting worse.

One evening while sitting around the fire and finishing their scant evening meal, Resa put her hand on Tim's arm.

"I'm so sorry Tim, I can't walk tomorrow. My ankle is completely inflamed, and the pain is going up my leg now. I've been walking on it until it's numb and been pushing myself because I don't want to stop," she pulled in a ragged breath, "but I don't think I can do it another day. I'm afraid I'm going to cause more damage and how will we ever get home if I can't walk? An infection could mean death out here." Resa struggled to lift up the hem of her pants leg to show Tim her ankle. He couldn't believe how black and blue and swollen her leg was.

"Damn! Resa! Why didn't you say something earlier? We should've stopped days ago!"

"I just want to get home!!" she howled. "I couldn't make myself stop! We have to get there! I have to get home!" She began sobbing. "All this time Tim. All these months and the steps we've walked and our struggles and for what? For me to slip on a stupid rock and be stopped again. I just can't…" Tears poured down her face as she continued to cry in pain and frustration.

Tim moved over and put his arms around her shaking shoulders until her tears stopped. "Resa, we'll get there. I promise. We'll get there."

"I'm sorry Tim. I just don't know how I can go on." She wiped her nose on her sleeve. "I miss tissues," she added with a damp smile.

"Look, I'll find a place for us to stay and you stay here and keep your foot up. And then after you rest, and the swelling goes down, we'll get started again. So when I find a house it'll have a driveway to a main road. And we'll be back on track!" Tim wasn't sure he could come up with that house, but he had to do something. Without Resa limping painfully behind him, he could move faster and cover more ground. "I'll start in the morning. And you keep your foot up all day. Ok?"

Resa sniffed again. "It's the best chance we've got, I guess. Thank you." She turned slowly and crawled into her tent.

Tim left early the next morning, waving goodbye to Resa and Max. Max pulled at his leash, not understanding why he couldn't go with Tim, but they'd decided that Max would stay with Resa for protection and company. Tim left her with a supply of firewood and some of his food rations. He could travel lighter and faster without having to worry about carrying water and food for both him and Max. He thought back to the hot sweltering days of summer. Some of that heat would be welcome right now! He'd never been so cold and didn't like it.

After a few days of climbing up and down valleys and following up false leads on small gravel roads, Tim finally found a small house and barn sitting back off a long driveway. He hid in the bushes and watched to see who was there. He knew people were living there from the soft white smoke drifting up from the chimney. Tim heard a cow moo. He saw an older man come out of the house and walk to the barn, probably to do chores. Then an older lady came out and followed the man. They looked about 60 or 70 but he wasn't good at guessing ages. He wanted to go back and tell Resa right away and they could plan what to do next. But first he needed to talk to these people. And he was really hungry. He'd eaten very little lately and needed food. He waited for the couple to go back to the house.

Tim took a deep breath. He knew he needed to go talk to them, but he was a bit afraid. Would they shoot him on sight? Would they turn him away without hearing that Resa needed help. Or maybe they wouldn't even care that Resa was hurt. For all they knew, he was lying. Well, he had no choice. He had to go and knock on their door and ask. Please don't shoot first and ask questions later, he thought.

He hadn't even made it to the front steps when a man holding a rifle opened the front door. A dark-weathered face peered suspiciously at him.

"Stay where you are! Don't take another step."

Tim stopped abruptly, stood still, and raised his hands to shoulder height.

"Who are you and why are you here? We don't tolerate strangers here," the man said coldly.

"My name is Tim and my friend, Resa, she's an older lady, well not exactly old, but older than me, kinda about my Mom's age, and she's hurt her ankle and she can't move and I'm afraid she's going to freeze to death. And maybe starve. We were running away from some guys who stole our car and she twisted her ankle and now she can't walk and we don't have any place to go and I don't know what to do. And I saw your house and was hoping you'd help us. But if you can't, can you tell me where I can get help? I can't leave Resa out in the cold by herself much longer. She'll freeze and die," Tim blurted rapidly. "Could you please help us?"

A woman stepped around from behind the man. She was almost as tall as her husband, but Tim thought her eyes didn't look as mean as his. "Tell us again who you are and slow down this time. Lorenzo won't shoot you, at least not till we know more." She smiled encouragingly at Tim. "Start again."

Tim found it difficult to explain the whole story with a rifle barrel pointed at his chest, but he did his best. He was so nervous his story jumped from one place to another, the beginning of his long hike in Arizona to leaving Sierra in West Virginia back to Kansas. The lady had to prompt him several times to get back on track. She finally stopped his rambling plea for help.

"Where is your friend and how can we bring her here?"

Chapter 20

February and March - West Virginia

The sun rose slowly in the distance. Resa sat on the porch of the 'shouse' wrapped in a blanket and watched the steam rise from her mug. It was chilly in the mornings, but she knew the sun would soon bring some warmth to the day and the lambs would stretch their legs in the sunshine.

The word for the building they were staying in was funny, she thought, but it was true. A shed-house. She and Tim were grateful to have their own space even if it was attached to the barn. Amani later told Resa how Lorenzo had built the shouse so he could sleep close to the animals when they were birthing. It was one room, but they could heat up food on the wood stove and use the portable sink for water. She watched Amani step out the back door of the Harper's house and make her way across the brown winter grass. Resa appreciated Amani's company in the mornings. It distracted her from feeling unsettled and impatient. Resa had been walking and helping with chores without pain for over a week or so now. Her ankle was still sore at night, but it wasn't swelling anymore. Those first weeks of lying around or hopping on one foot had been torture.

She was thankful Tim had found this place. She couldn't imagine trying to push their way through the woods and crawling over rocks with the pain she'd been in. And not just physically... Something had finally broken down inside of her when her ankle gave out and she couldn't go on. She had sunk into a deep dark hole of self-pity, anger, and overwhelming sadness when Tim was gone. She could barely bring herself to eat and drink. She had been sad and frustrated before, but being hurt, cold, alone, and stuck really made Resa believe she wasn't ever going to make it out of that valley. The grief had surrounded her with the weight of a rockslide. Taking care of Max had been the one thing that kept her fighting against the smothering darkness.

Curled up and shivering in the tent one afternoon, Resa had heard the snapping of twigs and the sounds of footsteps get closer and closer. She waited for the sound of gunshots or unfamiliar voices. But instead, she heard Max's excited barks and Tim's soft voice.

Tim described the kind and generous couple he'd found who would take them in. Resa could barely utter a word when they packed their belongings. They tied their packs together so Tim could drag them while he helped Resa climb slowly up from the depths. When they reached the road, Resa saw the pile of rocks Tim left as a marker. Then to her surprise, Tim had pulled out Lorenzo's flare gun and shot a flare straight into the sky.

"Isn't it dangerous?" Resa had said fearfully. But soon, Lorenzo's truck appeared over the rise of the hill, and they left the valley behind.

When they arrived at the Harper farm, the wood stove had been warming their small sleeping quarters and there was food waiting on the table. The Harpers had given them space to rest, but they gradually began to visit more often and share meals together. Amani and Lorenzo were grateful for Tim's help with chores and his more flexible knees. Tim had stood a little taller when Lorenzo made comments about how strong and broad-shouldered Tim was and Lorenzo was right. Not only had he started growing out his beard, Tim finally looked comfortable and self-assured in his own skin. He'd also helped clear some fallen trees, replenished their wood supply, and had been learning how to care for the animals. There were two sets of twin lambs, a couple of goats, some chickens, and a few cattle. Max had taken it upon himself to keep the goats and sheep in line and would yip at them sternly if they ventured too far away from the house. The Harpers had lost their old farm dog this past winter, so they welcomed their new furry friend. Resa had been helping Amani set up raised garden beds and make goat's milk cheese. It felt good to work and be helpful. The days had turned into weeks, sometimes creeping, sometimes flying by like the wind.

This morning Amani brought over boxes of pictures and photo albums. She said she'd always bought albums with the intent to organize family memories, but she'd never had time.

"You never know how life will change in an instant," she told Resa, sorting through pictures of smiling faces, "I know some people thought K-Pox was the end of the world, but I still think God has the notion to guide us through. Even though I don't know what the future will hold, we still have to have dreams for the journey ahead." Amani always spoke kindly and softly about life and her unwavering belief in hope.

Amani and Lorenzo had two daughters. Evangeline lived in Florida and their other daughter, Hope, lived in California.

"Evangeline goes by Angie at work," Amani said, rolling her eyes, but still smiling, "Not sure why she wanted to shorten her beautiful name, but I guess kids have to make their own choices eventually."

Resa smiled, noting Amani always talked about her girls in present tense. It was hard for Resa to think about what she might find when she actually got home. But resting here, she finally faced the demons she hadn't been willing to face before. Maybe, just maybe, she could walk through her fears and let courage lead her. She told Amani about how she was afraid of what her family might have experienced since she had lost contact.

"What if I get home and the house is completely overgrown with weeds? What if there's a skull sign on the door? What if...what if the house is empty and I never find out what happened to them?" Resa didn't stop the tears from sliding down her cheeks. It seemed that before they had been stopped by her injury, she had just been pushing ahead. Not thinking, just shoving the grief aside so she could keep moving forward. But she was so tired now. Tired of being strong. Tired of feeling weak. Tired of constantly getting delayed. Tired of fighting. And tired of wondering and waiting to find out what was happening with her family. Even though the time to leave was close, she was so very tired of putting one foot in front of the other.

"You know, one summer we took a trip to the Hoover Dam," Amani said, leaning back in the rocking chair and refilling her mug from the kettle resting between them on the small table.

"Lorenzo had just lost his job and we were NOT doing well. We were broke and weren't able to keep the apartment we were staying in. Lorenzo couldn't find any work and had slid into a mood where he barely said anything, and some days didn't even get out of bed. I know now he had a touch of depression, but we didn't talk about those things back then. We just thought people should be able to power through no matter what. So I was spending lots of time with my other mom friends, complaining about how our husbands weren't worth the paper our marriage licenses were signed on.

Lorenzo had a cousin who was an engineer and worked on the dam. He was the one who invited us out to stay for a few weeks. To be honest, the last thing I wanted to do was ride in a car with one small child, pregnant with our second, and a husband I didn't even want to look at." Amani gave Resa a side look and Resa nodded.

"We drove for days. No AC in our car back then, mind you. Across a hot desert. It was so hot and sticky! And I can't even tell you the frustration and turmoil spinning inside me as the tires were spinning on the road. I wanted to scream. I wanted to run. I wanted to break out of my skin just to escape the place I felt I was trapped in. Then suddenly, there it was." Amani's gaze looked off into the distance.

"We came around a bend in the road and the dam stretched across what seemed like the whole horizon. Evangeline had been whining as I tried to balance her on my lap, but all of a sudden, it was quiet. We were all mesmerized. And I was...terrified." Resa furrowed her brows and gave her a curious look. That's not the twist she was expecting in the story.

"Oh, yes, ma'am I was! Scared clear through to my knickers! We drove across that bridge and there was a river on one side and a drop off on the other. I couldn't imagine how this wall of cement, just plain ol' regular cement, was holding back what appeared to be a flood of water that could potentially wipe out everything in its path for miles around. It was like facing a giant of destruction and we were the tiny speck in its path."

Resa knew Amani may have been talking about the dam, but the feelings stretched deep inside her heart. K-Pox and the ripple effects had been the giants of destruction for the past year, but her own personal terror clawed at her too.

"When we finally arrived and parked, Lorenzo's cousin was waiting to take us on a tour. We went down INTO the dam to see the energy turbines and how everything worked to keep the overwhelming pressure of Lake Meade under constant control." Amani shook her head slightly, like she still didn't quite believe it. "Did you know they started building the dam during the Great Depression? They employed a bunch of people needing jobs. The Colorado River frequently flooded then and destroyed everything around it. And now the dam, the very thing that terrified me, was the one thing protecting everything around it and giving back life to the people living there." Amani shot Resa another look. "Sometimes in the depths of what we find to be the most terrifying, when we face what scares us the most, we realize there is always a way to look at our surroundings in a completely different way. Nature is a powerful force, but we are a part of that power too. When we realize we are still part of a greater connection of life and the energy of all things, we can see we are never truly alone and that fortifies us in our struggles. Even the most challenging situations can be met with endurance and healing. It was after the tour when I realized that Lorenzo and I had to have some hard conversations to straighten things out."

"There was nowhere for us to run in the desert you know," Amani chuckled. Away from all the distractions, they'd finally had the opportunity to say out loud how scared they'd been of their marriage, their family, their LIFE falling apart. They talked about their fears, but also ways they could be brave. They decided to make things work with what little they had left.

As Amani talked, Resa realized that what she'd really been afraid of, beyond losing her family, was that so many things had changed, and she wouldn't be able to get her old life back. But she also realized she had changed too. Nothing stayed the same and it wasn't necessarily a bad thing, just a different thing.

Resa knew Amani was a woman of faith, but her faith emphasized the relationship of all life and people. Amani had told her the connections of beauty and value in everything was more important than holding on so tightly to rules or expectations we make up as human beings. Better to be open to all the ways we can love and grow. Resa liked this gentle embracing of life and generosity of spirit and Amani's words settled in her bones like a calming salve on her restlessness and fears.

"You never know what opportunities you might have now, even though this world has flipped on its head. We ended up on this farm because we were open to doing something hard and growing from it."

Resa felt her spirit re igniting and for the first time in a while, she knew no matter what she had left of her family when she got there, she would face it with courage and embrace it with hope. If human beings could create a dam to withstand the pressure of a river, she could figure out how to face overwhelming possibilities. Look what they had overcome so far!

As they grouped and pasted pictures of family vacations, birthday parties, and family picnics, Resa talked about Sam, Meg, and Mitchell, and Tim, Sierra and Journey. She was relieved to be almost done with her travels, but also sad about walking farther away from the family she had left behind.

"It would have been hard to travel with a newborn baby, and Sierra being so young herself," Amani said.

"Yes, absolutely. We'd all agreed we wanted Journey to be safe. Sierra had formed a strong bond with Ann too. Sierra has been through so much loss and such incredible pain in her young life. The

225

need for stability and security is really deep in the core of who she is as a person. I think it only increased as she became a mother. Having someone truly care about you and someone to care for changes things," Resa replied.

Resa remembered feeling that way when Meg was born and then Mitchell...a deep, internal need to protect them from any harm. She would have roared back in a grizzly bear's face if it kept her kids safe.

"It was especially hard for Sierra to choose to stay. It was hard for all of us, but we sat down and talked about it and what would be best for everyone. I knew I'd be traveling on. I actually thought Tim might like to stay. He'd connected with the other young adults and, honestly, there might have been more of a future for him there than on the road with me. But I was relieved when he decided to keep going. I would have died without him."

"That boy isn't leaving your side," Amani said. "We could see the determination on his face when he showed up on our doorstep."

Resa smiled, looking down at what must have been a picture of a 13th birthday party of one of the girls. "It's been amazing to watch him grow through all the chaos and challenges we've faced. When we first met, he seemed like a lost little boy that needed someone to tell him where to go and what to do. And after losing his whole family, of course that was true. But now," Resa paused to reflect, "what an honor it is to see him shift into a mature, self-confident young man. If he hadn't taken the initiative and had the courage to go off on his own, to find help so many times, who knows what would have happened to us. His family would be very proud of the man he has become."

"Life is such a mix of struggle and delight. It's quite the experience to witness how people walk through it," Amani said. She held up a picture of their family standing in front of Jelly Fella jellybean factory. "I still hope and believe, no matter how much K-Pox has taken away, there's still a fantastic mix of all kinds of people out there who are rebuilding. Even though we'd like them all to be sweet, you're gonna get a few who will take you by surprise, and a few more who make you want to throw up. You just have to have the patience and openness to see how things will mix together and grow into something new from all this."

That evening, Tim sat down with Resa in their shouse to make final plans for their departure.

"Lorenzo said he'd take us to a truck stop about an hour away from the house and close to the Pennsylvania border. He's traveled that way a couple times looking for supplies and it's been safe. He said he can't take us further since he has to save enough gas to get back," Tim said.

"They've done a lot for us already. After what we've been through, all the miles we've crossed, the people we've met, the hard choices we've had to make in difficult situations…it's incredible how kind and compassionate people can be even in the midst of awful circumstances." Resa smiled at Tim.

They took the next few days to carefully map out their route then pack their bags. Resa couldn't believe how short the line was on the map between here and home. Finally, she thought. Finally.

Morning at the Harpers dawned clear and crisp, with the edges of frost still clinging to grass. Resa had drawn Amani a map with Outtatown and Laurel marked clearly.

"Just in case you ever decide you want to rejoin a community. Hopefully, I'll be able to get word back to you somehow when we get home. And if you head to Outtatown, please tell Sierra we love her and give Journey a big hug from us."

"Of course we will. We could pop by for a vacation," Amani said, smiling. Resa knew they were hesitant to leave their home in case their girls tried to find them, but she hoped their paths would cross again one day.

On the drive, Tim chatted with Lorenzo about the sheep and what would happen with them in the next couple of months. Amani had let him sit in front with Max while she and Resa sat behind. Amani left Resa alone with her thoughts.

"Make sure Toby behaves himself with those new fence posts we replaced," Tim was saying. Toby was the Harpers' bull. "I saw him looking at the fence like it was a challenge the other day." Lorenzo and Tim laughed.

"Sometimes it's hard to change nature when it wants to run its own way," Lorenzo said.

Before Resa knew it, they were pulling up to the deserted truck stop. Long grasses had grown through cracks in the pavement, and the light poles and gas pumps sat dusty and unused. Lorenzo pulled out his rifle from behind the seat as he got out of the truck. Even though the station looked deserted, one could never be sure. Tim and Lorenzo walked around the perimeter of the building until they were satisfied they were alone. Lorenzo and Amani said they might search for supplies on their way home and look for a stray dog that needed a home. They would miss Max.

Resa gave Amani a long hug, thanking them for everything they had provided and all the support they'd given. Lorenzo gave Tim a firm handshake and wished them well. Amani put her hands on Tim and Resa's shoulders.

"May God guide you safely and lead you towards peace. May you be rescued from hands who seek to cause you harm and may you always remember you never walk alone."

After one more hug and thank you, Resa, Max, and Tim turned north. Their boots crunched on the gravel as they started down the side road, and once again, headed towards home.

Chapter 21

April - Pennsylvania

Tim couldn't believe it. Pennsylvania! Finally! It only took a couple of days to hit the border and now they were within 300 to 400 miles of getting to Laurel. They figured if they walked an average of 15 miles per day and Laurel was approximately 300 miles from where they were (though it was probably more than 300 miles and there were still these mountains to get through, ugh!) it would take about 20 days. Twenty days. Tim sighed. This journey never seemed to end. How could they be in the correct state and still have 20 days to go? It didn't seem fair. When they saw the Welcome to PA highway sign Resa gave a loud yahoo and danced up the road, a big smile lighting up her face. Tim had never seen Resa this happy. They both laughed and ran as far as they could, Max bounding along beside them, packs banging against their backs, before they ran out of energy and slowed down to a more sustainable, but still quick pace.

"I can't believe we're finally here! Finally in Pennsylvania! And we'll get there soon!" Resa said, still smiling.

Tim watched her out of the corner of his eye. He liked seeing her this happy, but he wondered what she'd do if her family weren't alive. Or they couldn't find them. It did seem family members who didn't get K-Pox seemed to be immune so maybe her family didn't get it. He knew he probably wasn't immune. His whole family had died. He felt that sick deep grief he always felt when he thought of his family. There were days he missed his mom and dad so much he could hardly stand it. And his grandpa. He missed watching football with his dad and grandpa. Dad had been in a fantasy football league, and it made all the games interesting to watch. Their favorite team was the Cardinals but watching other games was fun when their fantasy players were playing. Occasionally Mom would sit with them and cheer on the Cards, but she didn't really get into the fantasy games. "Too many players to remember," she'd said. They'd eaten snacks and watched games and cheered and it had been wonderful. What he'd give to have those days back again.

He fell behind and watched Resa as she bounced up the road ahead of him. She was so happy now that she was close to Laurel. And the closer they got, the more aware he was of how far away he was from his home. It was hard knowing that he'd never go back. Never. And what if, when they got to Laurel, Resa's family was alive and decided they wouldn't want him. What if they were allergic to dogs and wouldn't want Max. He wouldn't desert Max. Even though they'd had their arguments these last months, Resa had been a sort of mom for him on their journey. What if, when they got there, she was so caught up with her real kids, she wouldn't want him hanging around. He didn't want to go to Maine anymore, but what if she was expecting him to leave, so she could spend time with her real family without him. It made him want to cry...thinking of being by himself and on the road again. He could go back to Outtatown, but he really hated traveling now and didn't want to turn around and walk back. Walking, walking and more walking. It never seemed to end. And now their destination was so close, and they were finally in the actual state, would he have to go on? He hadn't talked about Maine in months and months, so maybe Resa had forgotten about it. He hoped she had. How would he respond if she asked when he'd be leaving? Could he say he wasn't going, and he wanted to stay in Laurel? Maybe her family wouldn't be there, and she'd want him to stick around. He hoped her family would be there. But maybe they'd gone to look for her or they'd moved somewhere else for safety. How would he and Resa find them? Anyway, he wanted to meet her family. They sounded nice. She'd been honest about how she and her husband, Sam, had been having troubles before she went out to

California, but she still loved him. She'd talked about Meg and Mitchell pretty much every day all across the United States. He felt he already knew them. He wanted to know them in person.

He shook his head and picked up his pace to catch up with Resa. Whenever they got to Laurel, whether her family was there or not, whether he stayed or left, he'd find out eventually. Right now, they had to deal with the here and now. They were coming to an exit off the 4-lane and had decided this would be a good place to get off and take the smaller roads headed in their direction. It was starting to drizzle, and the dark gray sky threatened more rain.

"Here's our exit and we need to find shelter. Looks like it's gonna rain harder."

Resa looked up at the sky, blinking as rain got in her eyes. "Maybe it won't last too long."

"Still, it's better if our clothes and packs aren't damp when we start walking again. Walking with wet clothes is so uncomfortable! There's gotta be some place close by to get out of the rain."

"Yeah. You're right, of course. Let's see what's dry around here."

This was not one of those exits where there were a multitude of fast-food places and gas stations crowded together as you left the freeway. This was one where signs proclaimed food was several miles away. Tim was glad they weren't looking for a fast-food place miles away. They just needed shelter close to the highway. They saw an abandoned house and approached it. Max's tail was wagging when they approached the front door so Tim and Resa felt secure. He was friendly enough when he saw his people relaxing, like he did eventually with the Outtatown people. When he was a puppy he loved everyone. Now he was slow to warm up to strangers and didn't like new people getting too close.

Max noisily padded through all the rooms, nose to the floor, his nails clicking on the wood floors as he checked things out. It apparently was safe as Max lay down and started licking his paws.

Tim and Resa smiled at Max. "I guess this place is ok. Max approved," Tim said.

Most of the food was gone, but there was some powdered milk, canned sardines in mustard sauce, Shredded Wheat, prunes, an assortment of spices, and pickled pigs' feet.

"Well, we have interesting things to eat, but it's better than nothing," Resa said with cautious amusement.

Tim wondered if Resa's family would be eating lots of mustard sardines and pickled pigs' feet or if they'd have normal food.

They spent a restless night listening to the pouring rain and imagining the roads and creeks flooding. They had hoped to be on the road the next day, but the rain continued to bucket down in such torrents they knew they'd be in for a while. They spent their time napping and browsing through the few books which lay about the house. Whoever had lived here before had liked romance and nonfiction books about conspiracy theories. Tim looked at the strange titles of the books and picked up one that looked really farfetched, about aliens being in the White House and Congress. As he read, he called out to Resa, "Hey, listen to this!" and they both laughed at the craziness of the author. "How could anyone believe this?" Tim questioned. They continued laughing and reading until it was too dark to read.

The rain continued throughout the second day and night. Tim didn't think they'd be able to get back on the road the next morning, and his thoughts were confirmed when he woke up and heard the rain still beating on the roof. Day three and still stuck here. He walked into the kitchen and saw Resa standing at the window looking out at the rain. She turned towards him as he walked into the room.

"How about Shredded Wheat with warm powdered milk for breakfast again. And syrup for sweetener. Yum!"

He could tell she was trying to make the best of the disappointing situation. She got out the small cook stove and heated up the milk. At least staying in a house made it more convenient to make hot food.

Tim hadn't eaten Shredded Wheat growing up and this house was his first experience with it. He decided it wasn't his favorite, but it was better than nothing. And the warm milk and syrup made it ok.

When he finished, he put the bowl on the floor and watched Max lap up the flavored milk. At least one of them was perfectly happy with breakfast. Tim wiped milk off his beard. He was trying to decide if he liked it. It kept his face warm and looked cool, but he had to keep food out of it. He didn't want to decide now so figured he'd keep it til they got to Laurel and decide then if he'd shave again. And he might even consider a haircut now that his hair was below his shoulders.

That day and those following continued with rain pouring down in buckets and if it did stop for a few hours, it started up again just about the time they were ready to throw on their backpacks and hit the road. They watched the small rivulets run down the driveway and across the yard, mingle together and turn into larger streams. They could only imagine what the rivers would be like. Everything would be flooded and make for messy traveling. Hopefully the sun would come out soon. When it did, he thought they might have to stay where they were to let the water recede before starting out again. When Tim mentioned this to Resa, she disagreed. If they get sun, they will start.

"Even if we only walk two miles it's two miles closer to home. We're so close! If we could walk in the rain, we'd be out there right now. But I know it's not safe." Resa sighed. "I wonder if it's raining back home. Maybe they're playing board games like we did on rainy days when the kids were little." She looked out the window as if seeing them through the raindrops. "I wish I was there."

"What do you think you'll do first, after you say hello and get all the hugs out of the way?" Tim asked.

Resa smiled, "Don't forget all the kisses too! I don't care how old they are. After…," she trailed off. "I don't even know. Maybe I won't even get past the hugs. I don't think I'll ever be able to let them go. I'll want them next to me every minute. Not that they'd like it, but I may never want them out of my sight again." She closed her eyes. "What would we do *after* that? I don't know. I hope they've been able to find food. Maybe they have a garden and a system for saving food through the winter like Outtatown, and maybe they have some animals so we don't have to keep scavenging. I would love to stay in ONE place forever after this."

Tim nodded. "That'd be great, not leaving! I wonder if they're going to be like Outtatown. Like, maybe there'll be more people and they'll have a little community just like them. That'd be cool."

He and Resa talked about Laurel and what type of farming and animals could be raised there. Since it had been a small town it'd be different from the wilderness of Outtatown. Tim listened for Resa to mention his participation in this new home that she hoped would be there. She did talk about him being a part of it, but what if she was just being nice and she was waiting for him to bring up Maine.

Finally he couldn't stand it anymore. He had to ask. He had to know what he'd be doing and where he'd be going. "When we get there, to Laurel, like, do you want me to stay, or should I go on to Maine or back to Outtatown? I don't wanna be in your way. I mean, you'll have your family and everything. You won't need me around. I'm not your kid or anything."

Resa looked at Tim with disbelief. "Oh Tim! I'd never want you to leave and certainly not by yourself! Absolutely not! I mean, just look at all the things we've endured! I'd worry about you the whole time! No. Of course, if you wanted to go back to Outtatown, that'd be up to you." Her face softened. "You ARE family to me now. You and Sierra. Of course, if you still want to go, I would hope you'd let me help you plan your trip very, very carefully. But I'd hate to lose you after all this time and everything we've been through. Losing one more person would just be too much." She got up and put her arms around him in a big hug. "I know I'm not your mother, and I can't replace her, but I feel like you are one of my children. You are family. Don't ever think I don't need or want you around. Ever!"

Tim put his arms around her and held her tight. "Thank you. I wanna stay with you too. Besides, Max would miss you."

Max heard his name, padded across the room and bumped his cool nose into Tim's hand to demand attention. Tim and Resa both laughed at Max, and Resa patted Tim's cheek gently as she released him. Tim took a deep breath of relief and moved to the window to look out at the road. He was going to Laurel and hopefully everything there would be ok, and he and Max could both stay. A great big extended family with at least one dog. Sounded great to him.

The rain finally stopped on the fourth day. The sun peeked above the horizon through cloudless skies. The temperature was mild. Cool enough for a brisk walk but warm enough not to need extra layers of clothing. They excitedly pulled on their packs and ventured onto the soggy wet driveway. Trees were still dripping rain, and the air smelt damp and fresh. Leaves were pushing out on all the vegetation, and the grass was starting to grow. It was spring! After five minutes of bounding through the yard and up and down the road, Max was soaking wet from his floppy ears to his dirty paws. He was having a wonderful time!

They hiked happily for two days through sunshine and drying land. They saw rivers in flood stage and were glad the bridges they crossed weren't flooded. They planned on keeping to whatever highway led them to Laurel with the fewest miles possible. They wouldn't be in the mountains much longer, just another day or two and they'd be in the foothills, which Tim was very pleased about. They were making good time, walking quickly and stopping only when they needed a break.

They were climbing what Tim had hoped would be one of the last steep slopes of this mountain range, when they walked around a corner and froze. Part of the mountain had broken off and a landslide covered the road ahead with rocks, dirt, brush, and fallen trees. The destruction went all the way down the mountain. As they stood motionless in shock, a small boulder rolled loose from above and crashed its way down the already piled up barricade.

"NO! No no no no no! I don't believe this! I DON'T believe this! NO!" Resa yelled loudly at the blocked road. "We are just days away from home and there's a FREAKIN landslide! What the HELL IS HAPPENING?!" Resa's voice kept reaching a higher and higher pitch. "This can't be right! What in the name of BLUE BLAZES are we supposed to do now?!" She looked at Tim wildly and as she began to speak again, another boulder bounced noisily down so close to them, they both backed up in alarm.

Tim said, "We need to move back! This landslide isn't finished yet." He hoped Resa wasn't going to insist on clambering over the rocks. It was not safe. Max had run ahead and started climbing up the pile of debris.

"Max! Come!" Tim yelled. He didn't want to lose his dog this close to home. Max turned and looked at him. "Come!" he ordered. Max reluctantly turned from this new wonderful smelling experience and trotted back to Tim. "Good boy!"

Tim absently patted Max's head while shifting his glance between Resa's angry face and the rock covered road. He decided to be quiet while Resa silently fumed at this latest obstacle.

She took a deep breath, ran her hand across her eyebrow like she always did when stressed, and slowly exhaled. "I guess we have to go back and find another road. I don't want to but I don't want to die either." She turned and walked quickly back down the mountain.

Tim followed quietly behind. When they got to the next turn off, he'd get out their map and they'd discuss which route to take, but there was no sense in talking right now. Let her cool down first.

It wasn't long before they reached an exit and chose another route. It would take a day or two longer, but it would get them there. Resa said, "As long as the creeks aren't going to take out all the bridges between here and there, we should be good. Fingers crossed."

Fortunately, the road they chose was still in good condition. At first every time they turned a corner they'd scan the road ahead to see if something was blocking their way—water, rocks, whatever... Eventually they relaxed. The rivers receded, the spring temperatures provided good hiking conditions, and it didn't rain all the time. They kept walking on the days when it sprinkled lightly and at night they lit a campfire to dry out their clothes.

They talked sporadically now. When they did it was about the next day's travel plans, or Resa would talk about her family, or their conversations would drift to the people they'd met along the way, especially Sierra. They missed her company, her goofy laugh and how she teased Tim all the time. She had annoyed him at first, but soon he had liked having her around and they'd become best friends. It had been nice having someone his own age to talk to.

And soon they'd know if there would be more people to talk to. He hoped her family liked him. He'd find out soon enough.

The days went slowly by and finally they were close enough to see Laurel on the road mileage signs. Resa saw the first sign.

"Look!" she pointed to the green highway sign. "Laurel is only 36 miles away! Just two days away! Just two days!" She and Tim picked up their pace.

Chapter 22

June - Pennsylvania

Resa couldn't believe it. NINE MILES! She had awakened from a restless sleep at dawn and made what she hoped was her last instant coffee on the road. Her body was incredibly exhausted, but her mind could barely shut off. Nine miles. That was all there was left. Nine!

They had pushed and pushed to get here and last night they finally had to surrender to the long day and their aching bodies. Resa's ankle had started to swell again from overexertion and even when she gave in to Tim's plea to stop, her mind had struggled to shut off. They had stopped to rest by an abandoned gas station which is how Resa knew exactly where they were. She used to stop here on her way out of town. She'd fill up the gas tank, grab a coffee, or if she had the kids, she'd buy them a snack so they wouldn't fuss while she ran errands. This is the place where she and Sam had bought ridiculously large slushies to celebrate their first house. Her heart beat faster at the thought of those memories.

She packed quickly and she walked anxiously back and forth in the early morning air with Max sniffing around her feet. The weather had warmed up quite a bit during the day, but mornings were somewhat less humid and sticky than the afternoons.

She heard Tim stir behind her. It was one of the few times she had woken up before him. She tried to stay quiet, but she knew her energy was buzzing and humming all around her, shattering the peace of the rising sun.

"Is it morning already?" Tim asked, blinking and stretching as he sat up.

"Just barely. Sorry I woke you. Well, sorry, not sorry. I'm feeling eager to get going."

Tim nodded and blinked hard, his face showing recognition of where they were. "Today's the day," he said, looking at her with a determined set of his mouth.

"Today is the day," Resa answered as she stopped pacing and returned his resolute stare. She watched as he got up, grabbed a bite to eat, and quickly packed.

"Ready," he said. Resa closed her eyes to take a deep breath and fell in step with Tim as they left the gas station behind.

As they drew closer to town, Resa felt her shoulders tense and tighten, yet it was good to see familiar landmarks. There were farms in the distance, and she saw a wind turbine slowly revolving in the lazy wind. They passed by small groups of houses on the outskirts of town where some were pockmarked with the awful skull and crossbones signs. Resa saw roads where friends had lived and she listened for any sounds of life in the distance, but there was no noise except for birds and the scuttling of animals in the undergrowth. Branches and leaves littered the sidewalks and grass sprouted up between cracks in the road. It seemed abandoned in some ways, but not dead. Nature seemed to keep going along its own way. Resa held on to that feeling of possibility.

Welcome to LAUREL
Voted Most Friendly Small Town 2018

Here it was, Resa thought. The official town sign. Her feet slowed and faltered to an uncertain stop before the wooden landmark which was still anchored in the ground next to the road. The carved sign sloped and curved around the letters marking this place. They had made it, but...

"Tim."

Tim turned to look at Resa, his forehead creasing. "You ok?"

"What if...What..." The hope that she held onto only a moment ago slipped away like vapor. Resa could barely bring herself to speak. Her hands shook and she felt heat rising into her cheeks.

"What if only my memories are left? What if..."

"No," Tim said firmly and planted his hands on Resa's shoulders and looked her in the eyes. "We've made it all this way so you can hug your family and I can meet them. And we're doing it today."

"Yes," Resa whispered, "Today is the day we find them." She said more firmly, "Today is the day."

Tim nodded and Resa straightened her shoulders. She was amazed at how confidently he stared back at her. No longer an awkward teen, but a great support and genuine friend. She looked down at Max waiting for them.

"You ready, Max? Let's go!" Max wagged his tail in response.

As they walked through town Resa pointed out the highlights. Her stomach was tied up in knots. At least giving Tim a tour of their favorite spots was distracting her from throwing up or passing out, which is exactly what she felt like doing.

There was Albee's Diner where they'd had the best hot chocolate and key lime pie. And Sav-More Foods where Ol' Ms. Fox always had something impolite to say about your purchases. There was the dentist's office and the small boutiques. She wondered what happened to all the people who used to make up the story of this town. She pointed into the distance.

"The bigger, more expensive houses are on the other side of town. It's really not too far away, but sometimes it seemed like a world apart."

Resa stopped briefly as she faced the playground at the beginning of another neighborhood. She pointed to the swings swaying next to each other in the light breeze.

"I used to bring the kids here to play in the mornings. When Mitchell was four, all he would do was wake up and beg to swing. So we'd load up his wagon at 6:30 every morning and walk down here. Most days we were the only ones here until the rest of the sleep-deprived parents started showing up around eight. In the summer, Meg loved to join us. She liked to watch the way the sun shimmered off the dust as we walked, and she tried to catch the sparkles in her hands. She still did it when she was older and thought

240

I wasn't watching." Resa's feet picked up speed as she led Tim through the neighborhood. They walked to the right around a bend, then a left, and another right.

"I live on the next street," Resa said, her voice cracking. Her knees were shaking and her heart was pounding. Resa felt fear swelling in her chest like a dam about to break, but she squared her shoulders. She could do this. She HAD to do this. They walked down the block and finally stood in front of a blue, two-story house with gray shutters. The gutter had fallen and dangled like a broken arm over the front windows. The lawn was overgrown and the blinds hung in awkward angles in the downstairs windows. Resa and Tim didn't say a word, but Resa knew Tim was thinking it too. It looked abandoned.

"There isn't a K-Pox sign in the window," Resa said looking at Tim hopefully. Max sniffed around what was left of the flower gardens next to the front step. Resa flashed back to moments when her family would pick out annuals and share lemonade once everything was planted. She shook her head and walked up to the front door. Her feet stumbled over the step.

"Sam? Meg? Mitchell? It's Mom. Are you there?" Her voice grew louder with every word. "Sam? Kids?" She twisted the handle, but the door was locked. Resa and Tim peered in the windows and continued to knock and call out. No answer.

The pounding of Resa's blood in her ears threatened to block out her hearing.

"Let's try the back," Tim suggested, nudging her elbow.

Max ran ahead of them as they walked around the side of the garage to the back door only to find it locked too.

"Oh! The key!" Resa ran to the garage side door that opened easily. Max sneezed as he sniffed dusty boxes and cobwebbed sports equipment. She grabbed her flashlight from the side of her backpack and shone the light over rows of jars sitting on the shelf. They were filled with nails, screws, nuts, bolts, and washers. Resa soon spied what she was looking for in the back row. She picked up a jar filled with different sized keys and poured it out onto the workbench.

"How do you know which key it is?" Tim asked.

"Because it's the same blue as the house," Resa said, smiling. "Sam always left one out here because the day after we moved in, we got locked out and we had to break a window. Aha!" she exclaimed, picking up a key the same dusty blue as the house.

Tim and Max followed Resa and watched as the key slid easily into the lock. There was a satisfying thunk when it opened, and the door peeled back from the weatherstripping. They stepped inside and the dim light revealed a view that made Resa's heart sink. The kitchen cupboards gaped open, a dish was broken on the counter, chairs were overturned, drawers were open, and a small breeze from a cracked window fluttered the sheer curtains in the living room.

With Max on their heels, Tim and Resa stepped through the rooms carefully. Resa had seen ransacking like this before. The house had been looted. The only sound was the ticking of the bird clock on the wall.

"Well, that's interesting," Tim muttered.

"What?" Resa asked distractedly, blinking back tears.

"The clock is still running," he said slowly, "and I think…" Tim bent his head to look at his watch. "Yeah. The time is right." Resa and Tim exchanged puzzled looks.

"Either those are some super long-lasting batteries, or someone's been here to change them."

Resa felt the glow of hope flick up a notch in her chest. She narrowed her eyes at the clock.

"You know what else is weird," she said looking more closely at the room, "besides the plate broken on the counter, nothing else is broken. I mean it's like the chairs were set gently on their sides and the drawers are open, but only far enough so they won't fall out."

"Hmmm, like it's been staged," Tim said.

"And look!" Resa exclaimed, getting more excited and pointing above the sink and into the cupboards. "The saying I had above the sink about good moods being sponsored by coffee….and my grandma's vases were always right here. Those are strange things to be missing."

Tim wandered into the living room. "And there's huge spaces on the bookshelves. I know Sierra probably isn't the only person in the world who loves gathering books, but there's no way thieves would take so many unless they're librarian criminals."

"Something's not right." Resa walked over to the stairway and took off her backpack at the bottom of the stairs. "All of our family pictures are gone from the walls too."

Resa and Tim stared at each other for an instant before Resa turned and took the stairs two at a time. She paused at the top.

"Well, Mr. Flopsy, what are you doing here?"

"Mr. Flopsy?" Tim asked from behind her as he dropped his pack on the floor with a thud.

"He's the cement rabbit that sat outside in the flower garden. This is not an accident. Someone put it here."

"Resa, look." Tim stepped around her and pointed into the large bedroom off to the side of the stairs. The couches from the basement had been brought up and made into a living area.

Resa started to cry. They had been here! They must have made it through the initial wave of K-Pox. They must be alive. But where?

Resa ran to the kids' rooms. Similar to downstairs, all the special things they'd loved were missing. Pictures, clothes, Mitchell's fox lovey he'd had since he was a baby, Meg's fluffy blanket she used to curl up in on rainy days…all gone.

"The toothbrushes are gone from the bathroom and there's no deodorant or soap in there either." Tim announced.

Resa noticed new pictures had been plastered all over the walls in Meg's room. They were drawings, pictures cut out of magazines, and storybook pages of otters. Resa frowned as Tim walked in behind her.

"Ummm… Did your daughter like otters?" Tim asked curiously.

"Otters were a family thing. When the kids were little, there was a book we used to read over and over about Ozzie the Otter. He

243

floated downstream, reminding all his friends not to worry because the stream took care of all their needs. He always said not to worry about what was behind us, but to keep looking forward. But none of these pictures were here before."

Tim and Resa walked across the hallway to Mitchell's room. The wall next to the door was completely decorated with framed maps and map cutouts.

"These were not here before either," Resa said as she ran her fingers over the pieces, looking for an X or some way to figure out what it all was supposed to mean.

"Remember how Amani said if she and Lorenzo had to leave their house, they'd leave a coded message for their girls so they'd know where to find them?" Tim asked excitedly. "They must have had to leave, but they wanted you to know where they were going. The otters mean not to worry, so a map to where they are has to be here somewhere. There's gotta be more clues!"

Resa turned back to study the maps lining the walls. "Come on my loves, tell me what I'm supposed to see…," she said out loud.

She gave an exasperated huff and ran into the master bedroom. She put her hands on her hips and stopped to look at the couches covered with pillows. Sam had even brought up the game table they'd never used before. She could see how he'd taken good care of them…IS taking good care of them, she corrected herself. She heard Max's nails clicking in the master bathroom and his sniffing as he explored all the new smells. Tim walked towards the bathroom, and she followed after him.

"Find anything Max?" Resa asked Max. He tilted his head as she spoke.

"Look!" Tim said.

Glancing up from the floor, Resa saw a note stuck on her side of the mirror.

My dearest Resa, Mom, Mommy,

We hope you had a nice trip and your flight was on time. We decided to go to Grandma and Grandpa's house for the night so we could watch a movie. We love that buttery gold popcorn, don't you? If you get home early, come over, so you don't miss the movie. We are going to watch McMansions, the one about the Bennetts.

Hope to see you soon!

Love you lots,
Vince, Delilah, and Ben

"I don't understand," Tim said, "Who are those people? And why would they leave you a note to come watch a movie?"

"It's their middle names," Resa said softly. "Samuel Vincent, Margaret Delilah, and Mitchell Benjamin."

"Do your parents own a house where they would've gone?"

"My parents are dead," Resa said slowly. "But it sounds like they wanted me to know they were going somewhere…Wait!"

Resa grabbed the note off the mirror and ran back to Mitchell's room.

"Yes! That's exactly it. Buttery GOLD popcorn Tim! Gold!" She pointed to an old map of the town with an otter sticker in one corner. It had a gold heart in the middle of its chest. "THIS is what they mean. Remember I told you the fancy houses were on the other side of town? We used to joke and call it McMansion Heights."

"That's the movie in the letter," Tim said, understanding.

"This must be where they went. And the Bennetts did live there. They owned the art gallery."

"Let's go!" Tim called out.

Resa and Tim rushed down the stairs, grabbed their packs, and stepped quickly out the back door. Max gave a loud, sharp bark behind them like a battle cry.

Resa locked the door and replaced the key in the jar in the garage. She shook it so the keys jumbled together then hid the jar where she'd found it. They closed the garage door behind them and took off through the backyards towards the northwest corner of town.

"So smart." Resa was beaming as they ran and walked. She knew it was a couple of miles across town and she wanted to conserve her energy for when she got there. Maybe there would be more searching and clues to solve.

Tim and Resa turned left at the small doctor's office where the staff used to hand out lollipops when you had a shot, even to the adults. As they turned into McMansion Heights, there was noticeably more damage to the houses. Large tree branches blocked the road so there was no space for a car to go through. The houses were overgrown and unkept and the ones at the entrance were littered with burned out garbage cans and broken-down cars. Tim looked at Resa.

"Do you get the weird feeling of things being staged again? Maybe to keep people from looking further?"

"Yeah…Fear keeps people out, right?" Resa's eyes searched the landscape curiously, looking for signs of people. Tim was looking around too.

"You never know if there's scouts around like the other places we've been," Tim said. They walked past the wreckage. Even though they were getting deeper into the neighborhood, it still looked like things were abandoned a long while ago.

"The Bennetts lived a few blocks down this road," Resa said, turning a final corner. Abruptly Max's ears pricked up and he started sniffing into the wind.

"Resa, look down there," Tim said, pointing to the next block where lawns had been mowed.

"Tim…the houses."

All of a sudden, it was as if they had entered a completely different world. Flowers were tended and growing, houses were tidy, and they could see bicycles leaning here and there against garages.

"Listen!"

246

What had sounded at first like the wind or birds, they now recognized as people in the distance. Windows were open with voices flowing into the street. There was also hammering and the thud of something hitting the ground, like a shovel breaking up soil.

"Do you hear voices?" Resa asked Tim as tears pooled in her eyes.

"People laughing! What do you think, Max?" Tim said, looking at Max who was panting and wagging his tail with his ears perked up.

They instinctively started to jog up the street to search for people. Resa knew the Bennetts had lived to her immediate right, but there was something pulling her forward. She dropped her backpack and began to run while Tim and Max kept pace slightly behind her. At the end of the street was the huge house that had belonged to the Haverstroms. It gleamed white in the late morning sun, looking as pristine and as grand as ever. Now, however, there was someone working in a large garden in the side yard.

Resa wasn't sure her legs would cooperate with her anymore as she slowed.

"Go on," Tim said, nodding encouragingly. He knelt down to loop his hand through Max's collar to hold him close. Tim smiled up at her. Resa knew they'd be there waiting.

As Resa walked closer, the figure stood up with head still bowed as they tended the garden. They stopped to stretch and walked with the shovel towards the end of the row.

That walk. Resa's hand flew to her mouth. She swallowed hard and tried to catch her breath, now shallow and fast. She'd recognize that walk anywhere. She had seen it so many times across the playground or in the school parking lot. Resa started to run and her voice rang out.

"Meg!"

The tanned, beautiful young woman turned and Resa's feet faltered as she came to a stop. In that moment, Resa was sure that no matter what the world brought with its broken and crumbling fingers, goodness and redemption would always stretch further.

Tears streamed down Resa's face and she clasped her hands over her heart. In a daze, she walked unsteadily off the road and onto the grass. She reached for her daughter. Meg dropped the hand she'd been holding above her eyes to shade them from the sun and rushed forward into Resa's arms.

"Mom! I knew you'd come home."

Discussion Questions

If, after a worldwide catastrophe, you were left with only a small number of people, would you travel to another place or stay where you are? Why would you want to leave? What reasons and safety concerns would you want to consider?

There are several instances where Resa and Tim take supplies or do things that could be considered stealing (the gun at the motel, GW's ATV, food and clothes from houses along the way). Do desperate times justify desperate measures? Are crimes still crimes when situations change?

If you started a new community, what rules do you think should be required? What rules would rate in your top three of required rules? Should there be any rules at all?

What or who would you miss if you lost your whole community? Are there any groups/clubs that you would miss and want to start again if you had the chance? (e.g., church, art, sports, etc.)

How do both Resa and Tim change through their journey? What would be the hardest part of change for you? How do your external circumstances influence your changes and personal growth?

Throughout the book, the wind is present in many different ways (blowing across the plains, bringing the smells of carrion and fire and carrying the sounds of motors, crying, and gunshots, and new people). How does the wind connect the pieces of the companions' story?

Sounds can elicit different emotions depending on what they are or when they are heard. For example, an ATV can be fun or be someone chasing you. Or the sound of Tim burying his mom's jewelry, digging the grave for Nana and, at the end of the book, the sound of a shovel in the garden. How do the same sounds represent different emotions or experiences?

Acknowledgements

We could not have done this book without the support and encouragement from our readers of The Meek Shall Inherit. We thank you so much for your kind comments and questions about the "next" novel. Here it is. We hope you enjoy it as much as we enjoyed writing it.

We also want to thank Rebecca Chedester Dussault for the huge amounts of time she put into beta reading, even though she was working overtime at her real paying job and she still had a family who wanted to see her occasionally. We can't thank her enough for her meticulous attention to detail, not to mention her assistance with editing and formatting. We also want to thank Amelia Rakestraw, Cassandra Weidman, and Gail Franklin for their valuable input during the editing process. All of these remarkable women who took time away from their lives and families to support us in our creative journey, we appreciate you more than words can express. Thank you for accompanying us, helping our story become stronger, and being our support as we toiled and walked the process. Also, thank you to Laura Myers for seeing our vision and designing the beautiful covers for both books in our series.

Any mistakes belong to us and not to the people who graciously donated their time and effort to our project.

Thank you Julia. I have so enjoyed going on this writing journey with you. As we have traveled across the U.S. with Tim, Resa, Sierra, and Max, we have gotten to know each other better, and with each year we write together I get to know and appreciate you more. It's been a privilege. I was a little sad knowing we had reached the end of The Meek series, but then I felt less sad when I began to wonder what projects we might work on together in the future.

Cindy, it has been an honor. What started off with lunches and a playful banter of ideas has blossomed into an amazing partnership. I have truly valued the time we have spent laughing, writing, and working so hard to hash out how to navigate this journey. It has been an incredible adventure, not only on paper, but in our lives. Thank you for helping me grow as a writer, teaching me about the wonderful world of quilting, and always pushing us forward. You are a true companion and a dear friend.

About the Authors

Cynthia Siira has always loved writing and has written numerous short stories, song parodies, and poetry. She also has several unpublished books including a memoir about growing up in Libya which will be her next major writing project, hoping to prepare it for publication in the next year or so. Fingers crossed! She wrote an article about teacher retention for The Virginia Journal of Education and also wrote book reviews published in The American School Board Journal. Cynthia is a retired high school/middle school teacher with a Ph.D. in Special Education from the University of Virginia. A keen interest in art has Cynthia pursuing textile art design and exhibiting her work throughout the state.

Julia White is a passionate storyteller and has a deep love of sharing the gift of words with others. She has published seven Advent devotional and enjoys embracing the world through a variety of imaginative lenses. Outside of writing, Julia finds joy while spending time with family and friends, creating art, cycling, taking leadership roles in community organizations, and supporting others. She earned her B.S. from the University of Illinois and is a Licensed Clinical Professional Counselor, a Certified Rehabilitative Counselor and also has an M.S. in Criminal Justice from Illinois State University.

Cindy and Julia both chose to counsel and support teens and young adults in their move towards adulthood, enjoying the teens' varied personalities and unique views of the world. Together Cindy's and Julia's work has given them an in-depth look at social and family interpersonal dynamics as well as individual growth during tough seasons of life. Their experiences have also given them unique perspectives when creating these realistic and engaging characters and the communities in which they live.

Check out our Facebook and author pages for exciting updates and events!

Julia Website:
https://sites.google.com/view/jcwhitewrites/home?authuser=0

Julia Facebook: https://www.facebook.com/jcwhitewrites

Julia Twitter and Instagram: jcwhitewrites

Cynthia Facebook: https://www.facebook.com/The-Meek-Shall-Inherit-117286506853251

Cynthia Website: https://sites.google.com/view/cynthia-siira-author/meet-cindy?authuser=2

Cynthia Twitter: TMSICindy

The Meek Series

https://www.facebook.com/The-Meek-Shall-Inherit-117286506853251

Before you go!

We would love to hear your reviews on Amazon and Goodreads!

Made in the USA
Middletown, DE
23 May 2023

30822463R00146